LORD OF THE DEAD

Richard Rippon

Lord of the Dead
Copyright © Richard Rippon 2017

The right of Richard Rippon to be identified as the author of this
work has been asserted by him in accordance with the Copyright,
Designs and Patents Act 1988.

This book is a work of fiction. Any resemblance between these
fictional characters and actual persons, living or dead, is purely
coincidental.

Published by Obliterati Press
2017

www.obliteratipress.com

ISBN: 978-1-9997528-0-4

About the Author

Richard Rippon has been writing since 2007, when his short story, *Full Tilt*, was long-listed for a Criminal Shorts award. In 2009, he won a New Writing North Award for his first novel, *The Kebab King*. Since then, he's had a number of short stories published in newspapers, magazines and articles. In 2012, he was commissioned to write a short story (*The Other One*), which appears in the *Platform* anthology. He lives on the North East coast with his wife and two children, where he works as a social media manager in Newcastle upon Tyne, and in 2016 was one of the masterminds behind the Twitter sensation #DrummondPuddleWatch.

For Dani, Celia, Lana, Mam, Dad, family and friends.

With love and thanks to:
Uncle Jim, Guy and Jane Morgan, Kev Lynn,
Sam Harwood, Craig Devlin, Sue Carney,
Mindy Tucker, Susan Llewllyn and
New Writing North.

For your invaluable knowledge, skills, advice and support.

LORD OF THE DEAD

AL NITAK

CHAPTER ONE

Atherton did a double take.

His wallet was open on the bedside table and his University ID photo stared up at him. Back when the picture was taken, he'd thought he looked old, fat and tired. Now, nine years later, it was quite the opposite. He thought he looked fresh-faced and optimistic.

He turned away from it and Louise stirred beside him. The phone rang once more and he floundered to retrieve it from his trouser pocket on the floor. Louise's eyes flicked open and she moaned in protest.

"Sorry," he whispered.

"S'okay," she mumbled and smiled sleepily.

"Jon Atherton," he said, when he finally located the phone.

"Jonny?" It was Myers. He recognised the voice. "You up?"

"I am now. Kind of," said Atherton. "What time is it?"

"Early. What's your availability like this week?"

"Well, we've just broken up for Christmas. The little bastards are back home or away up Machu Picchu or some such shite. I've got stuff to mark, but other than that..."

"We've got...there's something for you. If you were interested. If you were up for it."

Atherton sat up, rubbing his eyes.

"I'm available," he said and cringed at his own eagerness. "I mean, I can probably move a few things around."

"Great. I want you to see the scene while it's fresh."

"Lovely."

"I wouldn't call it that," said Myers. Atherton could hear him dragging hard on a cigarette.

"Where is it?"

"Bottleburn," he said. "I'm en route already. I'm texting you a map link. How soon can you get going?"

"Pretty quick," said Atherton, sitting up and rubbing his scalp.

There was a pause.

"Do you want me to send a car?" said Myers.

"No, I'm good to drive," said Atherton and clicked off the phone.

He stretched out his left arm and clenched his fist a couple of times. He could usually get an indication of how it was going to behave on any particular day by how it felt first thing in the morning. The leg was different; it could feel great at the start of the day, but by afternoon or early evening, it could feel leaden and unresponsive.

He dressed as quickly as he could, sniffing the armpits of a shirt before throwing it on. He opened the door quickly, knowing it creaked less that way. On his way out, he stopped at Hannah's room, gently opening the door a fraction to peek in. She was sound asleep, her head just visible at the top of the pink duvet. He tiptoed silently in and placed a gentle kiss on her head.

Downstairs, he buttered some bread, put it on a plate and carried it out to the car. The air was cold and the sky the colour of bruised concrete. When he backed off the drive, he noticed Louise at the bedroom window, her dressing gown just visible through the venetian blinds. He raised his hand from the wheel and waved. She returned it, wiggling her fingers, and placed a hand to her head with the thumb and little finger extended: *call me*.

He nodded.

Balancing his phone on the steering wheel, he followed Myers's map and directions. Forty-five minutes later, he turned onto a farmer's lane and pulled in behind a large white van, which he recognised as SOCO. The rolling snow-capped Cheviot Hills loomed to the north. A plain-clothes officer approached the car and waved. Atherton wound down the window.

"Myers?" he said.

"At the riverside. There's a path down to the bank."

"Thanks. Richards?"

"Rogers."

"Sorry. I'm just thinking, is this the closest the road gets to the scene?"

"I think so. Possibly," he replied.

"Then it could also be where someone else parked up last night and we've got cars all over it. Can we get everything backed up at least twenty metres from here? Tape it off, too - it's part of the crime scene," said Atherton.

Rogers nodded.

Atherton checked his camera had power and stepped out of the car. Another young uniformed officer looked up on his approach. He was used to his gait attracting attention; the way his left leg leaned in at the knee gave him a limp that was pronounced on some days. This was one of those days.

"Have you never seen a hungover cripple, son? You should have seen the state of me last night," he said. The officer blocked his way.

"Just a second, sir," he said.

"I'm here for Myers," said Atherton.

"Do you have any ID?"

"I'm his psych expert from the Uni. He invited me to the picnic," said Atherton. He fished out his laminated University ID and showed it to the officer, who stepped back from Atherton slightly as a quick exchange on his radio followed.

"Go right ahead, Doctor Atherton. Sorry for the inconvenience," he said.

"That's quite alright, my friend," said Atherton and smiled. The officer returned it, uncertainly.

The young cop pointed down the lane, where Atherton saw Myers already emerging from the undergrowth, talking animatedly into his phone. Atherton picked up on the conversation when he walked within earshot.

"...guy walking his dog," said Myers. "We've taken him in. A mess, understandably. There's a car on the way to pick his wife up. Other than that, we don't think anyone will have caught wind.

We'll probably have an hour or two before we have any media problems."

He saw Atherton and nodded. "Sir, got to go now and I'll call you back in half an hour." He pocketed the phone. "Jonny," he said. "This way."

Atherton followed Myers down an overgrown path, which meandered through the trees toward the river. Already, he could see a large SOCO tent.

"Jesus, Paul, what is this? A wedding reception?" said Atherton.

"Sue told me it was the biggest bloody tent they have," he replied. "It's bad. I've never seen anything like it."

Myers took his time on the path. Leather soles were no good on this terrain. Atherton thought Myers's suit seemed a little tighter on him, his hair now a little more salt than pepper.

"So, how are you doing, Jon?" said Myers, short of breath.

"Fine. You?"

"Still doing it. How's Louise?"

"Good, thanks. We're good."

They continued down, until Myers stopped suddenly, blocking the path.

"I've got to tell you, Jonny; it's not a pretty picture in there."

"I'm okay with it Paul, if that's what you're getting at," said Atherton.

"I'm not getting at anything, I'm just telling you that it's about as bad as it gets."

"And I'm telling you I'm okay."

"Fine. Knock yourself out."

The two continued silently to the riverside, where the trees thinned and frosty grass spanned to the tent. Myers stopped short of the boundary tape and pulled out the phone once more.

"I'll be out here," said Myers.

A man in a hooded white forensics suit held open the tent door for Atherton and he stepped inside.

It was as if someone had exploded. Red-brown blood covered virtually the entire internal floor area of the tent. His eyes were drawn immediately to the decapitated head. Scattered around were other body parts, some identifiable, others not. There was an awful combination of smells in the air: blood, like that of a butchers shop, with a vague hint of human shit.

Atherton removed a menthol nasal inhaler from his pocket and took two sharp hits to each nostril.

"If you vomit on my crime scene, I'll tear *you* apart," said a nearby voice.

"Hi, Sue, where's good to stand? Here?"

Sue Cresswell was recognisable only by her large rimmed spectacles. Several other people moved slowly and deliberately around the tent, all wearing identical white coveralls.

"Stick to the perimeter, you should be fine. There are some booties at the back of the door there," she said.

"Ah-ha," said Atherton and slipped blue shoe covers on. "I must say, I like what you're wearing today. Is it new?"

She laughed.

"Aye, fresh out of the packet," she said. "I just wish it had more of a lining. I'm bloody freezing."

"What do you know?"

"Dismembered body of one female." She pointed to various areas of the tent. "Eight pieces altogether. Head, you can see. We've got upper torso over there...left arm...right leg, liver...looks like lower intestine there."

"Fucking hell," whispered Atherton.

"Hell is right," said Cresswell. "That pile over there?" She pointed to a pile of yellowing skin and glistening viscera. "That's the rest."

"And there?" Atherton pointed to an area close to one corner of the tent where several wired flags had been inserted.

"We'll get to that," she said. "We need to do some analysis, but this looks really fresh to me. Like eight or nine hours old."

An awful thought occurred to Atherton. They were miles from anywhere. Screaming didn't matter out here.

"Could she have been alive when he cut her?" he asked.

"Now you're asking. We're looking at a large volume of blood here, but I can't see anything which tells me her heart was still beating. I'd expect to see more evidence of arterial sprays. From the amount of blood, I'd say the dismemberment happened here, but it could have been post-mortem. We can check her arms for defence wounds too, when we pull them out of the pile. There's a sizable wound to her head, which we'll need to take a good look at. He could have killed her elsewhere and carried her down."

"Assuming it was a guy of course," said Atherton.

"It is an assumption, but whoever was responsible was strong. The victim's femur is a good size. I think this was a big girl. Maybe five-ten, five-eleven. Anyway, it's always a guy."

"I thought you people didn't make assumptions?" he said.

"I thought you guys waited for reports?" she answered.

"Touché. So what about the flags over there? Pitch and putt, Sue?"

"Indentations," she said. "Four in a square formation, which could have been a chair and three in front of that from something else."

"Camera? You think he photographed it?"

"Maybe. Something on a tripod would be my guess. From the depth of the indentation and the soil's water content, we might be able to make a stab at the weight of the equipment on top of it. Ditto the chair. We'd need to take the ground temp into consideration, too," she said.

"You can tell us the weight of the killer?"

"*Assuming* he sat on it. Ballpark only, you understand. We'll do casts to see if there's anything else identifiable about the legs. Likely to be a pretty generic portable camping chair, but you never know."

"What about the way he…"

"Chopped her up?"

"Yes."

"Fine-toothed saw, it looks like."

"Okay. A proper bone saw or a workshop hacksaw?"

"I'll get back to you on that. We'll need a bit of lab at some point, or do you want me to put you in a taxi and take you to a suspect right now?" Her eyes smiled.

"If you could please, it would save a lot of time," said Atherton. He looked across the tent again; the scene was surreal. "What about down by the river? Whoever did this would be covered in blood. You think he went down and washed himself?"

"Maybe. The water would have been like the Baltic, but that's what I might have done, although right here there's quite a drop down to the water," she said, pointing to the tent wall hiding the river. "Which isn't to say he didn't use it, but there's a better place to get in downstream. We've taped fifty metres in either direction, so we can check it out once we've finished here."

"Thanks, Sue. Do you need anything else?" said Atherton.

"Just a wood fire, a latté and a nice maple syrup and pecan pastry, please."

"If I find them, they're yours."

Atherton took a few photos of his own. It was a habit he had; to record how *he'd* seen it rather than anyone else. As he stepped outside, he felt a wave of dizziness suddenly strike and he took a moment until it passed. He walked to the riverbank. Alongside the crime scene, there was indeed a good four-foot drop. Not easy to climb in or out of, he thought.

He glanced downstream and could see the more accessible area of shale, which Cresswell had mentioned. He strolled down to it, following the natural curve of the river. At the shale, he dipped under the tape and put his hands on his knees so he could crouch and get a better view of the ground. He became aware of Myers at his side.

"We need to get more people out here, Paul," said Atherton. "We should be covering all this ground. The river, all of this, right the way up to and including the farmer's lane we have umpteen squad cars parked on."

"It's already happening. We're bringing in another six guys from Newcastle," he said. He watched Atherton as he scanned the pebbles. "What do you think?" he said, finally.

Atherton ignored him for almost a full minute, until his eyes fell onto a minute splash of dark red blood. He pointed at it and looked up at Myers, who nodded.

"I think we need to catch this fucker," he said to himself and crouched down to take a photograph. "Here we go up the river again."

CHAPTER TWO

The head had a name.

Focus Room 1 was bathed in natural light afforded by the floor-to-ceiling windows. In one corner was a separate office, also glass, with vertical blinds on all sides. In the middle of the room was a large H-shaped configuration of desks, with black monitors and various exposed network and power cables for laptops.

"Ellis Brampton," said Myers. He'd breezed in with a young, flustered IT support guy who was trying to upload an image to one of the main monitors. "Twenty-nine. Account manager at the Menshen Insurance Company. Lived in Jesmond."

The various occupants of the room stopped what they were doing and gathered around him. A large display screen lit up with a photograph. A shot of the girl in walking gear. One foot on a rock, hands on hips, with lush, mountainous terrain in the background. Her cheeks were flushed with exertion; calves tanned and toned in cut-off denim shorts. Her hair was drawn up and tied with a red bandana. She had pretty, Mediterranean looks, mid-length dark brown hair and a glint in her eye. Her face was a welcome change to pictures of body parts and blood, but also served as a reminder of the hideousness of the crime. A beautiful young girl reduced to meat, casually discarded in a field.

"Boyfriend's statement says he was working a night shift, so he's unlikely to be a suspect," said Myers. "Came home in the morning and thought she'd already left for work, so didn't start calling round for her until later. We've got a match for the description, height and estimated weight. We're waiting for DNA and prints as confirmation, but unless you hear otherwise, this is our victim. She was last seen leaving work at around 5.20PM on Monday night. This is confirmed by her work swipe card. We've already got someone to look at CCTV footage both inside and outside her building."

"Car?" someone said.

"The building has parking across the street, so we're checking to see if it's there or in the vicinity," said Myers. He scanned the room to see if there were any other questions. None came. Ellis Brampton's smile beamed out at them from the screen. Atherton stared back. "You all know what you should be doing, so crack on. There'll be another briefing at 8.30AM tomorrow morning or sooner if something else develops. Keep your phones on and yes Walsh, I am looking specifically at you. Jon, can I have a word?"

Myers led Atherton into an adjoining huddle room and closed the door.

"Paul?"

"Jon, we're bringing in Kate Prejean on this," said Myers. Atherton gave him a pained look. "I know, Jon. Not my decision, but one I happen to think is a good one. You work well together and they saw your last collaboration as a success."

A success.

Two young boys, dead.

Success?

"I can't work with her, Paul," said Atherton, trying to control his voice. He felt uncomfortably aware of the rest of the team on the other side of the glass partitions. "You know what happened. This whole place does. Louise and I are just starting to get somewhere."

"She's great at what she does, Jon and so are you. You do want to catch this twat, don't you? I don't know if you remember but we had the body of a prostitute turn up at an abandoned warehouse last year. The scene was similarly graphic. I want you and Kate to take another look at it in relation to this case."

"I'm not interested," said Atherton.

"What are you planning, Jon? Mark papers and read essays, with this on your doorstep?" Myers held his palms face up. "You can't wait to get stuck in. I can see it in your eyes."

Atherton raised a finger and started to say something, but was interrupted by a knock on the glass.

"Are we finished for the time being, Jon?" Myers said, gesturing to the person outside.

Sue Cresswell walked into the room as if she were on a field trip, a file and various papers clasped tightly to her small breasts. She was less imposing, Atherton thought, without her coveralls and hood, her small nose barely capable of supporting the large frames of her spectacles. She ran her hand through her cropped, blonde hair and smiled at Atherton. She took a seat at the table and Atherton sat beside her to better see the evidence file. Myers remained standing.

"Okay, Sue, what we got?" he said.

"Nothing too surprising. One female, as we thought. DNA is a match for the hair samples obtained from Brampton's flat. She wasn't on the print record, but prints match those taken from her vanity mirror. So, I think we can say with certainty that this is our girl."

"Okay. We'll need to take that to the media team. See how they want to deal with things," said Myers.

Atherton noticed that Myers had thought of this point before he'd thought of how best to inform the girl's family. This was the way of things now.

"Blood was O rhesus negative. We sampled from twenty-five locations at the scene, which I've indicated on the display. Only one blood type, all the victim's," said Cresswell. She paused to bring up a picture of the scene on a tablet computer; the large area of dark red on the grass. "The body was most likely dismembered in this area here. We think she was already dead by then. We put the time of death between midnight and 3AM."

"How accurate do we think those timings are?" said Myers. He was doing the management trick of not engaging eye contact. When you're the boss, you don't have to.

"The dismemberment makes it more difficult, but I think we can be quietly confident that's pretty much on the money," she said. Atherton glanced at Cresswell's notes. Her handwriting managed to be both neat and elegant. Not for the first time, Atherton wondered what it would be like to take her to bed.

"About the dismemberment," said Atherton. "What can you tell us?"

"The few marks on the bone tell us he was using a fine-toothed saw," she said. "Again, no surprises."

"Only a few marks?" said Myers. This was, Atherton noticed, the only insightful thing he had said so far.

"Only a few, because he didn't cut much bone. Most people, when they first come to cut a body up, they make a right meal of it," said Cresswell. She put the edge of one hand on her forearm. "They go straight for the bone. They're usually in a panic and don't realise it's like sawing through pine. This leaves what we call *chatter* marks, where the blade bounces along the bone. It's badly done, time consuming and obviously messy." She mimicked sawing on her arm. "This guy went for the major joints wherever he could. You get it right, you cut through skin, muscles and tendon and the bone just comes away."

"He knew what he was doing?" said Atherton.

"No master butcher, but he had an idea," she said. "He'd either done it before, or was well researched."

Myers looked as if he was mentally digesting something. Cresswell used the moment to adjust the position of the papers on the table.

"No chance of prints?" asked Atherton.

"From the suspect? There's not much to go on. If there was clothing, we might have something. Bring me a belt or a purse and we could have a try at a print, but otherwise, you know...it's the middle of a field. We're struggling for a good surface," she said.

"I'm going to ask a stupid question," said Atherton.

Cresswell smiled at him. She hadn't heard him ask a stupid question yet.

"It looks as if the head was moved." He slid the tablet so it was on the table between Cresswell and himself. "If the body was chopped up here and the head was left way up here...what's that; fifteen feet away? He's obviously touched the head quite a lot. In fact, it's fair to say he's touched every part of her. Is there anywhere on the body we could maybe get a print from? Eyeballs, or maybe from makeup?"

"We did dust the eyes. Nothing. I've never known a successful print from makeup," she said.

"It was the makeup which got me thinking."

"What about it?" said Myers.

"Just...she's wearing quite a lot of it." Atherton took the tablet and scrolled through to a picture of the head. The cheeks were rosy with blusher and the eyes were generously decorated with mascara and eye shadow. "Let's say she was taken as she left work. That's a lot of muck to have on your face for a normal day in the office, wouldn't you say?"

"Unless he took her at home, or on her way out," said Myers.

"Boyfriend said she didn't have any plans that he knew of," said Atherton.

"We need to find out if the statements are in from the girl's colleagues. I want to know what she looked like when she finished work yesterday," said Myers.

Atherton placed his thumb and index finger on the tablet screen and moved them apart to blow up the image of one eye. The eyeliner wasn't very well applied and there were sizeable lumps of mascara on the eyelashes.

"Would you go out like that, Sue?" said Atherton.

"I never go out, Jon," she said. "But I can see what you're getting at."

"You think our man made her up?" said Myers.

"Looks like it to me. Unless he forced her to do it before he killed her," said Atherton.

Sue Cresswell looked at Jon. She loved the way he didn't mince his words. Not for the first time, she wondered what it would be like to take him to bed.

CHAPTER THREE

Atherton rolled the food around his mouth. He couldn't work out whether the temperature of the chiller had done something to minimise its taste, or if it was quite simply a bad sandwich.

He found the new police headquarters disorientating. Each area had the same colouring and it was difficult to get a bearing, with each space looking much like another. The exterior was all glass and metal cladding, finished just before the austerity cuts had begun to kick in. Myers had pointed him towards the coffee snug and given him vague directions to the exit.

Atherton thought Myers had gained in professional stature – if not rank – since their last meeting. He had a directness with his team which Atherton respected, though he seemed to make little allowance for those who were not his subordinates. If any of that was pointed his way, Atherton knew he would tire of it quickly.

The idea of meeting Kate again troubled him more. His thoughts of her generally followed a familiar, well-trodden pattern. An intertwined combination of the highly pleasurable and the deeply disturbing. Whenever he thought of their physical relationship – the taste of her lips, the firm grip of her ankles on the back of his thighs – he knew it would inevitably lead to darker images.

The wardrobe where he'd kept them.

The chicken wire.

The two pale, naked bodies; hands reaching out to each other, unable to touch on the bloody, threadbare carpet.

And at the end of it all, there was always the guilt.

Not getting there in time.

Being too slow, in every way.

And of betraying Louise.

Myers strode suddenly into view. Behind him, Rogers tried his best to look purposeful.

"Jon, sorry, I knew you thought we were done for today, but something's come up," he said. "We might need your opinion on something."

"Sure," he said. He put the half-eaten sandwich back into its plastic triangular container and dropped it into the bin as he passed. He followed Myers and Rogers down the corridor and into a small meeting room, where Sue Cresswell sat next to a young man with cropped brown hair and a short goatee beard. Atherton recognised him from earlier in the focus room; he stood nervously when they entered.

"This is Doctor Jon Atherton, from Newcastle William Armstrong University, who's going to be helping us with this case," said Myers. "Jon, this is Mattias Klum who...Mattias, you better explain what it is you do." They all followed Myers's cue to sit.

"I work in the communications team," said Mattias. "Doing social media outreach." He spoke with a European accent, which Atherton could not quite place. Scandinavian maybe. Mattias read the confused look on Atherton's face. "We use a variety of social media platforms to reach out to local communities, update them with crime detection rates, issue warnings regarding burglaries. That type of thing."

He plugged a lead into the back of his laptop and clicked on a wall-mounted TV using a remote on the desk. "When there's been a big event, a crime or so on which we know is going to reverberate through the community, we monitor to see what people are saying on social. It's usually to gauge opinion on police performance."

A series of short, continuously changing messages scrolled down the screen. "We hadn't exactly been briefed yet to do this," he said, "but I heard about the death in the countryside, so naturally I looked to see what people were saying about it."

Mattias's fingers moved fluidly over the keys, as if barely touching them, and clicked enter. A new series of messages appeared with Bottleburn displayed in bold.

"Lots of people talking about it online, of course," said Mattias. "It was fairly new at this point. Most people saying 'what's happening?', 'there's police in Bottleburn, what's going on?' and so on, but then I found this...one moment please." He scrolled down the messages and clicked on one so that it increased in size:

A night in Bottleburn.

"It had this photograph," said Mattias and clicked on a link. The picture filled the screen. It was the top of a woman's forehead; a couple of inches of skin with a dark, prominent freckle and the dark roots of her hairline. The background was almost in complete darkness. Atherton could see immediately it was Ellis Brampton.

"Sue, Mattias is going to email you this photo," said Myers. "Do whatever you need to do to verify that this is the victim please."

"Sure," said Sue.

"Was it light when the dog walker found the victim?" said Atherton.

"Yes," said Myers. "So unless someone took a snap and didn't bother to call us, this was taken by the killer."

All eyes fell on Mattias.

"If you look at the user's profile, it doesn't tell you an awful lot," said Mattias, clicking on something so the profile page appeared with the username *@SonOfGeb* in large font. "The account was opened a month ago and as you can see, there's no profile picture or home location listed."

"Just a question," said Atherton. "Can we send him a message privately, so no-one else can see?"

"Unfortunately, it doesn't work like that. To send him a private message, he'd need to follow us and we'd need to follow him," said Klum.

"What about the photos; are they...what's the word?" said Myers.

"Geotagged? No such luck," said Mattias. "Also, this is the only picture and we know where that was taken."

"What about tracing the IP address?" said Myers.

"We can't trace him. I asked the Online Fraud guys for some help on that front," said Mattias. "The IP address associated with the message is in San Antonio, Texas, so it looks like he's using a basic zombie mechanism. Fairly standard stuff, but effective to hide your location. They're looking into it for me, but I doubt very much you're going to get anything this way."

"So who's seen the photo?" said Myers.

"Well, as you can see, the user only has ten followers and the message and photo would have dropped into their newsfeeds, but there are no guarantees they actually viewed it. When we look across the accounts following this user, they're mainly businesses, brands or people trying to boost their numbers with reciprocal follows."

Atherton looked at the list of followers on the screen. The first was for a roller-door company and the second for a hip-hop artist from Bristol. "My feeling," he said, "is that until pictures of the victim are released, no-one would ever link the photo to the murder."

Atherton became aware that Myers was staring at him.

"What does this say about him, Jon?" he said.

"We already suspect he likes to record things. It looks very much like he took a tripod with him for a camera. He wants a visual souvenir. That's one thing," said Atherton. "The other is that he might want to start telling people about it. He's taking baby steps, but why use social media if you don't want to be social? He wants his work to be seen."

"Do you think this is how he found Ellis Brampton?" said Myers.

"On social media? It's definitely something you should check," said Atherton. "But what this tells us, really, is that he's got quite an ego. This is useful, significant information."

Myers nodded, apparently satisfied. "Here's what I think we should do," he said. "We do nothing to indicate we've seen any of this. We watch and we wait to see if he puts up another message. Mattias, you'll raise the necessary alarm bells if this should happen?"

"Of course," said Mattias.

Mattias kept on talking, but Atherton had zoned out and was looking at the photograph once more; the skin on Ellis Brampton's forehead, the dark freckle and the expanse of blackness behind her.

"Any ideas what 'Son of Geb' might mean?" said Myers to the room.

"I googled 'Geb'," said Mattias. "He was an ancient Egyptian god. God of the Earth and father of all the other Gods, such as Osiris. Osiris was known as King of the underworld and..." He flipped over his notepad, looking for something.

"Lord of the dead," finished Atherton.

*

The empty wine glass tumbled onto its side, rolled across the counter and smashed onto the floor. Louise jumped a little and giggled at herself, pushing her skirt back down self-consciously.

"Oh," said Atherton. "Shit." He kissed her once more and she ran her fingers through his hair. "You'd better stay there."

He left her perched on the kitchen counter top and left the room, emerging moments later with a red plastic dustpan and brush. He crouched awkwardly and began to sweep up the glass, offering Louise a view of his thinning crown. He put too much product on it, she thought, so it made his scalp more visible through his hair.

"You're probably safe now," he said in an exaggeratedly deep voice.

"My hero," she said. He put his hands on her waist and lifted her effortlessly down. She still liked him physically; his strong shoulders, his neck and yes, his backside. She watched as he lurched ungraciously from the room, carrying the dustpan and heard him dump its contents in the bin in the room beyond.

He certainly still had *something*, a fact reinforced by certain comments from her female friends. Their husbands, of course, would have been baffled; surely their entire marriage was simply a sympathy fuck gone too far? As far as she could gather, he'd never had any trouble attracting women. When he talked about school or university, the names were all female, spoken with respect and affection. She'd built up a picture of a young Jon, precluded from the football pitch and spending his time sheltered in female company; a situation which had paid dividends at the onset of puberty.

When she probed, he'd deflect the question or simply offer a smile. She knew when they'd met, drunk at a mutual friend's party, and started to tentatively date that she was sharing him with at least one other. Back then, before he'd committed to her, it had seemed acceptable. Something attractive and dangerously bohemian to her. Now, since the affair, would she always be in fear she was sharing him?

Louise took the opportunity to remove her heels and rub her feet. She looked again at the cards on the shelf, lifting each one and reading the messages inside. She looked at Jonny's: *Happy Birthday* it said. *All my Love, Now and always.* She could remember last year's Christmas card, which had been quite different: *I'll try if you will.* He'd kept to this, but she couldn't help wonder what the upcoming 'festive' period would bring.

They'd been out to her favourite Japanese teppenyaki restaurant and sat right at the grill, wearing aprons bearing the restaurant's name. They'd watched as the chef sliced the lobsters lengthways and laid them down on the grill, seeing them curl slightly as they cooked, giving the macabre illusion of movement.

They'd both drunk too much wine too quickly, and Louise had succumbed to a fit of giggles the likes of which she hadn't experienced since before Hannah's birth. When Atherton announced to the chef it was her birthday, he'd encouraged her to join him behind the teppan where she was made to try catching an egg in the chef's hat, which he'd placed on her head. To her amazement, she'd caught it and the neighbouring diners had applauded. With a pile of frying rice, the chef had formed the number *29*.

"Your birthday. This is right, yes?" he'd said.

"If only," she'd said. "And the rest."

She'd eaten little. Before they'd gone out, she had watched the report on a rolling news channel at home; helicopter footage of the large tent by the river, played in a pointless loop, then a hastily assembled press conference, where she recognised Paul Myers in the background. When she'd asked where he'd been working, Jon had simply replied, "Bottleburn".

She knew all too well what would follow next; absence, moods and drinking. Withdrawal and irritability. They'd been following the counsellor's guidance: listen, acknowledge and then respond, and it had been working most of the time. The arguments had abated, but when they did argue, she didn't like the way he could detach himself emotionally. The way he spoke to her in that cool, professional manner. At those times, she felt as if she were simply an extension of his job and if he did finally lose his temper – a rarity now – it was short, explosive and something of a relief.

Later that evening, they made love and Atherton watched his wife rise and fall upon him as he held her, one hand on a breast, the other on a buttock, the way she liked. Behind her head, the light fitting cast a floral shape like a large halo, the features of her face hidden.

"It's the tablets," she said afterwards, in the darkness. "They stop me from coming."

"Do they?" he replied, spooning her. "I haven't lost the magic?"

"Anorgasmia," she said. "It's one of the side effects. I feel the urge and – don't get me wrong, I still love it – but I just can't come. There's still a little bit of magic, I suppose."

"You *suppose?*" he said. He could sense she was smiling. There was silence for a minute or more. Her breathing steadied and slowed and he was surprised when she spoke again.

"I think I'd like to start decreasing the dosage. Maybe take a tablet every other day," she said.

"Okay, if you think you're ready," he said.

"I'm not sure," she said. "What do you think?"

"I think..." started Atherton, knowing he needed to tread carefully, "you seem so much better now. Compared to last summer."

"Last summer? Last summer, I didn't think there'd be a *this* summer," she said, turning and putting a hand on his chest. "I know I put everyone through the wringer. Poor Hannah. And you."

"Me? I'll always feel so terrible that I didn't recognise what was happening," he said.

"You were busy," she said. "You kept things going, when I couldn't even get out of bed. I'm grateful for that."

"I've got a bloody doctorate in psychology, Louise. I should've known you weren't well. I should have been keeping my eye on you," he said.

She laughed gently. He sensed something unspoken in the silence which followed: *But you had your eye on her, didn't you?*

"It definitely started when Hannah was born," she said. "They should have spotted it then. All those appointments at the clinic."

His memories following the birth were a blur. Hannah had been born during an unseasonably warm spell in May, just before the examination period at the University. She'd been a terrible sleeper, waking every three hours through the night. He'd done his fair share of feeds; gritty-eyed fumblings with bottles of water and powdered formula. She'd been a poor feeder, too and was sick often, necessitating changes of sleep suits and bedclothes. He'd found himself stretched to the limit. He could recall afternoon tutorials when all he wanted to do was dismiss the students and lie on his office couch.

Louise had found it all so hard. Wandering around with a constant look of despair. Breast-feeding hadn't worked and the guilt she'd felt seemed to manifest itself in obsessive behaviour around the baby: room temperature, cleanliness, strict procedures for milk preparation and baths. Atherton had been brought to task on many things. Mother knows best, after all. Usually, he acquiesced, but the stolen hours of sleep left them with short fuses, little patience and frequent arguments.

Hannah's sleeping improved over the years and Atherton had felt the relief of normalised sleep, but Louise did not. No matter how many hours she slept, day or night, she felt no benefit and arose feeling the same level of exhaustion with which she'd laid down. She was constantly ill. Conversations always focussed on her various maladies and lack of energy. Sex was non-existent. Atherton felt himself grow distant from her and he let it happen, grateful of the breathing space. By then, his second book had taken off and his first was becoming accepted as recommended text for those investigating serial crime. The police started to consult him directly on cases and he took every chance he could get to travel.

And then there was Kate.

Now, lying in the spare room where he retreated when he couldn't sleep, and with the whisky keeping him warmer than the thin duvet, unpleasant images passed through Atherton's mind. He tried visualising the scene, the scattered body parts and the smell. A familiar feeling descended upon him; fear, apprehension and – yes – excitement. He listened to the sounds of the house. The creaking of floorboards and joists as they cooled, the ticking of the bedside clock and the occasional distant hum of the refrigerator in the kitchen below.

As sleep took him, and he fell gratefully into its dark warmth, he thought he heard something else altogether, which woke him briefly. It took him a moment to realise the screams he'd heard were in his imagination. Screams which had long since been silenced forever.

CHAPTER FOUR

Detective Sergeant Kate Prejean watched from the car as the light faded, turning the scant colour into greys and blacks. The bushes and trees had filtered the wind of fast-food packaging and other rubbish, which lined the edge of the industrial estate. Between the foliage, she could see the dark murk of the Tyne oozing its way steadily eastwards towards the North Sea.

She checked her eyes in the mirror, resisting the urge to delve into her make-up bag again. The insomnia hit only once or twice per month now and she held it at bay with exercise and a strict routine in the evening; winding down instead of stepping it up, as had been her habit. Her best thinking usually arrived at night, on a short-lived plateau, between glasses four and five, with her work strewn across all surfaces of the flat.

Eventually, Atherton's car rolled into view and he parked facing hers. She saw him smile awkwardly, his face partially masked by the reflection of the streetlight on the windscreen. She hoisted her heavy attaché case up, stepped out of the car and waited for him on the pavement.

"Sorry I'm late, Kate," he said as he opened the door. "Bit of poetry there for you, though." He noticed her expression remained unchanged. "How are you?"

"Fine. You?"

"Fine. Sorry, I'm late," he repeated.

"It's okay. Really," she said. "I've just got here."

"Top of the leader board on my list of inconveniences today has been this...bloody...leg." He struggled to drag his right foot out of the foot well.

"It's okay. Gave me some more time to read up on this," she said.

"You weren't here during the investigation I take it?"

"No," she said, almost elaborating and deciding against it. She didn't want to get into that quite yet.

"Come on, you swine," said Atherton, helping his leg out of the car with his hands. "So, why do you think we're here?"

"You know why we're here. To investigate whether or not there's a link between Bottleburn and this one from last year," she said.

"I read a little online. Do you see similarities? I didn't."

"Unlikely," she said. "Maybe Myers wanted to get this out of the way outside the confines of the station."

"This?"

"Me and you meeting again."

"Maybe. Like a first date?"

"Well, we never had a first date, did we Jon?"

"No. I don't suppose we did."

Once his legs were out, the rest of him followed quickly. He rose to his full height and smiled at her. He was dressed immaculately in crisp, dark jeans and suede desert boots. A perfectly tied paisley silk scarf sat outside his Harrington jacket. His dark hair had receded further up his forehead, she thought, and seemed greyer at the sides, but he was still presentable. She wondered how much of his late arrival had been due to him getting ready rather than his disobedient leg.

Getting ready for what, though? For her, or for his own vanity?

She shut the car door for him. "I think if we head around this way we'll see how he got in," she said.

"Lead the way, my dear."

She had missed the slightly sing-song nature to his voice. The cerebral palsy affected his right side, including his face, and consequently his speech. She knew he emphasised certain words, or pitched them higher in order to get them out, lest they be lost in a mumble.

They walked around the building, following tall vertical railings and when they turned the corner, were immediately confronted by a short, stocky man in black uniform and cap.

"Oh...sorry," he began. "Detective Sergeant Prejean?" he said, extending his hand to Atherton.

Atherton performed a sideways nod in Prejean's direction. "I am merely the valet."

"Oh, I'm sorry," he said. He gave up on the handshake altogether. "I saw you from up there." He pointed to a security camera high up on the wall, which rotated dutifully. "Of course, if that had been there when it happened last October, it might have made your job a lot easier."

At the gate, he produced a large set of keys and set to work on a padlock which secured a large bolt. "There're no more deliveries until tomorrow morning, so we lock the place up." He slid back the bolt and shuffled the gate open with effort. "I'm Ron, by the way. I'll open up the back door. I'll be inside, up the steps if you need me."

"Thanks, Ron," said Prejean, as he mounted some steps and disappeared inside.

"I think Ron likes you," said Atherton and she gave him a look which advised him to shut up.

They looked around. The huge brick façade was punctuated by three docking bays designed to receive lorries, each covered by metal roller-doors which spanned roof to floor.

"This is pretty much as it was," said Prejean. "Exterior at least. The place was taken over about three months after the murder, so the interior has been refurbished." She turned and pointed at the gate. "He cut off the original padlock with bolt cutters, but while he was in there, he put his own padlock on, so he wouldn't be disturbed. They found it discarded outside of the gate."

"Sensible fellow," said Atherton. "So he drove in?"

"Yeah." Prejean watched him chew on that fact for a moment.

"So, what about the car?"

"Van," she said. "One of the girls she was working with saw the victim getting into a van. Typical white transit. No markings, no-one saw the driver and the CCTV was a blank."

Atherton looked around the tarmac-covered courtyard.

"So he rolls in, parks up somewhere here. Any tyre marks or anything else to go on?"

"They bagged a few fag butts and crisp packets. Stuff that could blow in at any time. They printed them anyway, but nothing. Shall we go inside?"

Prejean lithely mounted the steps to the rear fire door. Atherton watched her. She looked as if she'd dropped a few pounds since he'd last seen her. He started on the steps, keen for her not to see him struggling up them, leaning on the wall to help his ascent. By the time he made it inside, he was slightly out of breath.

In front of him were several aisles of warehouse racking containing pallets of brown boxes. To his right were the docking bays; sunken ingresses designed to accommodate lorries so they were the correct height for forklifts to load directly from the dock. Prejean crouched and opened her bag to remove something.

"He must have subdued her in some way," he said, once he had caught his breath.

"Hmm?"

"If he'd driven up to an abandoned warehouse with her still conscious, I think a streetwise working girl would have had alarm bells ringing and put up a struggle."

"Good point. I don't know if they arrived at that in the investigation. Have you read the report?"

"No."

He caught her rolling her eyes. It made him smile.

"If it were me, Prejean, I would have picked her up, taken her somewhere quiet as if we were going down to get down to business, then zonked her out with something before I even thought about bringing her near the place."

"Makes sense," she said, looking at some paperwork. "Yes. They found ketamine in her system."

"Rather that, than leave a nervous pro in the car whilst I open the gate, drive in, tap in the pin number and so on. All that would be time she could get antsy and take off."

"No pin number," she said. "There wasn't a keypad at the time, just another bolt and padlock set up. The place was empty, so the security was minimal. Just 'Keep Out the Bums' type stuff. There were signs up for some half-arsed security firm or other, but when they looked into it, they hadn't been by for a week at the time of the murder."

"I see."

"All he needed were the bolt cutters. Snip and in."

"So...she's already out cold," said Atherton. "He gains entry to the yard, drives in, drags her up the steps. Then what?"

"Then...this." Prejean rifled through a stack of papers in her bag, pulling several colour photographs free. She turned and moved position a couple of times to get her bearings. "Body was here..." She indicated on the concrete floor. "Head facing north. Blood spatter here and here...pretty much all around here, actually." She gestured outwardly with her hands. "Multiple blows to the head with a blunt weapon. No wounds from self-defence, suggesting the victim was alive, but unconscious when attacked."

"What was her name?"

"Isabelle Lynch, twenty-three years old. Known as Izzy. On the game for two years. Known to the police for a few minor drug charges," she said. "Poor girl."

Atherton appeared behind her and looked over her shoulder. Prejean felt his breath on her neck, warm in the coolness of the warehouse. He reached out to take the photographs from her and there was a moment when their hands touched. His hand felt as soft as she remembered. She glanced around to him, but he was staring intently at the photographs.

"He really went to town," said Atherton.

The woman's head had been brutally battered, her features obliterated, leaving only hair and tissue like mincemeat. The blood spanned out from the head in an arc, like a huge scarlet halo.

"Horrible," he said quietly. Prejean noticed his face had grown noticeably paler. He handed the photographs back.

"This is cast-off," she said. "Here and here..." She pointed at two tendrils of blood, as if an artist has flicked red paint from his brush onto the floor.

"Cast off?"

"These trails came off the weapon when it was swung back and forth," she said. "Because it goes this way," – she cut through the air diagonally, from top-right to bottom-left with an imaginary weapon – "and not this way," – she swung the opposite diagonal – "it suggests that our man was right-handed and not left."

"That's pretty good," said Atherton absently.

Prejean's gauge of his sarcasm was a little off. It had been too long.

"Well, it cuts out about ten percent of the population who are lefties, so it's a start."

"Every little helps," said Atherton. The colour had entirely drained from his face.

"Want to have a closer look?" she said and held up one of the photographs.

"No," said Atherton, stepping away. "I get the general idea." He took deep breaths as surreptitiously as he could. "He must have been covered in blood?"

"Smears on the door, more on the floor. No prints. He was pretty careful, but they did get this." She delved into the bag once more and produced another photograph. "Partial footprint. Size seven or eight Puma trainer, from...there." She pointed to a spot between the door and the dock.

"Anything else?" he said.

"Let's try this."

Prejean took something else from her bag. It took a moment for Atherton to realise it was a small tablet computer in a rubberised sheath. She turned it on, selected an icon on the display and tapped in a password. She held up the tablet and the loading-bay showed up on the screen in front of them.

"There's an *aura* in here," she said.

"Well, I did detect a certain tension, my dear, but I was hoping we could work through it."

Atherton smiled. She worked hard not to smile back. The tablet appeared to register something and a rotating circle of petal-like segments indicated it was buffering.

"Augmented Reality. CID piloted it last year," she said. "Think they only used it here and one RTA on the coast road. Another shit-load of cash wasted which could have paid off my mortgage two or three times over."

"What does it do?"

"They take SOCO footage and tag it to a geographic location. When you come back later, you can replay it in-situ," she said. "The camera recognises features of the room, knows it's in the right place and links you to a secure URL for the playback," she said.

"We're through the looking glass now, Alice," he said.

Video began to play on the screen, which had been filmed from approximately where they stood. Prejean held the tablet a little higher to get the angle right. The body lay on the floor, legs bound together and arms extended to the side. A halo of blood extended out from her bludgeoned head in a large crimson arc. The camera zoomed in on various areas of the body: the obliterated face, the blood stained blouse, the short, dark skirt and ripped tights and one shoe hanging partially from her foot.

The view then moved upwards, performing a slow pan of the loading-bay. It had been a different place at the time of the murder. Back then, the concrete floor had been unpainted and littered with leaves and other detritus. Now it was painted a glossy grey with markings for forklift trucks. The walls surrounding Prejean and Atherton now were bright white, but on the screen, they were covered with layer upon layer of graffiti.

Prejean became conscious of Atherton, who had bristled to attention beside her.

"What?"

"Have they changed the lighting in here or did SOCO bring in lighting rigs?" asked Atherton.

"I don't know," said Prejean. "I could check."

"The walls are white in here now, but it looks darker *now* than it does back then," he said.

"It could just be the camera or maybe they put in new lighting. Daylight lamps?"

Prejean went over to where the body had laid and crouched down, fluctuating her gaze from the screen and the bare floor. Atherton watched her. She seemed more assured than he remembered, more confident. Physically, she seemed more toned, her dress more professional. She looked up quickly, catching his stare and forcing him to look away.

He took himself to the far side of the room and flicked a couple of light switches to observe the effect. He strongly needed to sit down or at least lean somewhere. His hips ached, with an incessant nagging. It was getting late and he felt like a drink.

Ron appeared at the door to his office. "Alright?" he said.

"Fine," said Prejean, not looking up.

Ron stood awkwardly for a moment, before retreating into the room with a firm click of the door.

"Is there anything else we should look at?" asked Atherton. "If we stay here much longer, they'll give me a job and those forklifts will play havoc with my disco leg."

"Yes. Actually there's another aura."

Prejean put a hand down where the body had been so many months ago and rubbed it back and forth on the surface a couple of times. She stood and Atherton joined her. She pointed to a box inset on the main screen, which Atherton took to be a map of the area. In the centre, a green dot indicated the position of the aura they had watched. Not far from it, there was a second luminous dot.

Prejean looked around the room. "Wait here," she said and moved briskly away, paused to refer to the screen, then bounded up the steps towards Ron's office. The clank of each step echoed loudly. She stopped, held up the tablet once more and watched the screen silently.

"Ah...this would explain the lighting," she said. She made her way down to Atherton and handed him the tablet. He watched the room pan from left to right on the screen once more, this time from the vantage point of the mezzanine. The view shifted, angled upwards and Atherton saw why the light had appeared so different.

"So there was no roof at the time of the killing," he said. "Interesting."

She nodded and he smiled at her, forcing her to break eye contact this time.

"I think this calls for a drink."

"I don't think that's a good idea, do you?" she said.

*

As they entered the bar, a group of girls surveyed them, looking Prejean up and down; hair, shoes and outfit. Prejean brushed at a patch of dust on her skirt from the warehouse loading-bay. It failed to shift.

The bar was busy, but comfortably so, occupied mainly by an office Christmas party crowd. The music was low, but a bespectacled DJ was poised ominously behind a pair of decks positioned on a bed of tinsel at the far side of the room.

"Are you still on the red?" said Atherton.

"Vodka. Slim-line tonic," she replied.

Atherton paid the barman and nodded to a quieter looking area. They negotiated a path through the congregation at the bar. Atherton's lumbering gait caused him to spill a little of his pint as he walked and he noticed one of the girls regarding him with thinly veiled derision.

"Are you dancing later, love?" he said. "I'm built for the floor, as you can see."

The girl turned back to her friends.

Prejean took a seat at a small table with a view of the quayside. A well-dressed couple walked past, huddled against one another, battling against the cold and a strong wind that barrelled down the river. Across the water, the Sage concert hall was lit from within, looking like a distended mirror-ball sitting on the south bank of the Tyne.

Atherton placed the drinks precariously on the table, spilling more beer in the process, and tentatively took a seat.

"You know, I pay for a pint and only get to drink a half," he said.

"You should get a half in a pint glass," said Prejean.

"Ah-ha!" he said and tapped his temple. "This is why you are one of the top murder detectives in the north and why they keep me locked up at the university."

She watched him drink hungrily from his glass. It was clear alcohol still played a significant part in his life. She felt some degree of smugness at this thought, quickly replaced with a pang of guilt.

She regarded him. His mobility seemed to be declining and his speech was even worse, the drawl making him sound intoxicated at best, unintelligible at worst. She knew he had good days and bad, but then again, didn't everyone?

There was a long silence during which Prejean stabbed at her slice of lemon with a cocktail stick. The alcohol rested warmly in her stomach and she felt a long dormant urge for a cigarette.

"So, how's it going, Kate?"

She took a healthy swig of her drink and fixed him with her eyes.

"You mean, how've I been getting on since you dumped me?" she said, calmly. "You feeling guilty, Atherton?"

"No, I mean how are you, Kate?"

"Tell me, what's the point in this?" she said.

"I thought..."

"You thought it would be good to clear the air since we have to work together. Get us back to that collaborative sweet spot Myers thinks we occupy?"

"Well, we do have a sweet spot. Didn't we find a sweet spot?" he said. There was a definite glint in his eye.

She glared back at him and considered throwing her drink over him. He seemed to register this danger, his eyes fixed on her glass. As if choreographed, the girls from the bar filed over and took the vacant table opposite them. The moment passed.

"Okay," she said. "Some ground rules. This is the first and last drink I'm having with you."

Atherton sat back in his chair. Prejean noticed the palsy-affected side of his mouth had dropped a little further, as it did when he was uncomfortable with a situation. *Good*, she thought.

"Secondly, you follow my lead on this. We follow the evidence, not the psycho-theory bullshit. It gets us nowhere fast. You can contribute your profiling as we go, but if you take us off on some pointless bloody tangent, I'll go over Myers's head to get you taken off this, you understand?"

"Okay, Kate," he said. "Jesus. This is...unnecessary."

Her last comment had stung him deeper than he had expected.

"And finally, you keep this fucking professional." She struggled to maintain her temper and volume. "Do you know how much shit I got into last time, while you flounced away scot-free?"

"I'd hate to disagree with you there, when you've got such a momentum going, but I wouldn't exactly say *scot-free*," he said.

"A few nights on the settee was it? They suspended me, Jon. I almost got demoted."

"I almost got fucking *divorced*." His voice was raised and he involuntarily spat a little on the 'F'. She resisted the urge to wipe her cheek and could sense the office girls tuning into their conversation. One of them began to show off her new shoes, extending her legs out to model them as the others cooed.

Atherton took several gulps of his drink. "Ten months of relationship therapy and counting, two months in the spare room, my own daughter not even talking to me," he said. "I think I've had my own share of punishment. I nearly lost my bloody family, so forgive me if I don't weep for the little note in your personnel file, love."

"You know what? Fuck this. I might have to work with you, but I don't have to listen to this shit."

Prejean stood up, downed the remains of her drink and struggled slightly to gather her things together. Atherton watched her leave silently. As she strode past the table of girls, she saw one of them whisper something to her neighbour.

"You've left the label on the bottom of your shoe, pet," said Prejean. "Forty percent off."

Despite everything, Atherton laughed and they all looked at him. He raised his pint and struggled to wink.

"Well ladies, in an unexpected turn of events, I'm all yours," he said.

CHAPTER FIVE

Prejean was at the station gym by seven-thirty.

When it was busy, the basement room became hot and sweaty, poorly served by rotary fans in each corner, but if she got there early enough, she was virtually guaranteed to have the place to herself and it was cool enough to be bearable.

She chose her usual treadmill and clipped her tablet onto the control panel, so she could read as she ran. She set off at a relaxed pace. The temptation was always to have that extra time in bed, but she never regretted it once she got started. The cardio shunted her body into action and – she liked to think – her mind in the process.

She swiped her finger across the surface of the tablet and pressed the email icon, opening a long message from Sue Cresswell. It was a summary of all the forensic activity from Bottleburn to date, with most sections having a postscript of *pending further analysis*. She touched the screen to scroll and read the rest:

Skull: multiple fractures and probable cause of death. Preliminary examination suggests repeated blows with a blunt weapon. Pending further analysis.

She clicked out of the email and opened up the folder of photographs from the warehouse loading-bay. She left it on a hideous shot of Izzy Lynch, her face pummelled beyond recognition. Perhaps both the riverbank and loading-bay killings had a murder weapon in common. She knew she was clutching at straws, but made a mental note to raise it with Myers.

The treadmill speed increased by an increment and she glanced at herself in the mirror which spanned the entire length of the room. She was happy with the person she saw there now; sleek in her black running leggings and matching top, she looked strong and purposeful, arms tanned and taut. She made a conscious effort to let her shoulders relax as the front of the treadmill lifted slightly and her thighs began to burn at the increased gradient.

She looked down at the screen again and flicked through a selection of pictures from the loading-bay. She looked at a wide shot of the body, the large halo of blood around the head. How pathetic Izzy's last moments must have been. Unconscious, unable to fight back, and the battle already fought and lost in the killer's vehicle. When the door behind her rattled open, she barely registered the noise.

"Most people just listen to dance music," said a male voice beside her, startling her somewhat. She looked over. It was the new guy from Myers's team.

"Richards, isn't it?"

"Rogers," he said extending a hand. "We've met once before, DS Prejean."

"Oh yes, I'm sorry," she said and they shook hands awkwardly across the treadmills. "It's pronounced *pray-john,* though. Soft 'J'. It's French."

"I'm sorry," he said quickly.

"That's quite alright. I'm sure it rattles off the tongue in Bordeaux. Anyway, I was just trying to get my head around some of this before the briefing," she said.

Rogers placed a gym towel over the rail on the treadmill and a water bottle into the plastic holder. Prejean stole another look at him: pleasingly athletic, if a little shorter than her. His running shorts revealed powerful thighs and his skin-tight top suggested a muscular upper body. She remembered where she'd talked to him before: a brief flirtation with him at the tail end of a birthday night out in town. Nothing overt; a playful look in his eyes and a couple of cheeky remarks. He'd been testing the water and she'd bypassed it entirely. What had stopped her then? More to the point, if he was still interested, what was to stop her now?

He selected a program and started jogging at a leisurely pace. Prejean clicked off the tablet, but when she looked up at the mirror, he was watching her again with piercing blue eyes.

"If only it were that easy," he said.

"What's that?"

"To switch off," he said. "I can't stop thinking about it."

"Is this your first homicide?" she asked.

He smiled. "Not exactly, but I've never seen anything like this."

"That makes two of us. Were you out at Bottleburn?" she said.

"Yes ma'am," he said. "It was awful."

"Don't call me ma'am. I'm sure your mother wouldn't like it," she said.

He smiled and appeared to relax a little. "Okay," he said.

"So, what did you think?" she said. A heavy frown creased Rogers's brow. "It's not a test. I haven't been out there yet. I wanted to know what you thought."

"In what way?"

"Scene, victim, evidence...what did it tell you about what happened?"

Rogers smiled. "So it *is* a test."

"A little," she said, smiling back.

"Well, I don't think you could describe this as a typical murder," he said.

"Go on."

"It feels ritualistic," he said, taking his first swig from the water bottle. "It was like...the way he laid out all the body parts was supposed to mean something."

"Like what?"

"I don't know. The way he'd positioned things like the head and other pieces of the body...it's almost arrogance. Like he's saying 'look what I can do, look at my power.'"

"Did you think the victim knew her killer?"

"I don't know. I'd hope not. It was like the body meant nothing to him, like it was just..." He searched for the right word. "Raw material...you know...stuff to do a particular job."

"I think I know what you mean," said Prejean. She'd already had her doubts on that front and would be surprised if the statements from family and friends came back with anything worth pursuing. "But couldn't it be someone she's rattled the wrong way? A spurned love can provoke strong feelings."

"Might be wrong, but I don't think so," he said. "The other thing I thought was what a nice spot it was. If it hadn't been covered in blood, I mean. I thought maybe that was important. The scenery. I know that sounds ridiculous, but it's just my gut feel."

"Hey, I don't think there are any wrong answers at the minute," she said, having to make a conscious effort not to sound out of breath. "So, you think we're after a National Trust member?"

He smiled. "Maybe. I've never trusted ramblers."

They both jogged in silence for a while.

"You didn't mention any of the physical evidence," she said.

"Well, there's precious little of it."

"Sue will have more for us later," said Prejean.

"Can I ask you something?"

"Sure." She was starting to build up a good sweat now. She licked her lips and tasted salt.

"What does Atherton think?" he said, looking at her in the mirror to gauge her reaction.

"He's working a profile, which he'll share with us when he's ready."

"But does he think the warehouse killing was the same guy? Could it be a serial killer?"

"The warehouse killing felt very different," she said. "And even if it was the same killer, it still wouldn't be a serial case..."

"Until there were three related murders, I know."

"If the scenery was an important factor, the warehouse was a little less picturesque, I'll tell you that much."

"Yeah. No. I mean, I've seen the photos too," he said.

"I think maybe it's a bit ambitious trying to link the two at the moment."

"And Atherton?"

Atherton's arse, she thought.

"I don't know what Atherton thinks yet. I'll no doubt find out when you do," she said.

"But you've...worked with him before?"

"I think you know I did, Rogers," she said. "I would imagine you know all about the affair I had with him too."

Rogers averted his eyes from the mirror, but nodded sheepishly.

Prejean tapped a button on the treadmill dash, slowing the pace down rapidly and she allowed herself to slide off the end. She grabbed her things quickly and headed towards the changing rooms.

"I just want to find the bastard," called Rogers. "I hope we can take him down before he even thinks of doing it again. That's all."

She turned and faced him breathing heavily, but his eyes were fixed on himself in the mirror.

"Okay. I'm sorry, Rogers," she said.

"Chris," he replied.

"Chris."

"Is it true that Atherton has a psycho's brain?" said Rogers.

"You're not far from the truth. You should ask him, but ask for the short version."

She pushed through the door into the corridor beyond, welcoming the cool air on her skin.

*

Harsh light woke Atherton.

He registered the stark white walls and turned over onto his side, away from the window. A spasm in his left arm precluded any further sleep. He was aware of movement elsewhere in the house; Hannah pottering about with her toy kitchen and exchanging muted chat with imaginary friends. If Louise was up already, he couldn't hear her.

He'd been in the midst of an anxiety dream, one which had recurred through the years since before his graduation. It always began with him struggling to get to an examination on time, through the busy streets of Newcastle city centre. His legs, and the crowds of shoppers slowing him down, but more than that, it was like walking through treacle, his limbs numb and useless, as if the palsy had spread throughout his entire body. Sometimes he made it to the examination hall, a converted gymnasium which merged with his memories of his high school. It was never as it should be. It would be locked, the other students staring out blankly at him through the glass of the door, or an impassable pile of junk would block the corridor. Whatever the impediment, he'd be forced to find another route, along deserted corridors and dead ends until finally he awoke with his heart racing and a hanging dread he'd always be too late.

The events of the previous evening slotted slowly into place: Kate walking out. Another drink at the quayside bar, until it became uncomfortably busy. Then a cold walk up the hill into town to his university local where he'd found a couple of well-oiled colleagues from the faculty.

He'd stayed too late. There was a sour, metallic taste in his mouth. Oh, yes; a trip to the kebab shop on the way home. He had vague recollections of struggling to stay vertical as he left the place, his leg misbehaving badly, not aided by greasy patches on the shop floor. And then a long walk home, with a number of people moving to avoid him on the path. Even without a drink on him, he looked like someone to be avoided, his walking problem and speech so easily confused with intoxication.

He checked the time on his phone and knew he had to get going. He would have to get a taxi to the warehouse to collect the car before he did anything and then double back on himself to get to the station in time for the briefing.

Pressure in his bladder compelled him to get up and he struggled to his feet, his left hip complaining painfully in the process. The palsy and the way it forced an overstep with his left leg – his 'pimp roll' as Louise used to call it – had led to excessive wear and pressure on the ball joint. A hip replacement was probably just a few years away. He walked up the hallway towards the bathroom, drawing level with Hannah's open door.

"Daddy!" shouted Hannah, a broad smile spanning her face and she ran forward, hugging his leg. "Do you want a cup of tea?"

"Well, that would be lovely," he said.

She released him, pirouetted back to the wooden kitchen and busied herself with some minute porcelain teacups bearing a kitten logo. The floor of her room was littered with random items of clothing, cuddly toys and various bits and bobs made of brightly coloured plastic.

"Do you like some cheese for breakfast?" she said, placing a bright yellow piece of plastic cheese onto a plate.

"Yes, please," he said, taking the cup and plate from her and pretending to take a drink.

"I had a bit of a bad dream last night, Daddy," she said, looking at him with a well-practiced look of forlornness.

"Oh really? I'm sorry to hear that, love. What happened?"

"There was someone up at the window, scratching to get in. I think it was a monster," she said.

"Well, there are no monsters allowed around here. Do you know why?" He cuddled her close.

"Why?"

"Because Daddy is the protector. It's his job to make sure no-one hurts you or Mammy."

"Or Giraffe?" She held up the scruffy soft toy which she refused to let them wash.

"Or Giraffe," he said. "Look here. You see this scar?" He rolled up his sleeve to show her the raised white scar tissue on his upper arm. She reached out with her tiny fingers to touch it. "That's where I fought off an ogre once."

"No you didn't, Daddy," she said, laughing.

"I did," he said, tickling her side and forcing her to writhe in giggles.

"What's he telling you, love?" said Louise, who was now standing at the bedroom door.

"He's making up porky pies," said Hannah.

"He better not be," said Louise. "Have you brushed your teeth?"

Hannah jumped up and ran past Louise into the bathroom and they heard the sound her small feet slap on the tiles, then water from the tap. Louise folded her arms and looked down on Atherton.

"Have you brushed *your* teeth?"

"I have," he said and showed her an exaggerated smile.

"How *did* you get that scar?" she said.

"I told you that. Didn't I?"

"No."

He put a hand on the bedpost to help himself up.

"It was an accident," he said. "Someone thought they could bunny hop over me when I was a kid."

"Bunny hop?"

"Jump over me on a bike. Come on, you remember bunny hopping and endos and three-sixties?"

"No," she said, raising her eyebrows.

"You're kidding me? Yeah, just a lad from school tried to jump over me and came down on my arm with his pedal. Ripped it wide open," he said. "It looked like I'd been shot. I was pretty cool for about a minute."

"No, I don't think you've ever told me that," she said, yawning. "I think I'd have remembered."

She turned away and Atherton heard her slippers padding down the staircase. He looked at the scar for a moment, trying to resist the desperate sinking feeling which always came with the memories, but it came anyway. One pimply face in particular came into mind, followed by a voice and the smell of cheap aftershave mixed with body odour. He could feel his heart rate begin to rise and a sweat form on his back. This was what his friend Osram talked about when he rambled on about implicit memories. Run of the mill memories get date-stamped and filed away as they should be. Traumatic ones remain unfiled and held in a mental staging area, where they can be all too readily reviewed.

Hannah came bounding back into the room.

"Why were you in the little room last night, Daddy?" she said.

"I got in late, sugar. I didn't want to wake up Mammy," he said.

"I was in Mammy's bed last night," she said proudly. "If you'd have come in you might have squashed me."

"Oh, I hope not," he said.

There was another spasm in his arm.

"Is your arm shaky today, Daddy?"

"It is a bit, love, yes," he said, smiling.

"Is it gone a bit disco inferno?"

He laughed.

"Yes. Thanks for my tea and cheese. I'm going to have to go to the toilet now, okay?"

"Okay, Daddy."

In the bathroom, he urinated and then moved to the basin where he washed his hands and face. He looked worse than he felt. Hangovers never hit him too hard. He unlocked the bathroom cabinet and removed a couple of boxes before returning to the spare room.

Sitting on the bed, he cracked open a sterile needle and secured it to a new plastic syringe. He shook a small ampoule of botulinum toxin, inverted it and stabbed through the membrane to draw in the colourless solution. He found a suitable spot on his arm and injected. He gave it a moment and curled his arm a couple of times. He became aware of Louise behind him.

"You shouldn't let Hannah see you do that," she said.

"I have to do it somewhere," he said, flexing his arm once more. "It's bad today."

"You sounded bad last night," she said. "Clattering around the place."

"I'm sorry," he said. She began to close the door. "What are you two doing today?" he asked.

"I need to get some Christmas shopping done," she said. "Home for lunch and we'll take it from there. You?"

"There's a briefing I need to be at. This thing in Bottleburn," he said.

"Do you think you'll be joining us at any point over the holidays?" she asked.

He looked at her but she seemed to be avoiding eye contact.

"You do know what happened out there?" he said.

"You're joking, right?" she replied. Ellis Brampton's face had been all over the TV for a couple of days now. Louise looked tired and pale. He wondered if she'd already started reducing her dosage.

How much of her mood was down to a genuine grievance with him and how much was biochemical?

"I've agreed to write a preliminary assessment and that's it," he said.

"A profile?"

"If they need one. If there's enough to go on," he said. He put the botox ampoule back into its box and cleared up the syringe. "I thought that since we'd be having a bit more money coming in, we could book a little holiday in the new year? Maybe just a week, before I go back to work?"

She raised a non-committal eyebrow.

"What about your marking?"

"I'll fit it in. It'll be okay," he said.

She turned and left him. A few moments later, he heard her talking warmly to Hannah and the creak of the banister as they went downstairs. He went into the bedroom and looked out the window. The sky was dull grey and the bare trees reached upwards, with branches like gnarled fingers. It was warm in the house and he was on holiday in the build-up to Christmas. A carol began to play brightly from the TV downstairs and he felt a sudden pang of guilt at his enthusiasm to get back to work.

*

If Paul Myers felt any pressure regarding the Brampton case, it didn't show. He appeared calm and focused, almost to the point of detachment. Prejean watched him as he talked on the phone. There were media challenges to overcome and most likely a press conference to organise; a moment for Myers to shine. Prejean had always found him strangely dispassionate, almost asexual.

She put a hand through her hair and found it to be still a little wet from the shower. Through the glass walls of Myers's office, she saw Sue Cresswell and Chris Rogers already talking in the briefing room, along with two of Myers's team she had never met; a black girl in her late twenties and a heavy set middle-aged man with a receding hairline.

"How did it go last night, Kate?" asked Myers, finally clicking out of his call.

"Good. We played the footage and got a feel for the scene," she said.

"Are we clutching at straws trying to link that one with Bottleburn?"

"Maybe, sir," she said. "But it's something we need to pursue at least. We don't get that many unexplained violent deaths."

"True."

"And if you consider the cause of death for both looks like head trauma, we could very well have a common MO."

"Let's see what Sue has to say about that," he said. Then, after a pause, "How was Atherton?"

"Taking it all in," she said. "You know how he is. He doesn't say something until he has something to say."

"I know he presents a difficult situation for you, Kate and if he becomes any sort of liability to this case or your ability to work it, he's out when you say the word," he said.

"Thank you," she said. She looked him in the eye. "I appreciate that, but in the meantime, maybe he can offer his perspective."

Myers tapped on the desk absently. Prejean knew he was already way ahead of this conversation and onto the next.

"Good. That being the case, I'd like you and him to go out to Bottleburn this afternoon to review the scene," he said. "Have the rest of the team do the donkeywork on statements and following up on anything else which comes out of the briefing. I want him back in that field while it still feels fresh."

"Okay," she said and felt a sinking feeling in her stomach.

"I should introduce you to the others and let you get started," he said, getting to his feet. Prejean stood and followed him out of the room. The team fell silent upon their approach.

"Introductions. Sue you already know, of course?"

Prejean nodded and smiled at Sue.

"DC Chris Rogers," said Myers.

"We've just met," said Prejean.

"This is DC Connie Amis, who transferred from somewhere awful down south, I believe," said Myers.

"He means Sunderland, don't you, guv? We'll see how cocky you are at the end of the season," she said and shook Prejean's hand, smiling warmly.

Prejean liked her immediately. Behind stylish glasses, her eyes shone with a bright intelligence and as Amis leaned towards her, she noticed the tiniest diamond nose stud glinting against her dark honey skin.

"And this is DC David Walsh."

"Hello. Nice to meet you," said Walsh. He had plenty of hair on the back and sides, but very little on top. That which remained on his crown reminded her of a baby bird; soft, thin and somewhat greasy. Mid-forties and a little pudgy round the middle, Walsh had a tired, washed-out look to his face. He shook her hand in a business-like manner and Prejean took a hit of stale coffee from his breath.

She stepped back a little from them all and Myers gestured to her that the floor was hers.

"It's good to meet you all and I'm sure it's going to be a pleasure to work together," she began. "Have no doubt that this is going to be a very high profile case, but don't let that distract you from the job." She glanced from face to face. "Let me and Superintendent Myers deal with all that shit."

"And it *is* shit," interjected Myers. They laughed politely.

"Last thing," said Prejean. "We're a team and I want us to act like one. We support each other until this case is done. There's no such thing as a stupid idea. I want to hear everything you've got. The only stupid idea is to keep something to yourself which could move the case forward."

"Thank you, Kate," said Myers. "I think all we are waiting for now is..."

And, as if on cue, Atherton appeared at the door.

"Sorry I'm late, chaps," he said.

*

Another board had been tentatively placed in the focus room next to that of Ellis Brampton; it held photographs of the warehouse murder and details of the victim, as if a link could be found by the proximity of the boards alone.

"Sue, you're top of the agenda, as always. What do you have for us?" said Prejean.

Sue Cresswell pushed her glasses further onto her nose. Although there was a stack of files in front of her, she didn't refer to them.

"Female victim. Late twenties. Confirmed as Ellis Brampton by tissue DNA and prior to that, fingerprints were found to be a strong match," she said, sharing eye contact between Atherton and Prejean. As she talked, Atherton couldn't help himself from glancing at the photographs of Izzy Lynch and Brampton on the boards at either side of her.

"Time of death estimated at 2AM, give or take an hour. I can confirm that we have a full body, if you'll excuse the irony," she said.

"A full set of internal organs?" asked Atherton.

"Yes. Everything accounted for. We have a bite mark to the neck with a small amount of missing tissue, but otherwise nothing missing," she said.

"No souvenirs, then?" said Walsh.

"No parts of the victim's anatomy, at least," said Sue.

"Her clothes haven't emerged yet," suggested Amis. "Bag, purse, belongings. The killer could still have all or some of them."

"Can you check on the statements so we are all very clear on what she left work with please, Connie?"

"Got it," she said.

"A souvenir doesn't have to be a physical item," said Atherton. "Sue, what can you tell us about the tripod?"

"A little bit." She pulled out a set of photographs from the pile. "We have two sets of indentations. One set of four and one set of three, suggesting he sat behind a tripod."

"So he filmed it?" said Rogers. Then under his breath, "Sick fucker."

"Or photographed," said Atherton. "Something to help him enjoy the memory of the moment. The enjoyment of his act."

"I've got someone looking at camping chairs and tripods," she said, "and we're having a stab at weight, based on the depth of the indentations. Don't get your hopes up on that one."

"Sure," said Prejean.

"Okay," said Sue. "Getting to the act itself. There's a total lack of defensive or ligature marks on Brampton's body, suggesting that she was unconscious before she was killed by several blows to the back of the head."

"What with?" asked Rogers. "Hammer?"

"No. Examination suggests a blunt instrument with a long area of contact. Something cylindrical with an approximate five centimetre diameter."

"Like a pipe?" said Rogers.

"Something along those lines," she said.

"So she was dead before he cut her up?" said Amis. Atherton looked at her; he was impressed with her bluntness.

"Yes, we can tell her heart had stopped beating from the blood pattern. It pooled here..." Sue turned and pointed to a photograph on the board, the bloody riverbank with a large dark red area. "And we don't have any arterial sprays or other spatter apart from a little cast-off from the weapon and drips from the various body parts."

"Moving on to Izzy Lynch. What was the murder weapon, Sue?" asked Prejean.

"You've stolen my thunder, Kate." Sue smiled grimly, as she stood up and positioned herself between the two boards. She pointed to the picture of Brampton. "We can measure the dimensions of the weapon with confidence here. There were only a small number of blows."

She took a moment to delve into the stack of papers and pinned up an x-ray photograph of Brampton's head. Alongside the areas of shattered skull were measuring scales.

"Lynch wasn't as easy to decipher, due to the severity of the injuries." She pinned another x-ray, this time on Lynch's board. The skull had been shattered like the shell of a boiled egg. She placed a mortuary picture of Lynch beside the x-ray and pointed to a purple mark on her pale white cheek. "Obviously, the victim was beaten with a blunt instrument, but this particular contusion tells us it was something cylindrical with an approximate five centimetre diameter."

"Boom. Same murder weapon?" said Rogers.

"Or very similar," said Sue.

Prejean saw Atherton's eyes light up. "So," she said. "We possibly have a common murder weapon. Let's not get too excited, until we can match other aspects of the MO."

"There's more," said Sue. "Bloods came back this morning and there appears to be a common drug involved. Ketamine hydrochloride, the horse tranquilliser. Controlled in most European countries, so therefore available anywhere, of course."

"David, is that something you could take a look at?" said Prejean.

Walsh nodded. He absently picked a large flake of dried skin from behind his ear, marvelling at the size of it before letting it drop to the floor.

"Injected into the neck in both cases," said Sue. "They'd not go down straight away, but I'm betting it wouldn't take long. I've called in some advice on this from a friend in the Met."

"Good. Thanks, Sue," said Prejean.

"The level for Brampton was almost twice the dose for Lynch," she said. "I'll need to get some pointers on dosage effects."

"Maybe he fucked up the dose first time around," said Walsh. "Maybe Lynch started to come around and he panicked. That's why the...what would you call that?"

"Carnage?" suggested Amis.

"Massive heard trauma," said Sue.

"What about sex?" asked Amis.

"Anytime you like, but perhaps you could wait until after the meeting?" said Walsh, smiling.

"My sides have totally split," Amis replied.

"No evidence of rape in either case," said Sue. "No DNA. No semen from the vagina or anus. No evidence of bruising in those areas, but, you might not expect so much of that with an unconscious victim."

"I thought sex and death went hand in hand with these guys, doc?" said Rogers.

Prejean noticed a playful look in his eye as he addressed Atherton. He took a moment to answer.

"*These guys?* I don't think that's helpful. Often there's a sexual aspect, yes, but it's not a prerequisite."

"So, two motiveless murders with mutilation?" said Rogers.

"No," said Atherton. "Don't be so naive as to think these crimes are motiveless. There is no such thing as a motiveless murder." He leaned on the table to leverage himself onto his feet; a slow process. He walked to Brampton's board. "What do you see here? A random act of violence? Chaos or carnage?" They looked at the photographs of Brampton's decapitated head, limbs and organs. "There's purpose and direction here, chaps. He's gone to an awful lot of trouble to get this done. He's taken this girl, undetected, from a place where hundreds of people work together every day and quickly and carefully dissected her in the open air. He put himself at quite some risk to do that. There's order and organisation running right through his actions. I'd say he was very motivated. Just because we don't understand it yet doesn't mean the motive isn't there."

"Okay, thanks Jon," said Prejean, after a heavy silence.

"Jean Paul Sartre called it *magical thinking*." Atherton struck a pose, with his hands extended in front of him. "He's thinking with his emotions, not reason. For example, there was a guy in the fifties who raped and decapitated a girl in Birmingham because he thought it would make him feel less anxious about sex. Our killer imagines that by killing, it will help him achieve something or address some perceived imbalance, or injustice in his life. He thinks by doing A, he'll get B. If we can work out what B is we can catch him, before he does more of A."

He looked on the verge of saying more, but grew silent and thoughtful. His attention was taken by the photograph of the Brampton scene: the dark patch where she had been dismembered, the various body parts strewn around. He looked at three pieces which formed a prominent line; the head, the heart and another organ he didn't recognise.

"What do you have to do to get a cup of coffee around here?" he said.

"Good point," said Prejean. "Let's break for five."

As the others began to leave the room, Atherton gently touched Sue's arm.

"Help me out here," he said. "What's this next to her head and heart?"

"You don't know what that is, Jon? You surprise me," she said. "It's the vagina."

CHAPTER SIX

The Range Rover swept them quickly away from the city, out to undulating hills and farmland. Atherton watched it go by. There was virtual silence: only the engine, the creak of leather and the radio, which was too quiet to hear properly, too loud to ignore.

"They seem like a good bunch," said Atherton finally. He'd been trying to absorb the scenery rather than look at Prejean's stockinged knee which rose occasionally to change gear.

"Oh really? How do they seem?"

"Amis is bright, inquisitive. Walsh...less so," he said.

"I hear he's good to have on follow-up. Tenacious," she said, checking the rear view mirror. "What do you think of Rogers?"

"Career man, isn't he? Thinks he's in a movie of his own life. You know how I hate ambition."

"I'm ambitious."

"Ah, but you have a range of other qualities, Kate."

Like what? The question arose to the line Atherton had cast, but Prejean resisted. "What did you ask Sue before we left?"

"The three pieces of Ms Brampton arranged all in a line. I didn't know what the last piece was," he said.

"Head, heart and vagina."

"Yes. Mind, soul and sexuality."

"The essence of a person? Of a woman?" she said.

"Maybe."

"You're the monster collector. Have you studied anything similar?"

"Well, you've got to go back to a great British original, like myself," said Atherton, becoming more animated. "Jack the Ripper's second girl. Annie Chapman. She was disembowelled in a backyard. He set the contents of her pockets around her very ritualistically. He was exposed, out in the open and could have been discovered at any time, but he took the time to arrange things just so..." Atherton placed imaginary items on the dashboard in front of him, with his good hand.

"And?"

"So, the arrangement of the body parts is important. It means something," he said.

"Like what?"

"Like, he never won at Scrabble. Who knows?"

"But you think our man's like the Ripper?" asked Prejean. She had an uncomfortable image of a *Northumbrian Ripper* newspaper headline, which she couldn't shake.

"You might want to think a little further South for a better comparison," said Atherton.

Kate sensed he was beginning to enjoy himself. "*Il Mostro*, the Monster of Florence, one of the few serial killers to use a gun. Most killers like to get up close and personal when they do their business, and therein lies the thrill. Il Mostro did too of course, but not before he eliminated any threat."

"He'd attack a couple, take out the man first and then shoot the woman, before getting nasty with her body," said Prejean.

"Well remembered. In fact, if our killer has similarities to any Ripper, he's more like Sutcliffe: a hammer to subdue them, knives to do the actual job. He's not in it for the struggle. I don't think that part excites him. He drugs them, kills them with a pipe or whatever and then gets down to the bit which is important to him."

Prejean thought for a moment.

"Do you think he's a small guy?" she said after some time.

"A size seven shoe at the Lynch scene certainly suggests so. Let's hope Sue can come up with an estimated weight. A little guy, with a thing for tall ladies."

She ignored this entirely.

"Your typical sexually orientated psychopath usually cuts around the genitalia, breasts or buttocks. Our man doesn't seem interested in that so much," said Prejean.

"Yes, that crossed my mind with the Lynch scene," said Atherton. "Arms akimbo, but not the legs? Sex may not be a driver for him," said Atherton. "Or it could be something he's building up to."

"Why do you say that?"

"I think he's refining his MO," said Atherton. "Look at Lynch, the working girl. Taken from an isolated part of town, unlikely to be missed for days, to a fairly secure place. Then, when he's experimented and knows what he's capable of, he comes back a year later, takes Brampton from her place of work and kills her right out in the open. Lynch was low risk, low gain. Brampton was high risk, high gain. He'll have even more confidence now. Unless there's a temporal pattern to his ritual we don't know about yet, I'd expect the next one to come sooner."

Prejean looked at him. Whilst there wasn't any apparent enthusiasm when he mentioned another victim, she didn't care for his stoicism.

"So, Lynch was a dry run?" said Prejean.

"Possibly. In a way," said Atherton. "He obliterated Lynch's features, but celebrated Brampton's with makeup. I think Lynch could have looked like anyone, but maybe Brampton was more like an ideal he was looking for."

"Dark hair, good looking, athletic?"

"Yep. He then left a long time between the first and second killings."

"He was getting ready?"

"Most definitely. If we consider organised versus disorganised behaviour, our guy definitely falls into the organised arena. I mean, *IKEA* organised. The scenes look chaotic and frenzied and the kills may be just that, but his preparation is anything but."

They pulled into the same spot Atherton had occupied several days previously and the lane felt empty without the fleet of police and SOCO vehicles. Prejean opened the door and grabbed her bag from the rear seats. The cold air hit his lungs and he saw his breath escape in a plume as he exhaled. He took a moment to remove a pair of leather gloves from his jacket pocket and put them on.

"Of course, your boys pissed on their own chips to a certain extent with regards to physical evidence here," he said. "There could have been some nicely frozen and traceable tyre tracks available had they not driven right over them."

They started down the path, with Atherton struggling to keep up with Prejean's pace. Soon, the trees opened up revealing the meadow and riverbank.

"Long way down for a little bloke to carry someone," said Prejean.

"Or drag someone," said Atherton. "So, a little fella with big muscles. Shit at scrabble. We're narrowing the field, Prejean, every step of the way."

They made their way through the long grass to the scene. The place where Brampton had been found was now all but indistinguishable from the rest of the area. The remains had been meticulously bagged and removed and heavy showers had washed the blood from the grass. It fascinated Atherton how quickly nature recovered from the horrors inflicted upon it.

"So," said Prejean. "He carries...or drags...her, unconscious down from the lane, picks a spot, then bosh, back of the head. Why not the front, like Lynch?"

"He didn't want to damage her looks," he said. Prejean raised her eyebrows. "He's spent some valuable time on her make-up, to get her to her look the way he wants. It's important to him that she looks her best."

"I think you're right. Okay, so she's looking like Kate Moss, then he caves in her skull, cuts her up here and arranges the bits here," she said, making her way to the point Brampton had been found. "With her head, heart and privates lined up so conspicuously, like they're on parade."

"Pretty much. Then he goes down to the river to wash." Atherton pointed to the part of the river where he'd found more of Brampton's blood.

"You think he was naked? It's not quite the weather for skinny dipping."

Atherton nodded cautiously. She knew he was already thinking about something else.

"I'd hazard a guess he was. It was cold, but it would be practical if nothing else. He'd be absolutely covered in blood," he said, looking down. "And what's this?"

She joined him at his side. There was a hole in the ground only feet away from the crime scene.

"Sue's boys," said Prejean. "She got someone to bag up soil for the lab. They're loading up camping chairs with different weights to get an estimate."

"Whatever turns you on, I suppose," said Atherton. "My money says it'll come back that he's a little bloke. I think he's slight, or at least he's not confident in his strength. He needs them unconscious. He doesn't want to have to tackle them." He paused and turned three-sixty degrees. "Quite a display he left for us, don't you think?" Prejean looked puzzled. "This was very ritualised. This all means something to him. I just wonder if he climbed that tree to look down on it all when he was finished?"

Prejean looked up at the tall, bare sycamore.

"Why don't you get up there and have a look?" she said. He adjusted his stance, put his bad leg forward and gave her a sorrowful look.

"I honestly don't think I could manage that, Kate."

She sighed, dropped the bag from her shoulder and looked him in the eyes.

"Just touch me as little as possible, please," she said.

Atherton hunkered against the tree and offered up his cradled hands. She put one foot on them and Atherton boosted her up. As she reached out to the lowest branch, her blouse rode up to reveal a flat midriff, just inches from Atherton's face. He could smell soap and skin cream. She pulled herself up confidently and took a seated position amongst several of the lower limbs.

"Well," said Atherton. "First things first. Can you see a pub?"

Prejean ignored him.

"He'd get a good view from here, definitely. If the light was adequate," she said.

"It wasn't quite a full moon that night. A waning gibbous, if you will, so the ambient light wouldn't have been too bad. There's one streetlamp too, up there at the start of the path. If he had a torch or IR goggles, I don't think he'd have to use them much."

Prejean surveyed the area. It would have given an ideal plan view of the scene. From the elevated position, she could see the water in the river, flowing off to the west and rippling in the fading light.

"Any signs that someone else might have been up there?" said Atherton.

"You were expecting to see a name? Bob was here?"

"Or a muddy boot print, or fibres. You know, Detective Sergeant; physical evidence I think they call it," he said.

She took several minutes to give it a thorough examination.

"Not a thing," she said, finally. "What now?"

Atherton began rifling through a supermarket plastic bag, which Prejean hadn't noticed he'd been carrying.

"I was hoping you might help me eat these." He produced a couple of pre-packed sandwiches. Prejean checked her watch.

"You'll have to get me down from here first," she said.

*

As they ate, they looked at the crime scene photographs, each anchored to the grass by a pebble. Prejean arranged them so that each was positioned in the correct orientation corresponding to the crime scene. She couldn't help but check the path to the road and the riverbank periodically for people walking, fearful their macabre picnic might be interrupted. Atherton chewed enthusiastically and obliviously on his lunch.

"Myers will start pushing for a profile," said Prejean.

"He can have one by tomorrow's get-together," he said.

"And then what?"

"And then it's over to you, and I go back to marking essays."

"Okay," she said.

"I'm around if you need me, but I know all this makes you uncomfortable. Maybe I should be at the end of a phone, not in your briefing room," he said, not meeting her eye.

Prejean took another bite of her sandwich and chewed it slowly.

"Does Louise know we're working together?" she said.

"We haven't exactly discussed it, but I think she has a fair idea," he said.

She looked at him, but he was lost in the photographs.

"I'll talk it over with Myers," she said. "If you can give us a strong profile, he'll probably be happy enough for you take a back seat."

Atherton stopped chewing. His mouth dropped slightly and he placed a firm hand on her knee. She instinctively grabbed his wrist and began to prise his hand off her.

"Jon..."

"Shut up," he said. "There's someone over there."

He pointed and Prejean looked across to where the row of trees marked the beginning of the incline to the road. She just caught sight of the dark figure of a man disappearing into the foliage. Atherton was already on his feet, throwing the remains of his lunch back into the bag and the two of them covered the fifty metres to the treeline. Prejean made it first, but the man was gone, seemingly having climbed the steep embankment in little time. Presently, they heard the sound of a car engine. Where they stood was a rarely-used dirt path, all but covered with grass and weeds. Atherton's eyes scanned the ground and he crouched forward awkwardly to get a better look.

"Cigarette butts. Three at least. They look reasonably fresh," he said.

Prejean pulled out her phone immediately.

"Fuck it. No signal," she said. "It's okay, I have evidence bags in the car."

"He was watching us," he said. His tone was almost gleeful, childlike. "He was watching us."

Prejean started to answer, but something caught her attention and she stopped, bolt upright, looking over Atherton's shoulder.

"Look," she said and pointed to the trunk of the tree behind him. Atherton turned.

Carved into the bark of the tree were two elaborately drawn eyes.

CHAPTER SEVEN

Paul Myers clicked off his phone and placed it back on the charger.

He glanced at the yellow note on the desk, reminding him to ring his sister about maybe meeting for lunch. It was too late though, now. She would understand, but it still made him feel bad.

The Family Liaison Officer he'd just spoken to was among the best. Tasked with liaising with Brampton's family and keeping them up to date with developments and formalities, his secondary concern was to ascertain if there were any indications that the boyfriend – or other family members – had anything to hide. There was nothing: the man was inconsolable and his alibi was solid. Myers felt confident there was nothing to be gained from probing further in that direction.

The situation at Brampton's work was another matter. He didn't envy Amis and Walsh, who'd been given the job of obtaining statements from up to one hundred and eighty office workers who shared the building. He picked up the phone again, found Amis's mobile number in the contacts list and called.

"Amis," she answered.

"Amis, it's Myers. Prejean is offline until later, so I'm just checking in."

"Just stepping out of the interview room, sir," she said. Myers knew that Menshen had let them use an office in the building. In the background, he could hear Walsh's deep voice talking to someone. "Sir?"

"How's it going?"

"Okay. We've done the ground floor and started on the first. Top floor is an IT company with a contract for Menshen Insurance and the call centre across the road."

"Brampton's colleagues?"

"In shock. The usual story; well liked, can't think of who would do this kind of thing."

"Alarm bells with any of them?"

"Not so far. A duller lot you could not wish to meet."

"What about contractors?"

"They've got one of those office management companies which cover most things, like the canteen, cleaning and security."

"Could be more who aren't covered by the office management contractors. Maintenance people, gardeners, delivery guys. I want you to find a senior manager, someone who pays for all the bills, he'll be the best person to tell you."

"Sir."

"Get him to give you a comprehensive list, then you and Walsh take a couple of hours to sense check it. We can't miss anything."

"Got it."

Myers could hear her scribbling notes and gave her a moment.

"Okay. Tell me about security footage."

"We've got her leaving the building on Menshen's CCTV and then about three seconds of her crossing the road and that's it."

"Crossing the road?"

"Yes," Amis sighed. "Here's the thing. Menshen's carpark is well over-subscribed. There's a vacant building over the road and they unofficially use the underground parking there as an overflow. The business park management let them use it to keep Menshen sweet, but of course..."

"No security and no cameras."

"Exactly. You come in late, you'll end up parking there. More often than not, that's where Brampton parked."

"Alright, when you get your list of security people from Menshen, I want you to ring fence them and go through them first."

"Got you."

"Add anyone else you think might be savvy to the carpark security situation."

"No problem."

71

"Briefing at eight tomorrow. You're doing a good job. How's Walsh?"

"Needs a drink."

"I'm buying when this is over, Amis. Keep your eye on the ball."

"On it like a car bonnet, sir. See you in the morning."

He hung up and immediately called Prejean. There was no answer. Hardly a surprise. Mobile coverage wasn't one of Bottleburn's strong points. He twirled a pen between his fingers.

The pairing of Prejean and Atherton came with a risk. Atherton's contribution could be useful, but he feared the press would pick up on it. Myers wanted a completed profile on the table sooner rather than later and before his presence could become a distraction.

He dialled one more time, with the same result and replaced the handset. He trusted his DS and felt a sliver of guilt for inflicting the situation upon her. Spending time with Atherton would be no picnic.

*

As soon as her phone picked up a signal, Prejean called Sue, balancing the phone between her shoulder and cheek as she drove. She agreed to send a SOCO officer out to cover the area properly.

Her next call was to Amis, who explained she'd just spoken to Myers. Prejean told her to get a list of security and maintenance people to Rogers, who was reviewing the files on Lynch at the station. Her call to Rogers failed to connect.

Atherton held the zip-lock bag of cigarette butts delicately in front of him as if they were in danger of decomposing before they made it back to the city. Prejean hid a smirk by looking out of the side window.

"You could probably put them down somewhere, Jon," she said.

He carefully lay them on the dashboard, but remained silent.

"So," said Prejean, after several miles without conversation. "What was that all about?"

"I think that could well have been our man, paying us a visit."

"Jesus fucking Christ," she said. "Why did he draw the eyes?"

"An audience," he said. "Some killers like the pretence of people watching them in the act. It's part of the fantasy. They'll position dolls, photographs, even corpses so they feel their performance is being observed."

"Lovely," said Prejean and they fell back into a comfortable silence.

By the time they got back to the station, a light drizzle had begun to fall. Atherton levered himself out of the car and stretched his leg. Anything longer than ten minutes in a car seemed to intensify the tension in his hamstring and it took a long time to walk off. Prejean started up the steps to the large glass façade.

"I'd better make my way back now, thanks Kate," said Atherton.

"You'll need to give us a statement on our sighting," she said.

"Can it wait until tomorrow?" he said. "I've got some work to do. Papers to mark, psychotic killer profile to write. That kind of thing."

"Guess so. You got everything you need?"

"I think so. Thanks," he said.

"Well...see you in the morning."

Prejean's mood seemed to have lightened, but Atherton couldn't work out whether that was due to him or the additional evidence they'd stumbled across.

"See you," he replied. He started towards the carpark and paused to look back, but she was gone. He pulled out his phone and found a text:

Don't forget – appointment. 4PM.

He looked at his watch: 3.15PM. He still had time.

*

Sue's eyes gleamed when she saw Prejean and she crossed the room to her with speed.

"Gimme, gimme, gimme!" she said.

Prejean handed her the evidence bag. "I got it logged as quickly as I could," she said.

"Who was on?" said Sue, taking the bag from her.

"I don't know, a girl with boots."

"She's good," said Sue, checking the Criminal Justice item label on the tamper-free bag and matching the details on the submission paperwork. She rolled out a fresh piece of paper bench coat and placed the evidence bag on top. Taking a pair of stainless steel scissors, she cut open the bag and gently shook the butts out.

"This is going to take a little time," she said, donning bright blue latex gloves.

"Happy to stay and watch if you can bear me looking over your shoulder," said Prejean.

"Used to it," said Sue. "Make yourself at home."

Prejean watched as she lay out the four cigarette ends and photographed them alongside a ruler. She made notes periodically.

"He's a pincher, like my ex," she said at one point. "Look at that one."

Prejean saw where the cigarette had been gripped, squashing the filter down in the middle. Sue then took a disposable scalpel, broke it out of its packaging and carefully began to cut off the paper from the last half centimetre of the filter. When it was free, she transferred it on the end of the scalpel to a plastic tube.

"One down, three to go."

"Are they good? Can we get a profile?" said Prejean.

"Oh, I'd think so. Dog-ends are DNA gold. It'll take us eight or nine hours."

Prejean punched the air behind Sue's back. "Sue, I could kiss you."

"Ha. Thanks, but I'll pass. Where's that good-looking friend of ours when you need him?"

"Atherton?"

"Yes. I wouldn't say no to that," said Sue.

Prejean wished she could have seen Sue's face.

"He still likes you I think, Kate."

"Yes, well...he can fuck off."

"I'm sorry to stick my beak in," said Sue, looking away from her work and into Prejean's eyes. "It's just a little obvious sometimes that you still like him too."

"No I don't, Sue," she said. "What happened last time was a bad mistake. I can't believe that I was taken in by him. Frankly, I think the man's an arsehole."

Sue looked at her over her glasses, with her eyebrows raised somewhat comically. "Neither of us are experts in behavioural science, love, but even I know that's bullshit," she said, smiling.

"He's manipulative, Sue, and...not to mention the fact that he's married with a kid."

"Hey, nobody's perfect. Just don't end up like me. All cats, PlayStation and crying into your Rioja. It's easy to turn opportunities down when you're young and you have this expanse of life in front of you, but when you get a bit older you start to realise there's not an ideal man around every corner."

Sue put a gentle hand on Prejean's forearm for a moment and then turned back to the bench. She picked up another cigarette end with tweezers.

"Right. Two down, two to go."

*

Atherton checked his watch again: 4.10PM. The receptionist smiled vaguely at him with a glazed look, which appeared to be a default setting. He glanced again at the home design magazine he hadn't been reading; a pristine modern kitchen, with a staged scenario; a mother at her laptop, the father cooking, the children happily running in from the garden. An adjoining door opened and a short, dark-skinned man leaned out.

"Hi, Jon. Would you like to come this way? I realise Mrs Atherton hasn't arrived yet, but I wondered if you mightn't be more comfortable in my office?"

"I can certainly give it a try, Doctor Dabbawal," said Atherton.

Atherton made his way down a short corridor to Dabbawal's office.

"Take a seat," said Dabbawal.

Two sturdy armchairs faced Dabbawal's leather-bound swivel seat. Atherton chose one and sat down on it gratefully.

"Can I get you anything?"

"No, I'm fine thanks," said Atherton. "Have you redecorated since we were last here?"

"No, not for a couple of years," said Dabbawal.

Atherton hadn't noticed the colour of the room before; a very light pastel green. Nice, calming and neutral. It reminded Atherton of a piece he'd read about a prison for the criminally insane in the US where they'd tried a similar technique to calm the inhabitants: apple greens, magnolias and rose pinks. Within two weeks, they'd picked off the paint, piece by piece and eaten it.

Dabbawal had just taken his seat, when his receptionist buzzed his intercom. "Mrs Atherton is here."

"Please send her through," he replied.

Atherton turned as Louise entered. She was smiling, but there was a slight redness to her eyes. She greeted Dabbawal and walked across the room a little gingerly to take the neighbouring chair.

"Hello," she said and Atherton caught a slight smell of alcohol on her breath.

"Are you okay?" he asked.

"Clare and I went out for lunch," she said. He looked into her eyes. She didn't look drunk. "I'm fine. Sorry I'm late. Shall we make a start?"

"Yes, let's," said Dabbawal, who'd used their exchange as an opportunity to position their notes at his side. "How have you both been since our last session?"

"Not so bad," said Atherton.

"Okay," said Louise, more tentatively.

"Oh." Dabbawal, looked from one to the other. "Is there a difference of opinion on that?"

Atherton suspected Dabbawal was an expert in body language and tonal shifts with the spoken voice. He tried not to give away any cues, but Louise was like an open book. She smiled nervously.

"It's probably to do with my job," Atherton said, when it became clear she was not going to speak.

"Ask him about his job," said Louise.

Dabbawal looked at Atherton. "Your job? Your position as a lecturer at the University?"

"No," said Louise. "His other job."

"I've been assisting the police in an investigation," said Atherton.

"With the woman he had an affair with," added Louise.

Dabbawal looked at Atherton, who suddenly began to resent the calm expression peering back at him. It bordered on nonchalance.

"She is part of the same investigation, yes," he said.

"Just remind me of this person please?" said Dabbawal.

"She's a detective sergeant leading a homicide investigation I'm involved with and yes, she's the woman I...grew close to when Louise and I were going through the worst of our problems."

"And how does that make you feel, Louise?" said Dabbawal.

The question seemed to wrong-foot her for a moment.

"It just rakes up the worries I used to have. Over Jon, over Hannah, over everything."

"How do you respond to that, Jon? We've talked at length about Louise's anxieties over trust," said Dabbawal.

Jon held up his hands in surrender.

"I took the job, completely unaware of her involvement on what is becoming an increasingly serious and concerning case and I think Louise needs to realise..."

"I should realise what? Just accept that you're going to be spending every day with her?" said Louise. "Have you mentioned where you went on holiday at the start of the summer?"

"I was in Quantico, Virginia at the FBI's Behavioural Analysis Unit. They had some courses which were incredibly useful to me academically."

"Yes, I have read about this place," said Dabbawal, looking genuinely interested for the first time. "But we've talked about how important it is to hit the right equilibrium of work-life balance. Is it possible this new assignment and your summer trip could push this off kilter?"

"We also need to hit the right equilibrium where we don't default on our mortgage," said Atherton.

Louise shot him a glance and then looked down to the carpet.

"I think this is a dig at my current work situation," she said.

"It wasn't a dig about anything," said Atherton. "Just financially accurate. If I didn't supplement my wages somehow, we'd be in trouble."

"I *will* go back to work, Jon," she said, looking at him, earnestly.

"Only when you're ready," he said.

"Do you think..." started Dabbawal.

"I've only ever wanted you to be better. The way things were before," said Atherton, ignoring Dabbawal entirely. "I'm sorry, Louise. I'm just trying to do what's best, but I don't know what that is. If I worked less, I'd be home more, but I don't know how we'd manage."

"I know, I know," she said. Her eyes fell to the floor again. He wanted to reach out and hold her hand, but the chairs were too far apart.

ALPHA DRACONIS

CHAPTER EIGHT

Atherton's hangover proved to be an exception to the rule. There was an all-consuming headache centred behind his eyes.

The room grew increasingly light, letting him know he was certain to be late. His mouth tasted vile, and he tried to remember what he'd been drinking; a couple on the quayside, a bottle of wine at the University bar, a brandy at some point and vague recollections of rummaging through cans in the refrigerator of a brightly lit corner shop. He could remember Louise had left the therapist's and gone immediately off to see her mother; some breathing time to gather herself after the session. It was a habit he had also begun to adopt, in his own alcohol-infused style.

He sat up and it felt as if there was a delay whilst his brain righted itself in the same orientation, as if it was free floating in its own juices. The house was silent and he concluded that Louise and Hannah were already out. His phone told him it was 8.30AM already.

He dressed quickly and ate a single slice of bread slathered with chocolate spread. On the way to the police station, he asked the taxi to stop for gum, water and paracetamol. He crushed the tablets between his teeth and swilled away the bitter taste with the water.

On his phone were two texts from Prejean and a voicemail saying only: "Call me, immediately".

Atherton had written nothing in preparation of a profile. Pulling a pad and pen from his bag, he started to record a few notes:

Sex: Male.
Colour: White.
Age: Mid to late thirties.
Marital: Single / divorced or problems.
Occupation: Blue collar. Electrician, plumber.
IQ: Average – above average.
Education: Low level. A-levels at most.
Crim. Record: Arson, sexual assault.
Personality: Asocial, quiet.
Traits: Speech impediment / missing limb / disfigurement / disability.

They had to stop again when Atherton realised he had no cash to pay the driver. By the time he finally reached the station, signed in, obtained a visitors card and took the lift to the second floor focus room, it was 9.10AM.

Amis, Rogers and Walsh sat quietly at the table, all eyes on Myers who was engaged in an intense telephone conversation within the confines of his fishbowl office. His expression was stony, brow furrowed. Prejean stood at the window, looking out on the grey morning. Outside, a window cleaner applied soapy water with a dull thud, soon followed by the squeak of a squeegee blade against the glass.

"Ah, sorry I'm late. Traffic and so on," said Atherton, taking off his jacket. He felt terrible. "I have some notes, if you'll just hold on a moment."

Rogers and Walsh kept their eyes to the table. Amis looked at him with something resembling pity.

Prejean spoke, but didn't turn around: "There's been another one."

"What..." started Atherton.

"We don't know anything yet, we just got the call," said Rogers.

Myers was nodding and seemed to be winding up on the phone. Rogers tapped Walsh's arm with the back of his hand and by the time Myers came out of the office, they were all on their feet.

"Okay. The scene is secured. We've got uniform officers in place and Sue's lot are already en route," he said. "Be warned, I hear there are some press down there. Don't engage, but if you're in a corner, please remember your media training. We're heading to Hillheads up the A1. If you don't know the way, follow me, but I'll be driving fast." Myers slid on his suit jacket as he walked.

"DS Prejean," said Atherton. "Should I just..."

"Rogers, can you take Doctor Atherton?"

"Sure," said Rogers.

*

Atherton could have picked out Rogers's car from the carpark without any pointers; a sharp-looking metallic grey Audi as well-kept as Rogers himself. Atherton glanced at him as they drove; he was alert and purposeful. It was hard not to profile people. Flash car, ambitious, a player with the ladies no doubt, probably captained a team at school; typical alpha male. Then an additional thought arose suddenly: *I bet he has designs on Kate.*

"Did they tell you anything about the scene at all?" asked Atherton.

"Nothing," said Rogers, his square jaw chewing enthusiastically on some gum. "We were talking about the cigarette butts you and the gaffer found when the call came in."

"What about the cigarettes by the way?"

"Oh, the good news was that we got a full profile alright. Sue was up all night, I think."

"And the bad news?"

"There was no match on the database," said Rogers. "So..."

"He hasn't been charged with anything or left his DNA at a crime scene since 1995?"

"Basically, yeah."

There wouldn't be a match, thought Atherton. *He would have been very young if he'd been caught doing anything and since then he'd been so very careful, hadn't he?*

"It's a good step forward," said Atherton.

"Yeah," said Rogers, overtaking a lorry with relish. "All we need is a suspect and boom, we've got him at the scene."

"At the scene, but not necessarily at the time of the murder."

"Aye, but you must think that whoever was spying on you yesterday killed Brampton?"

"Yes, I think that could well have been him," said Atherton.

There was a pause. Rogers drove, Atherton thought.

"Cheeky fucker. What makes a person capable of something like that?" said Rogers after a minute's worth of silence.

"A variety of factors," said Atherton.

"Have you studied this for long?"

"Well, I've just tipped over forty, so twenty years, give or take."

"You must have an affinity for all of this stuff?"

"How do you mean?" said Atherton.

"Is it true what they say?"

"It depends on what they say."

"They say you have the mind of a psychopath," said Rogers. Atherton laughed and Rogers cracked a smile. "So that's why you're so good at tracking these fuckers down."

"Not exactly," said Atherton.

"Not exactly?"

"Okay, let me give you a basic recipe for cooking up a psychopathic killer," said Atherton, slipping into a well-practiced routine. "There are three ingredients on the list and all are required to produce a killer, at least a killer of the type we're looking for here. Miss one of them and it doesn't work. No killer. It would be like...making an omelette without eggs." He paused for a moment to make sure Rogers was hooked. "One, you have to be born with a particular genetic makeup. They carry one or more high risk, violence related genes."

"A mutation?"

"Not really, usually just a particular version of the MAO-A sequence or *the warrior gene*, as it's sometimes known," said Atherton, rubbing his eyes. The pain behind them endured, though he felt somewhat better. "Next, you have to have a specific abnormality in the brain."

"No surprise there," said Rogers.

"Perhaps not. The orbital cortex in the brain of a psychopathic individual doesn't function properly and this is the part of the brain which deals with empathy, morality and conscience. It's also the bit which controls impulse. So, not only are they without apathy, they can't control themselves. Not the best combination."

"And what's the last ingredient?"

"What do you think it is?" said Atherton.

Rogers thought briefly.

"A dark, twisted soul?" he said.

"Abuse. Without exception, individuals who go on to exhibit this type of behaviour have been subjected to some sort of abuse; sexual, physical or emotional," said Atherton. "The kind of thing which could definitely lead to a dark, twisted soul, so you weren't far off the mark."

They drove on another mile or so. Atherton could see Prejean's car up ahead and wished he were in it with her. He knew the mention of press at the scene was the reason he had been relegated to Rogers's car.

"Do you have all those ingredients then?" said Rogers, who seemed to be spending more time looking at Atherton than the road.

"No. You'll be disappointed to hear I'm only two thirds a maniac."

"I'd rather you weren't even that. At least not while I'm driving," said Rogers.

Atherton laughed.

"I went to visit the FBI a few months ago. They're really starting to understand this a bit better and they've done genetic profiles and brain scans on a number of offenders. All had the three ingredients: brain, genetics and abuse. As a bit of fun, they decided to run profiles and scans on a couple of the course members to provide negative controls of 'normal' individuals." Atherton punctuated the air and immediately hated himself for doing so. "Guess what? Not so negative."

"You were psycho positive?"

"Nearly. I'm on the spectrum, as are most CEOs in multi-national corporations, I should add, but one vital ingredient was missing: no abuse," said Atherton. "Daddy didn't leave when I was young, giving way to a string of transient, abusive males in the house. Mummy didn't drink or resent me for her loss of youth, and they didn't lock me in the coal shed with the spiders."

"So if they hadn't taken you to the fair..."

"I could be eating your liver right now. Yes, I had a great childhood and my parents are thoughtful, kind and loving. My wife might disagree, especially at Christmas."

Rogers laughed.

"Thank you, Mr and Mrs Atherton," he said.

"Indeed. The FBI gave me a laminated certificate to prove I'm a psychopath. It's in my office at the University. They have a good sense of humour, which I think helps in their line of work."

"Official recognition."

"Exactly. I've finally made it," said Atherton. The road dipped down to a spectacular valley.

"So you don't have any feelings then?" asked Rogers. "You're a stone cold bastard?"

"No, I'm fucking delightful."

"You seem pretty normal to me," said Rogers.

"So do bona fide killers. If they all dribbled and clucked like chickens, they'd be easier to spot."

"I bloody wish they would," said Rogers.

"Okay. Let me give you a litmus test. Here's an example. A runaway train is hurtling down the track towards a group of ten people who will most certainly be killed in a horrible, bloody fashion. You're standing on the bridge above the track next to a switch. If you flick the switch, the train will be redirected down another track, where it will kill only one unlucky bastard who's working on the track. What would you do?"

"Flick the switch," said Rogers, after a moment's thought. "Ten versus one, right? It's not a nice decision to make, but it's the only one."

"Right, and most people would make that very same decision," said Atherton. "Okay. Now, imagine same situation. Same train, same ten people are going to die if you don't flick that switch, except this time, the workman is on the bridge in the way of the switch and he's not moving."

"Okay," said Rogers, his brow already creased in thought.

"If you don't throw him over the bridge to his death and flick that switch, ten people die. What do you do?"

"That's tricky," said Rogers. "It's different."

"It feels like more of a decision, doesn't it? It's more personal, less anonymous than the first example. You have to watch him die and know you're the one who killed him. You have to see the whites of his eyes, the shock and fear as you push him over."

"I don't know what I'd do. I don't know if I could do it."

"And that's the difference," said Atherton. "For a psychotic individual, it's still a simple equation and an easy decision to make. One will always be fewer than ten, every time."

Rogers pondered on this for a while, nodding slowly.

"So what would you do, Doctor?" he said.

Atherton gave him a broad smile, popped a piece of gum in his mouth and extended the pack to Rogers.

"No thanks," he said. "I think we're here."

Up ahead, Atherton could see Myers's car turning off to the right and a number of police vehicles through the trees which lined the road. Rogers pulled into a lane and then almost immediately into a small gravel carpark and stopped.

Atherton exited the car as quickly as his leg would allow and saw a large sign: Whitehough Butterfly Farm, the text surrounded by several poorly rendered illustrations of butterflies. It appeared to be a converted farmhouse with a large greenhouse at the rear. The front of the building had been cordoned off with bright yellow tape. Two uniformed cops, one male, one female, were on point. A young woman in her twenties and a middle-aged man with a camera loitered by the tape eagerly. Atherton followed Rogers as he flashed his warrant card, ducked under the tape and proceeded down a narrow passage toward the rear of the house. As he passed them, he saw the woman whisper something to the man and heard the *click-click-click* of the camera.

The butterfly house consisted of two identical cylindrical glass houses joined by a central rectangular section. As they approached, they could see white SOCO suits inside. Blood was spattered liberally up the glass at one side. Myers was talking to Prejean in hushed tones, with Amis and Walsh standing silently nearby. As they approached, Walsh coughed up something he had to swallow again. Amis looked away in disgust.

"Right folks," said Myers as he saw Rogers and Atherton. "I managed to call ahead from the car to secure a few more details. One female victim, discovered by the owner at opening time." He pointed to the farmhouse building. "That building operates as a coffee shop and the owners no longer live on site." Myers looked at each of them in turn as he talked. "Sue and the boys have done their photography and preliminaries, so we can suit up and go in." He turned away, remembered something and turned back again. "It's a bit toastie in there."

"Like a greenhouse," said Rogers, sarcastically.

"Indeed, Rogers. Also, there's an added complication; I'm told they have several rare species of butterfly, so mind how you go. If we can avoid marching out of here with anything flapping on the soles of our shoes, it would be appreciated, particularly with Lauren Schloss from the Evening Chronicle watching."

Atherton stuck to the back and followed them into a gift shop area filled with various butterfly-related toys and merchandise and an over-sized Christmas tree, where they donned suits and put elasticated paper socks over their shoes. A rush of warm air greeted them as they entered. It was oppressively hot, like stepping into an incubator, and he immediately felt uncomfortable in his multiple layers. To top it all off, there was that familiar awful smell of meat, blood and tissue. Atherton felt queasy and wanted to lean on something or someone.

"Alright, Jon?" said Sue.

"I'm okay. Too many lemonades maybe," he said. "Never mind that, how are you?"

"Hey, two hours sleep is enough for anyone, isn't it? I'm ready for Morecambe and Wise and a few sherries, though."

Atherton could see she was tired, eyes red and bloodshot.

"I wish we had a chance to catch our breath. Most inconvenient."

"Sue?" said Myers. "Can you talk us through the scene please?"

Atherton glanced at Prejean, who stood at his side, and noticed her body language was off; was she nervous in front of the boss?

"Sure," said Sue. "Single dismembered female victim. Body parts cover quite an area, as you can see. Fourteen pieces, all in all. Head looks like it has the same trauma to the rear. We have blood on the glass of the west wall, which looks like arterial spray, and we also have some on the ceiling..." Everyone looked upwards to see three streaks of spattered blood on the glass roof. "...which I think could be cast-off from the weapon."

"Thanks Sue," said Myers. "Anything else?"

"Lots, hopefully. This could be a different ballgame to Bottleburn. We have more to play with; an enclosed environment, lots of glass and other surfaces we could get prints or DNA from. We'll be here all fucking day in other words."

"Good work, Sue. Anyone want to add anything?" said Myers.

"Head?" said Atherton.

"Yes please, Jon," said Sue. There was a polite ripple of laughter. She pointed.

The SOCO crew had placed a low interior barrier of tape around the body parts. They did cover a much wider area than last time. Atherton counted the fourteen pieces, strewn across the floor, with the rest of the body; torso, intestines, skin, unceremoniously dumped together in one corner. Her head had been cut squarely and the neck pushed into the soft earth to maintain an upright position. Atherton knelt beside it. She had a close similarity to Brampton, the *same stamp*, as his mother would have said. Olive skin and dark brown, almost black hair. Atherton became aware of Prejean at his side.

"He has a type, wouldn't you say?"

"Same war-paint," said Prejean.

"Yeah, but he's getting better at it. He'd still struggle to get a job as a makeup artist, but there's an improvement."

The prominent eyeliner had been applied with more care, in an elaborate sweep towards her temples and the eyeshadow on her lids was a striking earthy gold.

"What do you think that is?" He extended a gloved hand and pointed to a small, pearlescent blob which had all the appearance of a tear under the girl's right eye.

"Semen?" suggested Prejean.

"No such luck," said Sue, who was photographing something nearby. "It's superglue. He glued her eyelids shut."

Atherton pulled at the neck of his SOCO suit in an attempt to let in some cooler air. He felt another rivulet of sweat roll down his back. Close to him, a large blue butterfly rose up from a palm leaf. It fluttered for a moment in his eye line and he noticed a fine spray of blood had decorated its wings.

CHAPTER NINE

"Looks like we have an ID," said Rogers, entering the focus room at pace. "Abigail Southern, twenty-five. She's a nurse at North Tyneside General Hospital." Prejean and Walsh looked up from their screens. "Shares a flat beside the hospital with another nurse on the opposite shift, who came home to an empty place and a blood stain on the wall. She dialled it in and the uniforms who went out took this from a picture she gave them." He held up his smartphone, which displayed a photograph; a young woman ready for a night out; pretty, with brown hair and brown eyes. Rogers placed the phone on Prejean's desk and Walsh leaned over to see it.

"It's her," said Prejean. "Are the uniformed cops still at the scene?"

"Yes, they've been there since eight," he said.

"Okay. You and Walsh get down there and seal the place off properly, but keep it low key. I don't want anyone making a connection to the butterfly house and turning it into a circus. Once everything's secure, call me and we'll get down there with Sue's lads."

"No problem," said Rogers. Walsh rose quickly and grabbed his jacket, leaving his chair spinning behind him.

Prejean lifted the phone from its cradle and pressed two buttons to speed-dial Sue.

"Engine room," she answered.

"Sue? Looks like we have an abduction scene for the butterfly girl. How soon can you get a team to North Tyneside Hospital?"

"Half an hour, tops," she said.

"Minimise the team please. We need it to be discrete and make it a priority to get DNA samples for ID purposes."

"Of course," she said. "See you soon."

Prejean hung up, just as Amis walked into the room, carrying a coffee.

"I'd put a lid on that if you have one," said Prejean.

"What did I miss?"

"I'll tell you on the way."

*

The flat was on the ground floor, one of many identical buildings surrounding a large quadrant, constructed from the same dark brick as the hospital it nestled behind. Walsh and Rogers had done a good job. The scene looked secure, but un-showy; one visible panda car and a SOCO van. Prejean and Amis climbed into white forensics suits at the rear of the van.

"I'm starting to feel like I live in these things," said Amis.

"I know," replied Prejean, zipping up the front of her suit.

Sue was immediately inside the flat, taking photographs and she stepped aside to let them see. There was a long streak of blood on the wall, leading from the edge of a doorframe diagonally downwards. At the bottom of the mark was a single dark hair stuck to the congealed blood.

"Hi," said Sue, taking another photograph for good measure.

"Hi, Sue," said Prejean. "What does this tell you?"

"No signs of forced entry, so it looks like she let him in. A brief struggle here, then she went down quickly, banging her head and sliding down to a seated position here," said Sue, pointing with a light-blue gloved hand.

"There's a peephole in the door," said Amis. "On her own at night, you'd think she'd have used it."

"Anyone in the neighbours' flats hear anything?" said Prejean.

"Rogers has being knocking on doors. You should ask him."

"The flatmate?"

"Through there, with Walsh. You'd better go and help him out."

"Will do," said Prejean.

"Before you go, you'd best take a look behind you," said Sue. "If this didn't freak her out, then that probably did." She pointed to the wall over Prejean's head. Prejean turned slowly. A large eye had been daubed in dark blood.

"Jesus Christ," she said.

*

Less than an hour later, Amis sat on an uncomfortable faux-leather chair in a lounge area of Menshen's offices. Across from her was a board displaying the words *Team Energise*, with details of the *Great Office Bake Off* and photos of recent efforts beneath. She looked at her watch, then across the office, where a maze of partitions covered the floor. The place was silent, but for the clattering of keyboard keys. Occasionally, someone would raise their head above the corporate parapets to look at her, to the point where she was ready for them, eyes raised suspiciously in wait. Somewhere, a phone rang and was answered in muted tones.

"Detective Amis?" A young, trim bespectacled man extended a hand. When Amis took it, his grip was surprisingly strong. "I'm sorry for keeping you. I have a conference call at this time every week and it often drags on. Everyone panicking to get things done before the Christmas break." He rolled his eyes a little effeminately.

"That's alright, Mr Douglas, I completely understand," said Amis. "I promise not to keep you long, if you've managed to get the information we asked for."

"Yes, of course, no problem at all," he said. "Let's grab a huddle."

Amis followed him into a tiny meeting room where he gestured for her to take a seat. He sat himself and placed a file on the table in front of him.

"Right, this is a comprehensive list of all the companies we pay for on site," he said, flipping open the file. "I've asked for a summary at the front. Ah, here it is. It breaks it down, company by company. Where they have regular employees and we know names, we've added them too."

Amis looked down the list. She was surprised by how many people it took to keep the employees of Menshen happy in their workplace. She hoped they'd get some help checking each of the company's employees against criminal record data.

"That's great, Mr Douglas," said Amis. "If you could email me an electronic version, it would be helpful."

"It should already be in your inbox," said Douglas.

"Perfect. I'd just like to thank you again for your cooperation and that of your staff," she said.

"That's absolutely no problem. Such a terrible, terrible business. Please let me know if we can help in any other way." His narrow eyes darted to the clock above Amis's head.

"Did you happen to know Miss Brampton on a personal level?" she asked.

Douglas's eyes fluttered in a rapid series of blinks.

"On a personal level? No...I mean, when her photograph was on TV, I remembered seeing her around the office. I've spoken to her line manager though, who said that she was a very effective worker and very well-liked by her colleagues," he said. "Such a terrible, terrible business."

His eyes flicked to the clock again.

"Okay, we'll be in touch," said Amis. She rose and shook his hand, finding it marginally less bone-crunching. When she left the meeting room, half a dozen heads quickly looked back to their monitors.

*

Walsh lit another cigarette and inhaled deeply. He took the full ashtray from the dashboard, dropped the window and threw the contents out of the car and onto the grass verge.

"Isn't that littering, officer?" said a female voice.

Walsh looked over and immediately recognised the reporter from the butterfly house. She smiled and raised her eyebrows. He couldn't help but let his eyes drop over her smart grey suit to the place where her skirt met her tights.

"Front page news is it?" he said. "What are you doing here?"

"Same as you. I'm interested in having a word with Mr Forrest." She nodded towards the detached cottage where Walsh had spent an unproductive hour talking to Forrest. "Did he have much to say in his statement?"

Walsh ignored her and drew greedily on his smoke.

"Lauren Schloss," she said. "Evening Chronicle."

"I know who you are," said Walsh.

"I know you too, Detective Walsh," said Schloss. "My boss remembers you pretty well. He said you sometimes helped us out in one or two mutually beneficial situations."

"He must be thinking about someone else," said Walsh.

"I don't think so, somehow," she said, levelling her icy blue eyes with his. "Just tell me if I'm wasting my time door-stepping the butterfly man over there."

"You're wasting your time," said Walsh. "All he cares about is getting the place cleaned up and open again. He had thirty-five school kids due tomorrow he's already had to cancel. He sees money fluttering out the window."

"Do you have a spare one of those?" Her eyes flicked to the pack of cigarettes on the dash.

"Help yourself. Then I really must be going," he said. He grabbed the pack and flipped open the lid with his thumb. She took one with slender fingers and placed it between her full red lips. He lit it with a disposable lighter. She drew deeply and exhaled from the side of her mouth.

"You don't seem to be in much of a hurry?" she said smiling. She twisted a foot casually on the ground and took another drag. "What does he do to them, Walsh?"

"The investigation is ongoing," he said and smiled back.

"What about Detective Sergeant Prejean and the Doctor? Are they back on?"

Walsh reached into the inside pocket and handed her a card.

"If I could just direct you to our media department, I'm sure they'd be happy to help you further, Miss Schloss."

"Come on, David," she said. "I'm not one for formalities. I doubt you are either." She ground out the cigarette beneath an expensive shoe and produced a business card from her handbag. She leaned inside the car and placed it into his inside jacket pocket, her hand brushing slowly against his cotton shirt. She whispered, her lips tickling his ear: "There's a monster out there, isn't there? I want to know all about him."

He took her hand from his chest and she stepped away from the car. The grin remained on her face as she turned and headed towards the path for the cottage. He couldn't resist watching her go.

She spun suddenly on her heel and winked at him before continuing down the path. He watched her until she was out of sight and twisted the key in the ignition.

*

Atherton woke suddenly at the sound of his office door rattling open. Peering around it was Doctor Neil Osram. Atherton's heart pounded in his chest and he looked quickly around the room and down at himself. Apart from his shoes, he was fully dressed. Osram glanced down at Atherton's feet where they overshot the couch. The toe of his right foot protruded from a hole in his sock. Osram's eyes beamed somewhat mischievously. He wore a green bomber jacket over a pale blue polo shirt, with wiry white chest hair protruding from within. It was clear his new girlfriend was dressing him.

"Fucking hell, Jon, have you been here since the end of term?" he said.

Atherton struggled to sit up. He had no gauge on how long he'd been asleep. It could have been an hour, could have been five. There was a clock on the desk, but it was obscured by several lofty piles of students' files.

"Just popped in to do some marking," said Atherton. "Thought I'd put my feet up for a little while."

"Oh yeah, I can see you've been ploughing through the work." said Osram.

Atherton noticed the golf bag on his back for the first time. He knew it was too big for the boot of Osram's sports car and he would never leave it exposed on the passenger seat.

"I didn't know people played golf in the winter," said Atherton. "I thought it was like cricket."

Osram threw him a mock-confused look.

"All you need is a thicker pair of gloves and a flask of something to keep the chill out," he said. "Just nine holes today, though. Thought I'd spin by and check my emails and I heard you snoring. Thought there was someone in here with a chainsaw."

"What time is it?"

He looked at his watch. "Getting towards three," he said, offloading the bag and taking Atherton's seat behind the desk.

"Fuck," said Atherton and quickly tried to think if he'd missed anything. He drew a blank. He clicked on his phone and tapped in the pin. There was only one text message: Kate.

"So what can you tell me?" said Osram.

"About what? Your appalling golf clothes?"

"About Bottleburn," said Osram. "They've had you up there?"

"What makes you think that?"

"If I was running the investigation, I'd have you up there, even if I had to drag you," he said, swinging two chunky, tartan-clad legs onto the limited desk space. "You don't have a whippet on your doorstep and race a Labrador."

"Nice analogy," said Atherton, rubbing gritty eyes.

"Thanks," said Osram. The room was growing darker and most of his face was in shadow. Atherton struggled to see him. A dull headache returned to his brow. "I'm surprised you don't get dragged into more stuff, what with your experience," he went on.

On the wall, to the left of Osram, was the joke certificate from the FBI. It read :

*Doctor Jon Atherton has passed all selection criteria
and is hereby certified as a grade-A psychopathic motherfucker.*

Beside it was a faded poster of a Venn Diagram which had been presented to him by one of his students at the end of the summer term, several years previously. Two large circles, one green, the other blue and a thin region of red where the two intersected. The key below it explained: *blue: people who like gory horror movies, green: people who like musicals and red: serial killers.*

"I'd have thought that's exactly why they might want to leave me alone," said Atherton.

"You still cut yourself up about that, don't you?" said Osram. His tone had dropped to a more measured timbre, which Atherton recognised as his professional voice. "Are you still talking to someone about that?"

"The police counsellor? Guy was an idiot," said Atherton. "Besides, I've plenty of therapy going on already, thanks very much."

"You could always talk to me, Jon," said Osram.

"Are you detecting excessive stress in my behaviour, Neil? Is it a while since you helped someone exercise..." Atherton struggled to remember the title of Osram's book, "...the seven-step pathway to an anxiety-free life?"

"No, it's a while since I had a drink and a chat with my mate," said Osram. He stood and loosened the buckle from one of the side pockets of his bag and teased out a large unmarked glass bottle.

"Jesus, what the fuck's that – moonshine?"

"Sloe gin. Medicinal. Rejuvenating. Invigorating." He beat his chest to each of these pronouncements.

"But is it a pathway to an anxiety-free life?"

"Most very fucking definitely," he said.

Osram's own sense of peace had come at the expense of an ex-wife by the name of Amrita, who'd taken their two teenage girls to Switzerland, leaving him to move in with his girlfriend. He smiled with grizzled jowls as he unscrewed the bottle.

"Okay. Let's do it," said Atherton.

*

By the time Prejean made it back to the flat, she was wiped out. She kicked off her shoes and headed straight for the kitchen, nudging aside the dishes so she could fill the kettle, and sat at the small table to check her phone. She found a pack of fresh pasta in the fridge and filled a saucepan with water, leaving it on the hob to boil.

Atherton hadn't returned her call.

Coffee made, she moved into the bedroom and placed her mug on a stack of packing boxes while she changed. Six months and she still hadn't unpacked. She wondered whether the flat had been a good move. It was an awful lot to pay for a place she felt she barely spent any time in, but she loved the river views and the runs she took along its banks at the weekends. Wearing a pair of soft cotton jogging bottoms and a T-shirt, she moved back into the kitchen and threw a handful of pasta into the pan.

The five o'clock meeting had been a miserable affair. There was growing pressure to have a formal press conference and behind Myers's stoic facade, Prejean detected a hitherto unseen level of stress in her boss.

She bypassed the bottle of red she'd bought on the way home, took a seat in the lounge, clicked on the TV to an innocuous Christmas-themed game show and opened her laptop. The screen awoke from hibernation with a low whirr and she spent several minutes browsing the riverbank scene. She paused on a picture of the tree, the eyes gouged deep into the bark. The sap hung beneath where it had bled and congealed, like tears.

A thought crossed her mind. She closed the folder and opened up one of the warehouse killing. In a wide shot, Izzy Lynch's body lay surrounded by its dark red halo. In the background, on the walls was a dark melange of overlapping graffiti. Prejean used the laptop touchpad to click on the small icon of a magnifying glass and hovered over the photo. The graffiti blew up on the screen; a mixture of hip-hop style tags, expletives and crudely drawn caricatures. She moved her fingers over the touchpad to reveal various areas of the wall in more detail. When she saw it, the hairs on the back of neck tingled to attention.

There were two small, but very clearly defined eyes, dark red in colour, looking out over the mutilated body.

In the kitchen, the water finally bubbled over the edge of the pan and onto the hob with an almighty hiss.

*

The drinking escalated quickly. It so often did with Osram. Nine holes of golf had left him with a thirst. The sloe gin had gone quickly in the office and they had then walked into the centre of town, eaten chicken chimichangas at a bright, modern Mexican place in the shadow of Grey's Monument and sunk a bottle of red between them. Then they'd found a snug at a quiet pub down the hill towards the quayside, for a couple of rounds of real ale.

Later, Osram dragged Atherton into a livelier bar, with a familiar wild look in his eyes. It was still relatively early, but there were plenty of people both inside and out.

Inside, Osram loomed over him, his bald, shiny head illuminated in an ominous red disco light. A deep rumbling bass rattled his innards and he smelled a curious combination of alcohol and disinfectant.

Osram shouted something at him. Atherton felt his hot breath hit his face, but couldn't make out the words. Osram leaned closer.

"Shots?" he yelled.

"No. That's a bad idea," shouted Atherton.

Osram said something in return and jimmied his way between two groups of people at the bar and Atherton saw him enter into a discussion with the barman. He looked around the room; young ladies in dresses and Christmas cracker party hats; guys with smart shirts and dark jeans. It was a young crowd and he should have felt totally out of place, but the booze was having the most wonderful effect. It felt as though everyone was on the same train with the same destination.

Osram nudged Atherton's arm, pulled him into a space which had appeared at the bar and shoved him a cocktail in an elaborate glass.

"What's this?" asked Atherton.

"Dirty Mojito," he said.

"Ah fuck, Neil. This is my last one. I need to get home."

"Bollocks," he said.

Atherton sipped through the straw, tasting the spiced rum and lime.

"I thought this was a counselling session?"

"Okay. Does that girl over there remind you of your mother?"

"Not exactly," said Atherton.

"Then you're cured. Drink your meds," he said and pushed himself off the bar, making his way over to two young women sipping drinks from elaborate, vase-like cocktail glasses.

He approached the taller of the two, who seemed a little shocked at the sudden appearance of Osram and took a step back. Osram whispered something in her ear. She listened, nodded and laughed in rapid succession, returning something in Osram's. He gestured to Atherton and the girl laughed again. Atherton glanced at the diminutive friend, who smiled coyly and hid behind her drink. Osram turned to them.

"Jon, this is Lisa and her friend Vickie," he said gesturing drunkenly to the taller girl. "They're going to buy us drinks all night as long as we sleep with them."

Lisa laughed and Vickie joined in after a moment.

"So, what do you do?" said Vickie, with a strong scouse accent.

"We work at the University," said Atherton.

"Are you teachers? You have that look," she said.

Atherton didn't correct her.

"What are you drinking?" he asked instead, looking at the brightly coloured umbrellas sticking out of her drink.

She shrugged. "*She* picked them. It's her birthday and she's hammered already. We're expecting a load more people, but they haven't turned up."

"It's still early," he said, lost for anything else to say.

"No, man. They're late," she said.

Atherton glanced at Osram, who'd draped himself over Vickie, visible beads of sweat decorating his forehead. Unbelievably, Lisa seemed comfortable with this, listening to his chat and taking occasional sips of her drink. Her occasional howl of laughter punctuated the music.

"What's wrong with your leg?" said Vickie.

"Lost it in the war," said Atherton.

"Is it one of them prosthetic ones?"

"Bionic," he said. "For body popping purposes."

"Oh, show us your moves then, love," she said.

Atherton performed a standard hip-hop move he'd mastered many years previously, a cerebral palsy-friendly version which focussed on the upper body, to distract from the fact that the lower was doing very little.

"Oh, he's off," he heard Osram say and Lisa laughed again.

The DJ seemed to sense their little pocket of drunkenness might hold the trigger to launch the party for the entire bar and began to spin a more funky number. Lisa began clapping her hands, splashing her drink and dancing precariously in her high heels. Vickie joined her in an uncommitted fashion and all four of them moved onto the nearby dance floor. Just then, several other young women spilled into view and a number of high-pitched squeals erupted as Lisa greeted her friends. Osram joined in with a low guttural howl, the sweat patches on his armpits and back ever expanding. Atherton continued to dance, with Vickie beside him, though not with him. He caught the confused looks of some of the other girls: *who are these old fuckers?*

One track segued gently into another and soon Atherton had built up a sweat of his own. Osram appeared with a tray of purple-coloured drinks in plastic shot glasses, which he distributed to all in his vicinity and he began beating the tray with his hand in time with the music.

Atherton clocked the security gorilla who had taken position at the side of the DJ booth. Osram spotted him too, flashing a large grin which was clearly not reciprocated by the man in black. Osram tried to spin the tray on one finger like a basketball player, until he dropped it.

A new song started and when the vocals began, many of the girls joined in. Osram tried to sing along too, replacing the lyrics with noises. He wrapped his arm around Lisa and the other around Atherton briefly, before he span off dancing. In one quick move, he ripped off his polo shirt, revealing a pudgy white torso, a pelt of grey-white hair and obscenely large nipples.

This was clearly the policy violation the bouncer had been waiting for and he pushed his way through the dancers who parted readily. Osram squared up to him.

"*Wharrayougonnadolike? Wharrayougonnado?*"

He put his fists out in front of him and the dancefloor cleared rapidly. Atherton stepped towards the pair with his hands up in front of him. The bouncer grabbed Osram's forearm and twisted it around and up his back. With his free arm, Osram made a delayed move to punch the bouncer, missed and swatted the air. A second man appeared and grabbed Atherton's upper arm with a steely grip.

"Outside," he said with a stern, yet bored finality and began walking him towards the door. A second hand clamped around the back of Atherton's neck.

"Okay, okay," he said.

"Leave him alone, you bastard!" Vickie shouted. "He's a hero."

Atherton began to laugh. The bouncer took this as some sort of insubordination and squeezed his neck harder, shoving him more forcefully through the bar.

Osram was struggling with his own man, his free arm flailing, but connecting with nothing. The bouncer pushed him out into the street, forcing him to run several strides to avoid falling on his face. He turned and raised his fists, bouncing from foot to foot like a boxer, his large belly wobbling in time.

Atherton was pushed out into the street to join him. The force of the push and his bad leg conspired against him and he fell onto the cold pavement, to the amusement of the line of onlookers queuing to enter the bar. Osram stood with fists clenched and chin raised obstinately, hurling abuse.

"Fuckin' pussies," he hissed.

"Jesus, Neil. Please pack it in," he said, struggling to his feet. He put a hand on Osram's bare, clammy shoulder and tried to lead him away. He resisted, but then began to move away with him.

"Next time," he said, pointing at each of the bouncers in turn. "I'm coming back for you two."

The bouncers looked at each other and broke into laughter simultaneously.

Atherton and Osram staggered down the hill in silence until they reached the quayside. The dark murk of the Tyne rolled silently by. Atherton sat down on a bench overlooking the water.

"We shouldn't do this anymore," said Atherton.

"We've got to," said Osram. "Otherwise what's the point?" He pulled out a battered pack of cigarettes and lit one up with a plastic lighter, blowing out a plume of smoke above his head. He shivered violently. "I wish I hadn't left my shirt."

Atherton removed his jacket and handed it to Osram. He struggled to put it on. It was too small and the sleeves rode up high on his arms. Atherton slumped, letting the wooden bench support the back of his neck as he looked up. Even with the light pollution from the city, the stars shone brightly in the dark sky above.

He breathed deeply, smelling Osram's cigarette smoke. His eyes flicked over the night sky, from one set of stars to the next, whilst others scintillated in his peripheral vision. He marvelled at the ability of seemingly empty areas of sky to hold an abundance of stars. You only had to look long enough.

He looked for the few constellations he could remember. There weren't many: Taurus, Gemini, Canis Major – the big dog – and two whose names he couldn't quite remember. He found Orion near the horizon, remembering it from the start of movies in his youth; the stars breaking free from their celestial shackles to form a rotating 'O' for the Orion production company. His eyes fell onto the 'belt' of the figure, three stars almost in a perfect line save for the third star, which was ever so slightly off, too high for perfect alignment.

He sat up suddenly.

"Fucking hell, Neil," he said. "It's Orion!"

"It's bloody something, I'll tell you that," said Osram.

"No, you don't understand. I need to get in a taxi now," said Atherton.

"You'd better get me one too," he said, flicking the cigarette butt into the water, the lit end leaving a trail in the air until it was extinguished by the black water. "I'm totally fucked."

*

The wine didn't remain unopened for long.

Prejean was on her second glass when she heard a series of loud knocks on her door. When she opened it, Atherton stood leaning against the doorframe, hopelessly out of breath. He saw her puzzled face and raised the palm of his hand until he was able to speak. Behind him, across the hall, a small elderly lady was peeking out from behind her own door.

"It's okay," said Prejean. "This one's relatively safe."

Atherton nodded to the old dear and smiled, drunkenly.

"Sorry," he said, when he could finally speak. "This can't wait."

"Come in," she said, holding the door for him. "Goodnight, Mrs Warren."

As Atherton walked past into the flat, Prejean could smell the alcohol on him. She closed the door.

"What are you doing here, Jon? Do you think you can just turn up pissed and jump into bed with me?"

"That's not why I'm here. Unless you're offering of course, but that's not it," he said.

He walked into the lounge, which was in a state of mid-decoration. One wall had partially removed wallpaper; on another was a large canvas print of Klimt's *Sea Serpents*.

"I like what you've done to the place," he said.

"Fuck off."

"Not got your decorations up yet?"

"Haven't got round to it."

Atherton could see where she'd been sitting; the only gap on the settee which wasn't covered in papers or files. On the TV, a reality show played on mute. He grabbed a magazine from the floor and his eyes darted around the room until he located a pen.

"What are you doing?" she said.

He started to scribble on the front of the magazine, scoring a large dot, then another and a third. He held it up to Prejean.

"Orion's belt, Kate. The constellation of Orion," he said, quickly adding the remaining five stars. She looked from Atherton to the magazine and back again. He pointed to each of the stars of the belt in turn.

"Head...heart...vagina," he said. "In the constellation, the uppermost star is misaligned. Remember Bottleburn? It's the same, Kate. It's the same." He smiled at her.

She dove to the files, quickly locating a picture of the scene, with the flags representing each of Brampton's body parts: three flags in a diagonal line, the uppermost misaligned with the others. She placed the picture on the floor and dragged her laptop from the settee onto the floor. She rapidly tapped the keys and in a moment, an astronomy website appeared. She searched and found Orion, blowing it up as large as it would go. She placed the laptop alongside the photograph and counted the stars.

"Eight body parts. Eight stars," she said. "Fucking hell."

Atherton moved a pile of files from an armchair and took a seat. "I said he was doing this for a reason. This is it – he's recreating constellations with the bodies."

Prejean changed the orientation of the photograph slightly. Although the photograph was not a plan view, it was clear that the flags corresponded with the stars.

"Why, Jon?" she said.

"I don't know. All we know is he's compelled to do it. He's mirroring the stars, honouring them. This is why he likes open spaces and why the warehouse loading-bay had to have no roof. This is why he doesn't give a shit about disposing of the body. The body is the whole point."

"A sacrifice?"

"Yes. Maybe."

"What about butterfly girl?" she said. Prejean rifled through another pile on the sofa and produced a photograph of the scene from the glasshouse.

"Wait," said Atherton. He joined her on the floor, flipped over the magazine and roughly scored the position of the body parts. There were more this time.

"Look familiar?" said Prejean.

"No," he said. "I haven't a clue."

She looked back to the laptop screen and flicked through a number of constellations.

"Hold on...this one?" she said. "Draco. Fourteen major stars."

Atherton counted the number of flagged positions in the photo.

"Bingo."

He smiled at her and she smiled back, reaching for her wine and taking a large swig.

"It looks like the right shape," she said. "Draco...blah, blah...circumpolar – that is, never setting – for many observers in the northern hemisphere. It was one of the forty-eight constellations listed by the 2nd century astronomer Ptolemy, and remains one of the eighty-eight modern constellations today."

"I think it matches," said Atherton.

"Me too. This is pretty fucking major," she said.

"It is," he said, looking into the middle distance. "But the warehouse killing. The MO doesn't fit."

"Ah, but it does," she said. She showed him a split-screen picture she'd knocked up of the eyes; painted at the warehouse and carved into the tree at the riverside. "It's like you said...Izzy Lynch was a trial run. He was building himself up. Asking himself questions. Could he kill? How would he go about doing it?"

"Is there any wine left?" said Atherton.

The following few hours passed in a blur of photographs and speculative internet searches. Prejean gave him a Spanish Merlot she'd been avoiding for months. He looked at the bottle label with curiosity, but drank it anyway. She was impressed by his ability to focus when drunk.

"So, you think you've got enough?" he said.

"Enough for what?"

"To be able to raise it with Myers and the Red Hand Gang tomorrow?"

"You mean you're not going to take the stage and get the glory?"

"I'm thinking I should make an appearance at home sometime," he said.

"Fair enough," she said. "But this isn't your style. What's in it for you?"

"What do you mean? Nothing's in it for me?"

"You think you'll score a few points with me, by throwing me a bone. Is that what it is?" She was still smiling, but her tone had an edge.

"No, Kate," he sighed. "It's just an idea. It might help, it might not, but I want you to have it." They stood up together. "If it makes you hate me a bit less then that's a bonus, too."

"I don't hate you, Jon," she said.

He wobbled slightly, nearly having to grab onto her for support. "I'd best head off."

"Okay," she said and a silence followed. Another word hung unspoken in the air, almost tangibly, as if they could reach out and touch it: *stay*.

He smiled at her for a long moment and headed for the door.

CHAPTER TEN

Rogers upped the treadmill speed. His knee, which had developed a slight niggle, was bearing up well and the small wall-mounted fan blew welcome blasts of air over his face and shoulders. His thighs already ached from the five-a-side the night before. He'd been sluggish on the pitch, making basic mistakes, much to the derision of his teammates. Later, at the pub, he'd been quiet and distracted, unable to get into the conversation. He knew it was probably too late for Prejean to make an appearance, but he found himself checking the reflection of the gym door nonetheless. He found her something of a conundrum; methodical, dogmatic and an accomplished detective, but somehow willing to risk it all with a career-limiting affair with Atherton.

He'd watched her in the butterfly house and noticed the shorthand between them as they'd talked. The rest of the team had felt peripheral, merely resources to exploit as and when required.

He looked at himself in the mirror. He was in good shape, dressed well and was good-looking. She'd knocked him back, but taken on the disabled shrink. What was that all about?

He pressed another button to increase the incline, felt the surface rise beneath his feet and, before long, his thighs burned with the additional effort. Afterwards, he showered, letting the steaming hot water run over his face for long minutes and when his watch beeped to herald a new hour, he ignored it. It could be his turn to be late.

He had barely sat down before the phone rang with an internal tone.

"Rogers," he said, taking a pen from a neatly organised desk caddy.

"Morning. We have a Mr Forrest about a video camera at his premises? He wants Walsh, but his line is busy," said a male voice.

"Okay. Thanks. Put him through," he said. He heard a dull click. "Good morning. DC Rogers, how can I help you?"

"Yes, good morning. This is Malcolm Forrest," he said, with a slightly nasal twang.

"From the butterfly house, yeah?"

"That's correct. I'm the owner and manager..."

"I'm sorry about the inconvenience sir, our scene of crime unit will be finished with it as soon as..."

"Excuse me, Detective Constable, if you'd let me finish, I'm not calling about that," he said tersely. "In fact, a Mrs Cresswell released the building back to us yesterday evening."

"My apologies, Mr Forrest," said Rogers. He noticed Amis watching him from the far side of the room He rolled his eyes for her benefit. "And thanks again for your assistance in the past few days. What can I help you with?"

"Well, I wanted to inform you that you've left one of your cameras here," he said.

"Ah, I see. I'm sorry, I'll arrange for that to be picked up. Thanks for..."

"Quite a liberty, I must say. I don't remember giving permission, or anyone even asking if they could attach a video camera to my mast," he said.

"Excuse me, sir, your mast?"

Rogers heard him sigh.

"You can't have failed to notice the mast I have at the rear of the property, which supports my security cameras?"

"Yes, sir?"

"Well, there's a new one on there, which isn't mine. I presume it's the property of Northumbria police service, DC Rogers?...DC Rogers?"

*

Mattias Klum sat uncomfortably in his bus seat. The girth of the man to his left meant his right shoulder stuck out into the aisle and was knocked periodically by other passengers. He could feel the onset of a cold. It was no wonder – he seemed to spend his life going from the freezing cold outside, to overheated buses and offices. Someone nearby sniffed. He struggled to free his phone from his jacket pocket, clicking on the home button and selecting a bright blue icon on the touch screen.

He loved the internet; the beating pulse of news, of humanity, of life. He loved that he could carry all this in a thin wallet-sized rectangle in his pocket, but it also meant his work came everywhere too. It was hard to switch off. His setup at work was pretty good; a social media client package, which allowed him to monitor multiple newsfeeds from multiple social media platforms and search items simultaneously. On the bus, he had to do it manually. He entered the username of a known burglar and thumbed back through his posts to find a photo of a skinny young man posing beside a new-generation games console. Mattias emailed the post to himself to cross-check later against recent burglary statements.

He tapped the magnifying glass icon once more and entered the username @SonOfGeb. It was the last thing he'd looked at before he'd fallen asleep the night before. The profile appeared, with the single post beneath it, the blurry picture and the message. He pulled down on the display with his thumb and a flashing sunflower-shaped image appeared to indicate the feed was refreshing.

There was another post.

He stared at the screen, the light from the moving image flickering in the reflection of his glasses. The bus was stuck in a long stream of traffic leading to a large roundabout. By his estimation, he was still around two miles from work. He got to his feet, pocketed the phone and mumbled an excuse-me to the college kids standing in the aisle. They made a few efforts to let him past.

"Can you let me off here?" he asked when he drew level to the driver.

"I can't mate. I need to be at a bus stop, or else I get a bollocking," he replied.

"Let me off here!" he yelled.

The doors hissed open. Mattias Klum hit the ground running.

*

"Egyptians," he said over the phone.

Prejean had run from the shower to take the call.

"What?"

"Egyptians."

"Egyptians?"

"They paid tribute to the stars, didn't they? Worshipped them?" His voice was somewhat more difficult to decipher on the phone. "And that *Son of Geb* account that Mattias has been tracking. I think I might be on to something here. Go with me on this. I'm taking you to see someone."

She made sure she was ready and waiting by the time Atherton rolled into the parking bay outside her flat. By the time Atherton had left the night before, it had been after 3AM and even at that late hour, her thoughts had conspired to keep her awake through her tiredness. In the end, she'd masturbated, bringing herself to a weak, perfunctory orgasm and sleep had taken her soon after.

"Hey," she said, getting in. The air was a mix of alcohol, aftershave and breath mints. In the rear, she noticed a bright pink booster seat decorated with princesses and fairy tale castles.

"Morning," he said. "Fresh?"

"As a daisy," she said, fastening her seatbelt. It had taken two cups of coffee to pull her around, but she felt surprisingly good. She had experienced it many times before; the adrenaline and excitement of a developing case allowed her to go without decent sleep for days or weeks, only to come crashing down when it finally ended. They took off at quite a speed and she suddenly remembered his driving could be a little on the erratic side.

"I wish I could say the same," he said. She glanced his way and caught a redness to his eyes and she wondered if he'd slept at all.

"So who are we going to see?" she asked.

"Well, I tried to get hold of the head of department, but he's out. That's the trouble with Egyptologists, come the holidays, they tend to piss off to Egypt."

"Best place for them, really," she said.

"We'll be seeing a..." - he glanced at scribble on the back of his hand - "Maude Quint, who I'm told will be more than able to help."

"Okay," she said.

"Guess it's a start at least."

Atherton knew the morning traffic well and when they slowed to a stop behind traffic, he turned down a side street which Prejean hadn't been aware of.

"Yeah, I did some reading of my own at breakfast. Wait there..." she said, pulling the tablet from her bag. He snorted in derision and smiled broadly. "What?"

"You rely too much on that trumped up chopping board," he said.

"Bollocks," she said. "And anyway, this might back up what you were saying. Here it is...'the Pharaohs of Egypt believed they were earthly representatives of God in the stars and, as such, were required to leave their mark on the world when death arrived to remind them of their mortality. To do this they constructed the monumental tombs which symbolise Egypt – the pyramids.'" She looked at him, but it was hard to gauge what he thought. "He's paying tribute to the Gods in this life before he passes onto the next," she said. He glanced down at the screen and saw she had already written an array of notes, with pictures and photographs interspersed amongst the text. "I wonder what would make someone skip Christianity, Judaism and all the rest of it and go for hokey star-gazing?"

"Magical thinking," said Atherton. "Something about it inspires him. Maybe he got a hard-on when they did Tutankhamen in history class. Who knows? Something about it clicks for him. Like I said, he thinks if he does A enough times, B will happen."

"Well, we know the A, but what's the B?"

"Work that out and he's ours," he said.

*

Prejean followed Atherton beneath the red brick arches of the University Fine Arts building and into a large quadrangle, which had a paved thoroughfare on one side and a well-manicured lawn on the other. Waist-height hedgerows rose from the borders and a number of disparate trees dotted the grass. Atherton nodded at a passing man with ridiculously thick lenses before passing under another set of arches into a much shadier square. He stopped, pointed in one direction and then spun one hundred and eighty degrees before heading off again. Finally, they approached a large doorway which displayed the university coat of arms: a blue Cross of St. Cuthbert with a red lion above, and the words *Dept. of Ancient Egyptian Studies.*

Maude Quint was much younger and more attractive than Atherton had anticipated. She greeted them from behind a large desk with handshakes and a transatlantic accent. He hadn't seen her at any university functions or at any of the bars. Where had she been hiding?

"Nice to meet you, Dr Quint," said Atherton, taking a seat before he was asked.

"Miss," she said. "I'm working on the doctor bit."

"Thanks for seeing us at short notice," said Prejean, offering up her warrant card.

"It's really no problem," said Quint. "In fact, by being here, I may be inspired to get some work done." Quint's desk reminded Atherton of his own; littered with books and files. A large mug of tea sat beside her. "Can I get you anything to drink?"

"No, thank you," said Prejean. Quint's pretty eyes darted to Atherton.

"Yes, please," he said.

She rose and moved to a dilapidated kettle in the corner of the room.

"I'm afraid I only have Oolong," she said.

"Oolong's my favourite," said Atherton. Shortly after, Quint placed a steaming mug in front of him.

"So what can I help you with, Dr Atherton?"

"Detective Sergeant Prejean is investigating a –"

"It's a crime. An ongoing investigation, which we can't disclose too much about, I'm afraid, but it's possible that our person of interest has a passion for ancient Egypt," said Prejean.

A little wounded by the interruption, Atherton took solace in a sip from his tea.

"Okay," said Quint, giggling pleasantly. "Well, you've come to the right place."

"The guy we'd like to talk to..." said Atherton, looking at Prejean and pausing for effect to see if she was going to interrupt, "seems particularly interested in Osiris and his relationship with the stars."

"Well, it's known that the ancient Egyptians based quite a lot on whatever the stars were doing. It's particularly relevant to Osiris," she said. "Now...what can I tell you?"

She reached behind her and took down a large volume from the shelf, put it on the table and leafed through until she found a page, turning it to face them. She tapped a picture with a well-manicured fingernail. The picture was very typically Egyptian in style: Osiris, in a seated position, being attended to by two females. His skin was green, with a long pharaoh's beard, his clothing a bright white. In his hands were two implements: a crook and what appeared to be a broken stick. Behind him was a bank of hieroglyphs set into columns.

"I like his get-up," said Atherton pointing to the bright colours displayed on his crown.

"That's an Atef crown with ostrich feathers," said Quint. She pointed to his legs. "See how he's wrapped in bandages here? He's partially mummified because he's ruler of the afterlife. Lord of the Dead."

"He sounds like a right laugh," said Atherton. Quint giggled again.

"Yes, well, it's the old skeleton tarot card scenario," she said. "It wasn't all about death per se. Osiris was associated with the hope of new life after death. Cyclic stuff, like the death and growth of vegetation and the flooding of the Nile. In fact, green was the colour of rebirth, hence the zombie look he's rocking there."

"What about the stars?" said Prejean.

"The stars were important. They were essentially their gods. The afterlife, to them, was to travel eternally amongst the stars. Quite a nice thought, really. So Osiris is heavily linked to the stars, the afterlife, everything."

"So is this why they built the pyramids to be a map of the stars?" said Atherton.

"Ah, well. That might be the case. Some say yay and some still say nay on that one," said Quint. "Welcome to the world of Egyptology."

"What about the pyramids at Giza though?" he said.

"Being a facsimile of Orion's belt?" she said. "Yeah, three in a row with one offset and the Nile to the east representing the Milky Way. The Orion Correlation Theory. More people buy that one."

"Do you?" said Prejean.

"Given ancient Egypt's obsession with the stars, I think it's possible. Mind you, I streamed a documentary one night which tried to tell me the pyramids were built to be some kind of electromagnetic speaker system to contact alien worlds." She giggled again. Prejean watched Atherton smile dopily back. "I think...well the point is, people continue to attach a huge amount of significance to the pyramids. How and why they were constructed."

"And what about the alignment of the burial chambers with the stars?" said Atherton.

"Who's been reading books from airports, Jon?" She smiled. "Yes, the shafts they found in the King and Queen's chamber, leading to the surface of the Great Pyramid...wait..."

She got out of her seat and turned, reaching to a high shelf. Atherton's eyes involuntarily fell onto her back and moved down to her trim rear. He realised Prejean was watching him. She raised an eyebrow. Quint placed the book on top of the previous one and rapidly located a page.

"Here," she said and pointed to a cross-sectional diagram of a pyramid. "So here are the two shafts. For years people thought they were air-shafts, for ventilating the place, you know? Maybe that's exactly what they were. Truth is, it's still not clear. Anyway, one hypothesis is that at certain times of the year, key stars would line up with shafts so they'd be visible in the chambers."

"For what?" said Prejean.

"No-one knows, but it's hypothesised it would likely be a specific rite involving the dead pharaoh's passage to the afterworld."

"The start of his voyage into the stars?" asked Atherton.

"Exactly," she nodded.

"So which constellations were involved?" asked Prejean.

"Orion, of course. Little Dipper, Draco and Sirius," she replied, tapping each in turn with a fingernail.

Prejean's phone sounded; a cartoonish series of robotic bleeps.

"Sorry," she said and looked at the screen. A text from Myers: *Something you need to see here asap.* "We're going to need to wind this up, Jon."

"Thank you so much for your time, Maude," said Atherton. "Is it alright if we contact you again if we need some more advice?"

"Absolutely," she said and scribbled onto a scrap of paper. "Here's my number and my mobile, if I'm not at my desk."

"Thanks," said Atherton, nodding to the files on the desk. "Good luck with that lot."

*

As soon as Myers spotted them from his office, he marched them down the corridor to a small interview room where Mattias Klum was already sitting. He mumbled a tentative hello to them.

"Kate, Jon, take a seat," said Myers. "*Son of Geb* has posted again."

"A picture from the butterfly house?" asked Prejean.

"Yes, but it's not like the last one," said Myers. "Mattias?"

"Okay, this was posted at around 2AM this morning."

Mattias dragged a screen from his laptop until it appeared on the flat screen monitor on the wall. Atherton saw the crudely illustrated picture of Osiris next to the username *@SonOfGeb*, with the text:

We Know Who U R

Beside the message was a URL link.

"We?" said Prejean.

"That's not the bit you need to see. Before you watch it, I want you to know, both of you, that we'll take every precaution necessary to..."

"Just click it," interrupted Prejean.

Mattias clicked on the link and a grainy image filled the screen. It took Atherton a moment to realise what they were looking at. It was the butterfly house, shot from above. Prejean and Atherton were clearly visible through the glass. It was a short, repeating sequence: Atherton pointed at something and looked at Prejean, smiling. Prejean returned the smile and raised a hand to her hair, letting it drop again when it touched the hood of her SOCO overalls. Six seconds from start to finish and then the sequence repeated.

"Motherfuckers," said Prejean.

*

"Not familiar with the model, but it looks like a fairly standard home security cam with auto night vision," the SOCO officer shouted down to Sue Cresswell and Chris Rogers at the ground below. "Lithium battery...WiFi hook-up, so you can watch on your phone or laptop. For people to check their sheds when they're away from home."

"We're going to need to get it down at some point," said Sue. "Do you think that'll be a problem?"

"No, it's been taped on with duct tape. Just give me the nod and I'll bag it."

"Okay. Thanks. You can come down for the time being," said Sue.

The SOCO officer descended slowly, with another man holding the ladder tight against the mast.

"What do you make of that?" said Rogers.

"Cheeky," she replied, taking another shot of the camera and mast from a different angle.

"Cheeky, alright," said Rogers. "He obviously likes to star in his own movies."

Sue nodded.

"It's pointed directly at the spot she was murdered," she said. "From that angle, it would have caught everything."

Sue took a step back to see if there was anything else to be taken before she had the camera removed. The mast was aluminium and far enough away from the wall to assume whoever had positioned the camera hadn't touched the glass: prints would be unlikely, but she'd try anyway.

"Think you'll get anything from this?" said Rogers.

She twisted her face. "Best bit is the camera itself. We'll take it down, print the arse off it in the lab and see what else it can tell us."

"What about tracing the footage? If it's been hooked up to the free cafe Wi-Fi, would it have left a trail?"

"You're asking the wrong person there love, but I'd say it's worth a try."

"The fucking gall of the bastard," said Rogers. He looked around as if looking to find a job to do. "I'd better go and tell Mr Forrest he'll still not be open today. Unless you want to, Sue."

"No," she said. "That's your job, kidder."

Rogers walked off towards the house, leaving Sue to take more shots.

A cold breeze picked up and caused the long grass to dance beside her leg. She pulled the hood up on her jacket and pulled the drawstrings. Nearby, a bird took flight from the undergrowth and flew past her, so close she could feel the displacement of air from its wings against her cheek. Her eyes were drawn to the undergrowth from whence it had flown. She looked up the path to Rogers; he had gone, leaving her alone.

But she had a disconcerting feeling she was not alone at all.

*

Atherton followed Prejean into the focus room just in time to see her kick over one of the display boards. It was an impressive swipe with the sole of her foot.

"Kate," he said.

"Fuck, Jon," she said.

Myers entered the room. He looked as if he was going to say something then thought better of it.

"I know," said Atherton.

"What the fuck does that mean? *We Know Who U R?*"

"He's just trying to mess with us," said Atherton. "He's trying to exert control..."

"Will you shut up with the psychobabble shite for one minute? What does it mean? Is he coming after us?"

"No, I don't think..."

"How many of them are there? *We?* That better be the royal fucking we." She was pacing the floor between Myers's office and the window.

Myers's face had begun to redden, in contrast with his white hair. He placed one hand on his hip and held the other out towards Prejean. Atherton saw his managerial mode toggle between authoritative and compassionate, unsure which side to land on.

"Kate, if you want to take some time this afternoon, please do. I'm not going to underestimate the gravity of this," said Myers. "I think we should give this the respect it deserves and view it as a threat. To all of us, perhaps. Jon, if you'd like me to make the necessary arrangements, I can have your family placed into safety by this afternoon."

"How many people have seen this?" said Jon.

"His followers haven't gone up any. He's got no idea that anyone is noticing this stuff, let alone the police."

"I don't want Louise to see that," said Atherton after a moment. Had he been looking her way, he would have seen Prejean roll her eyes at this.

"Sure, I understand," said Myers. "And if you need to back away from this case, I'd totally understand that, too."

"Do you, Paul?" said Prejean. "I don't remember you ever becoming the public focus of a case, or appearing on the cover of a newspaper, but it seems to be a regular bloody occurrence for me."

The room bristled with tension. An atmosphere which, despite the circumstances, Atherton found delicious. Myers's brow furrowed.

"I'm sorry this has happened, Kate. It's beyond anyone's control. If you want off this case, either or both of you, please let me know," he said calmly. "If you need me, I'll be with Amis, working on tomorrow's press conference." He left the room briskly.

Prejean folded her arms, moved to the window and looked out. Atherton righted the display board and pinned a photograph back in place.

"It's happening again, Jon," she said.

CHAPTER ELEVEN

"There," said Prejean, pointing to an 'Oncology' sign nestled amongst numerous others. He'd followed her into the heart of the building, struggling to match her pace.

Atherton hated hospitals. He'd seen enough of them in his youth. Labyrinthine corridors with sickly shiny orange floors and the stink, disinfectant over shit, the smell of illness itself. His parents had brought him, in his dad's rusting Ford Cortina, with promises to improve his walking. The doctors fitted him with a steel calliper brace of steel and soft leather buckles, which still managed to chafe his skin. It helped to an extent, but it clicked against the ground when he walked and made him look all too much like the collection box effigies seen outside paper shops. *Help Spastics*, they said. That word. How many times had he heard it or a derivative over the years? Whispered by giggling children or spat in his face in anger?

"Can we make this quick?" he said. "Hospitals give me the heebies."

He followed her in the direction of the sign and round a bend where the corridor opened into a reception area with a desk and rows of well-worn plastic chairs.

"Thank fuck for that," said Atherton breathlessly. "I was afraid you were going to have to find me a bed."

"You'd like that, wouldn't you?" said Prejean, avoiding his eyes.

In between the rows of chairs was a low coffee table covered in flowers; lilies, roses and carnations. Prejean knelt beside it, angling one of the wrappers so she could read it.

Abigail, our angel. You're back in heaven now where no-one can hurt you.

"There's more out the back," said a voice from behind them. "It's hard to know what to do with them all."

They turned to face a nurse wearing a bright green smock, with a balding head, which reflected back the strip lighting from above. "We've had to let some of the staff take them home," he said.

"It would be a shame to waste them. I'm Detective Sergeant Kate Prejean of Northumbria police." She extended a hand and the man shook it warmly. "This is Doctor Jon Atherton from Newcastle University."

"Yes, someone called to say we might expect you," he said. "I'm staff nurse Rick Shermer. Please take a seat."

Atherton sat, trying not to emit a noise as he did so, breathing out silently between pursed lips instead.

"Cerebral palsy?" asked Shermer, taking Atherton by surprise.

"Guilty," he replied.

"My sister has ataxic palsy," he said. "She's pretty much a full-time wheelchair user, but she's studying law now."

"Every power to her," said Atherton. "Would she know how to sue the architect of this bloody hospital? It's like a maze."

Shermer smiled.

"Can you spare us a few moments of your time?" said Prejean. "We just want to find out a bit about Abigail at work, particularly in the last few days. Anything which might have seemed strange or out of the ordinary."

"Well, I've already told one of your colleagues everything on that front," he said. Prejean noticed his rather hirsute hands as he spoke, a feature she found strangely attractive. "What can I say? She was well-liked. She was quiet. A bit naive maybe, but she was young, you know? She was good with patients; a good nurse. Everyone liked her. She left that day as normal." His voice cracked a little. Prejean placed a hand on his shoulder, finding his frame small but solid.

"It's okay. I'm sorry to keep going over things, it's just by doing so, it sometimes shakes something loose and helps you remember."

"We're all in shock over what's happened," he said.

"Did Abigail mention anyone new in her life?"

"Like a boyfriend?" he said. "No, but I doubt I'd get to hear about it. You'd be better off asking her flatmate that kind of thing. She works in the maternity ward."

Prejean nodded. "My colleagues are with her now."

A stooped, sallow-faced man entered the waiting area, looked up at them from beneath the peak of his baseball cap and gave Shermer a nod of recognition. He took a seat and emitted a drawn-out sigh in the process. The nurse put his hands on his knees as if ready to rise.

"We may have to call upon you again, I'm afraid," said Prejean.

"Sure, if you think I can be..."

"What about patients?" said Atherton, interrupting.

"What do you mean?"

"I mean, have you noticed anyone out of the ordinary visiting the ward?" said Atherton.

"Out of the ordinary?"

"Shall we say not normal, for the sake of brevity? Sometimes we can sense which birds need to be pushed from the nest."

"No," said the nurse, frowning. "The people we see here are generally in pain...afraid...and at various stages of illness. We see all types of emotions and behaviours over the course of a day here. I don't know how you'd categorise normal."

Shermer looked away from Atherton as if marking the matter closed and looked at Prejean, who smiled at him.

"I'm sorry," she said. "We won't keep you any longer. Thanks."

Shermer bounced to his feet.

"That's quite alright," he said, shaking her hand and, after a laboured moment, Atherton's.

They started to walk back up the corridor and Prejean waited until they were out of earshot before she said, "You need to work on your bedside manner, doc."

She watched him trying to come up with a snappy retort from the corner of her eye, until it became too late.

"Noted," he said eventually.

*

Sue Cresswell double-checked the figure she had in her notes. It was a bad habit she needed to work on. She knew the work her team had completed was good, she knew the methodology was sound, she knew the spreadsheet formulae she'd used for the final calculations were absolutely fine, yet still she checked everything repeatedly.

It was something which presented itself at home too. At night, she locked and unlocked the back door three times before she felt safe to go to bed. She thought there was at least some rationality to this: better safe than sorry right? She'd seen too many crime scenes to want to star in her own. However, she had a similar process with the light switch, counting seven clicks – off, on, off, on, off, on, off – before she climbed into bed. She knew what it was, but never referred to it by name, because giving it a name would mean it was something which needed to be addressed and she had little time for that.

Slowly, they filtered in: Rogers, Amis, Walsh and a minute later, Myers, Prejean and Atherton.

"Okay, Sue, what delights do you have for us?" said Myers.

"I don't know about delights, but I'm sure I have one or two things you'd be interested in," she said.

"Superb," said Myers.

"Well, finally, and after much deliberation, I think I'm able to give you an estimated weight from the camp chair indentations."

Sue tapped her keyboard and a picture of the marks from the riverbank appeared on the wall monitor.

"So, using dirt from the scene and recreating the moisture content and temperature of the soil in the laboratory, we were able to put an estimate of the weight of the individual who used the chair at approximately one hundred and fifty-five pounds."

"That's pretty light. Who said they thought it would be a little bloke?" said Amis. "We should have opened a book."

"Lightweight," said Rogers.

"Another thing was the murder weapon from the butterfly house scene." She tapped the keyboard again and several photographs of the blood on the glass roof appeared; bright red spatter in trails against the bleached-out skies above the butterfly house. "Having had a bit of time to consider these, I don't think these are as consistent with a simple blunt instrument as we first thought. See how there's cast off from the weapon all up the south wall? We know that this would essentially have been behind the killer. Now, if I'm positioned over someone with a short, solid metal pipe, beating the victim from above..." Sue leaned over the desk, with an imaginary weapon in her right hand and swung downwards several times to demonstrate. "...I would expect the cast off to appear directly above." She gestured to the ceiling. "Instead, we see multiple trails behind."

"So what does that mean?" said Walsh. "A different murder weapon?"

"I think so, possibly," she said. "The wounds on Brampton and Southern both suggest blunt force trauma with something five centimetres in diameter, but the cast off suggests something which isn't a completely solid pipe or bar. What it made me think of was nunchucks," she said.

"Or a flail?" said Atherton.

"What's that?" said Amis.

"An agricultural flail was used to strip grain in a field. Basically, two sticks separated by a chain. Pretty brutal as a weapon. In fact, the nunchuck probably developed from the agricultural flail in Japan."

"So what are we looking for," said Rogers, "a farmer or a ninja?"

Walsh and Amis smiled at this. Atherton cleared his throat.

"I have a theory," he said. "Bear with me on this."

*

"Wait," shouted Atherton, struggling to keep up with Prejean as she strode across the carpark. "Where are you going?"

She said something in return, but it was drowned out by the sound of a police van heading towards the exit. Prejean found her car, jumped in, started the engine and jammed it in reverse. Her foot was almost off the clutch when she saw Atherton filling her rear view mirror. She took her foot off the gas and he jumped in the passenger seat.

"What, Jon?" she said. "I need some time alone."

"Me too," he said. "Let's go somewhere."

She sighed and reversed out. They drove for several minutes in silence, heading out of the city centre. He watched as they passed by people in the street, noticing their uniform, stoic faces as they passed. How oblivious they looked.

They dropped onto the steep incline of Stepney Bank, heading down towards the Ouseburn. Prejean made a sharp left and parked up beneath the massive stone arches of Byker Bridge. Behind them was a second hand furniture shop, with various items – dressers, pews and wardrobes – spilling out onto the street. She turned off the engine and stared out of the window.

"How does this kind of thing not affect you?" she said after some time. She felt depleted, ground down, like wood sanded down upon a lathe until there was nothing left but dust.

"You mean apart from being exceptionally high on the psychopathic spectrum?" he said. "It's probably because I'm as cool as fuck."

"The killer has called us out personally and we're no further forward. How they ever thought I could run a team after last time..."

"You put a child-killer inside, Kate," said Atherton.

"Too –"

"Don't tell me *too late*. You think that was going to be a one-off for him? He was just getting started. He would have done it again and again and again, but you put him away."

"Based on your profile," she said.

"You ran the team and you caught the bad guy. Myers knows the best chance he has of catching this one is you. And don't say we're no further forward, because we are."

She looked away again and her shoulders began to shake in heavy sobs. He reached out and placed a hand on her shoulder. She shook her head and put her hand on top of his. He expected her to peel it away, but instead she squeezed it tightly.

"I can't do this," she said.

"You *will* do this," he said. "You can and you *will* do this. You can't walk away now, because you know what that would mean: some other girl being found in pieces in the countryside."

"I can't..."

"Who's going to do it? Myers? Rogers?" he said.

"No," she said. "Look, I should get back." She let go of Atherton's hand. "There's a press conference tomorrow."

"Fuck that," said Atherton. "That's Myers's gig. It isn't for you to worry about."

"So what do you suggest?"

"We go somewhere now, me and you, and we work on the evidence, then tomorrow, when the smoke has cleared, you can rally the troops."

She started the engine. On the way to her flat, they stopped at an off-license.

*

Rogers strode into the office with the newspaper under his arm. Walsh was already in his seat, deep in the midst of a low-volume telephone call. Amis nodded a greeting and went back to tapping her keyboard. Myers was already on the phone, his baritone voice audible even though the words were not. Rogers waited until Walsh had finished his call and picked up a plastic cup before slamming the newspaper down in front of him with a loud thump. Walsh jumped in his seat.

"What the fuck," he said, wiping spilled water from his shirt-front.

"Lauren Schloss is all over this," said Rogers. "Look."

Walsh unfolded the paper and read the headline: STARMAN: CRAZED KILLER'S OBSESSION.

The black text overlaid an aerial photograph of the crime scene at Bottleburn. He quickly read the front page and thumbed to the rest of the article, which spanned the centre pages; a large centre panel of text alongside photos of the victims.

"For fuck's sake," he said after a moment. "Who's feeding her this?"

"I don't know. Someone is and Myers will go ape-shit. Just you watch," said Rogers, looking briefly towards the DI's office.

"'Northumbria police believe the gruesome killer, dubbed *Starman* by investigators, has an obsession with mapping out the stars with the bodies of his victims'," said Walsh angrily. "No-one should know that. That's come from inside."

"Atherton?" said Rogers, throwing himself into his chair.

"You think? He'll be hoping to get a book out of this, so would he really spill anything to the paper?"

"Who knows, but it's going to get a little interesting around here, if you ask me."

Walsh put an elbow on the desk, cupped his chin and looked intently at the paper.

*

"*Sorry, I can't take your call at the moment, but please leave a message,*" said Prejean's voice, followed by a familiar beep.

"It's Myers. Call me back please, Kate." He was conscious of keeping his tone neutral. He paused for a moment. "We need to talk before the conference tomorrow."

He hung up, and sighed. "And my lead investigating officer has fucked off on me," he said to himself.

Myers caught a glimpse of himself reflected in the glass, his face disappointingly more rounded than expected. He was still slimmer and fitter than many of the schoolmates he met regularly at the pub, but he needed to keep his diet in regular check. He sighed again, and tried to brush down an errant strand of silver hair on the side of his head. There was a knock at the door. Amis smiled coyly through the glass and he beckoned her in.

"Hi, Connie, grab a seat," he said. She sat opposite him and arranged a notepad and pen neatly in front of her. He stole a glance; the conservative wool jumper only hinted at her figure. He sat down himself and pulled over his notepad, which was decorated in numerous notes, phone numbers and doodles.

"Okay, we're going to be talking to Callum Brown in external relations," said Myers. "He's out of the office...of course. You can tell he's a bit of a media luvvie type, but he's pretty good."

Amis dutifully jotted Brown's name on her pad. He tapped a number into the table-top conference phone and there was a loud beep.

"Hi," said a deep, male voice.

"Hello, Callum, how are you? This is Paul Myers and with me is DC Connie Amis." Amis noticed how he raised his voice and leaned down to talk; she found his mistrust of technology endearing.

"Hi Paul. Hi Connie," he said. "So we have a few friends from the media popping over tomorrow?" His confidence seemed to ooze through the conference phone speaker.

"We do indeed," said Myers. "I was hoping to have lead investigating officer DS Kate Prejean on the call, but she's following up on something related at this time."

"No problem. I'm up to speed on the salient points, I think," said Brown. "What are you trying to get out of the conference?"

Just to get through the bloody thing, thought Myers.

"We're getting a significant amount of media pressure, as you can imagine, so I think it's an assurance position we need to take. Do you agree?"

"I do and I suggest we keep it as short as possible. I'll do the introductions and let you do a statement – I can help you draft this by the way – let's keep it to the basic information, but draw it out a little to minimise the number of questions we need to field."

"Sounds good to me," said Myers. "I'm anticipating questions about the nature of the killings themselves and I don't think we really want to get into that."

"No, that's right. I suggest focussing on the abductions. You know, state the places and approximate times they were taken. Appeal for witnesses and it may help draw attention from the killings themselves."

Amis's hand ached from the notes she was writing.

"Okay," said Myers.

"I'll keep things ticking along and intervene if I think we're heading anywhere contentious," he said. "I know Lauren Schloss has already turned up at one of the scenes, so I'm ready for her, believe me."

"What about the evidence we have so far?"

"What do you have?"

"Not much. We have an approximate weight and psychological profile."

"No. Not worth giving any of this up at this stage. If anything comes back from the witness appeal: a description, a car reg or model, then that's when we think about roping in the press and only when it couldn't compromise your investigation."

"Understood," said Myers. "I don't know if this is worth mentioning, but neither woman was raped. I've been advised by Dr Atherton not to mention this detail in case it could infer the killer has a problem in that area and provoke him further."

"No, that's useful to know. So, we reiterate what has happened, call for witnesses, tell them public safety is our priority etcetera and fuck all else, basically."

"Fine, Callum. That's great. I'm going to draft a statement and get that over to you in the next hour or so," said Myers.

"I'm picking up emails all evening," he replied. "Now, one thing we need to discuss is DS Prejean and her previous run-ins with the media."

Myers looked over to Amis and their eyes locked for a moment. She thought for a second he was going to ask her to leave. He wondered if that would be the correct thing to do, but the moment passed.

"Yes," said Myers. "I think we need to be careful here on a number of counts."

"As I remember, the affair between Prejean and Doctor..."

"Atherton," said Myers, helpfully.

"Ah yes...was pretty widespread through the redtops at the tail end of the case and I can understand why. The combination of a pretty young cop and a – shall we say – unorthodox profiler was pretty compelling, so it's no wonder. Do you have any specific concerns this time around?"

Amis watched Myers inhale deeply as he considered an answer.

"In a recent development, we've intercepted social media messaging from what we believe to be the person of interest in this case," he said. "It appears that this individual has already latched onto the former relationship between Atherton and Prejean as some kind of...focus."

There was a long moment of silence from Brown's end.

"My recommendation is that you avoid any direct reference to Prejean leading the case. Don't mention Atherton in any capacity."

"Would you recommend any other steps?"

Another brief silence.

"If you're asking me whether it would be better from a public relations standpoint if she was off the investigation, I'd say probably yes. But it's your team and you'd have to weigh that decision against the chances of a positive outcome for the case," he said. "If you're asking if she should be at the conference or not, I'd give some thought to keeping her out of it."

Myers removed his glasses and rubbed the bridge of his nose.

"That's clear. Thanks," he said.

"Okay. Anything else right now?"

"No, I think that covers it," said Myers.

"I'll look out for your email," said Brown. "Bye."

The phone clicked and was silent. Amis continued to write. Myers took the opportunity to look at her neck: the delicate muscle where the fingers of her left hand rested, the milk chocolate brown skin there. After a moment, she stopped and looked up at him.

"So, how did you enjoy that?" he said.

"That was that, I guess," she said and smiled, her white teeth taking a sharp contrast against her dark lipstick.

"Yeah, External Relations is the only department to have grown in the past five years instead of being cut back."

"Maybe I should ask for a transfer," she shrugged.

"No, I need you right here," he said. "You ready to start this statement?"

"I think we'd better."

"Do you have plans tonight?" he asked.

"No, sir. Why?"

"Just in case we overrun a little trying to get this done," he said awkwardly. "Dinner is my shout, okay?"

"It's a deal."

He flipped open his laptop and failed to see the corners of her mouth rise into a slight, but undeniable smile.

There was a knock at the door: Walsh, holding a copy of the Evening Chronicle. Myers beckoned him to enter.

"You both need to see this," he said when he entered. He unfolded the paper to let them see the headline. Myers's face dropped and he released a long sigh, leaning back in his chair, resignedly.

*

The flat felt cold.

Prejean turned the dial on the wall thermostat and Atherton heard a boiler kick into action somewhere. He watched her cross the room and look out of the window, as he sat down in a nearby armchair, sighing with relief when the weight was removed from his hip.

"Do you ever feel like you've taken a wrong turn somewhere?" she said. "As if you've got on the wrong train and now you've got to ride it out to the end?"

"No," he said after a beat. She turned to him. "I think I've found my particular place." He watched her kick her shoes off and click on a table lamp. "So being the youngest, most celebrated DS in the region isn't your calling. Maybe you should have gone into interior design?" He looked around the room.

"I just have a bad feeling. I think this press conference is going to be a car crash," she said. "It was much easier before I was promoted." She watched the light reflect on the water as the Tyne lumbered by.

"Somehow, I don't think you'd like being ordered around by Walsh or Amis," he said.

"No," she said. "Maybe not."

"You excel at this, Kate. I can't think of anyone better," he said. "We're making progress. You just need to go keep going."

Prejean looked at the disparate people passing by on the promenade beneath: an old bespectacled man in a raincoat walking a dog, a male jogger in a hoodie, a couple in hats and scarves walking hand in hand, deep in an inaudible conversation. She removed her jacket and laid it carefully on the settee nearby and walked slowly towards Atherton. He watched her approach, her lithe body in a thin blouse, illuminated by the lamp behind. She stopped in front of him and he squinted in an attempt to see her face.

"Maybe we should get back to work," she said. "Coffee?"

"Please. Where do you want to start?"

"Selection," she said from the kitchen. "We think he's got a type and we know he's a voyeur. If he enjoys watching us – me and you – I think you can guarantee he's been following these girls and watching them beforehand."

"Without a doubt. At Menshen's, he knew exactly where the camera blackspots were and he knew exactly how to take the nurse; when she'd be alone and off-shift. How? Because he's been staking them out."

A few minutes later, she emerged with two steaming cups and placed one in front of him. He took a sip, found it too hot and put it back down.

"He's selecting these women based on his own pre-set criteria. They're all beautiful women of a similar height and look. They're all worthy. Worthy of his attention, worthy of sacrifice. He's honouring the gods, so he can fly alongside them for eternity, remember?" Atherton made a flying motion with one of his hands. "You don't honour deities with any old skank, you present the finest examples known to humanity. At least, I would. These women represent his version of perfection."

"So how's he spotting the talent?" she said. "Something he does brought him into contact with all three of them, but we found no links between Brampton and Southern."

"There is, we just haven't found it yet, baby. What did Amis dig up at Menshens?"

"Nothing much. She looked at security guards, catering, maintenance people, you name it. She didn't find any commonality between personnel at the insurance office and the hospital."

"Mmm," he said. "And the warehouse?"

"Ditto," she said.

"Actually, I've been thinking about the warehouse," he said. "Of the three, we've been classing it as the anomaly, right? A trial run which doesn't quite fit the MO?"

"Yeah."

"I started wondering why he left her with her arms outstretched and legs together," he said.

"He wanted to make it clear there wasn't a sexual motive. To show us he's above that. He was trying to tell us his act of killing operates above the base desire to rape and kill."

"Perhaps, but it also reminded me of this." He took a pen from the table. He struggled to find a piece of paper and instead went to the wall where the paper had been partially removed to reveal the plaster beneath. "Do you mind?"

"You can't hurt anything."

He drew a shape on the wall.

"What do you call that again?" she asked.

"An ankh. Osiris is often depicted with one. Very *de rigeur* in ancient Egyptian times and with Goths in the eighties, if I remember correctly. It's the symbol of life and birth." He pointed to the loop, crossbar and downward vertical shaft of the ankh in turn. "Womb, fallopian tubes and vagina. It's an actual diagram of the reproductive organs."

"So…you think killing Izzy Lynch represented birth?"

"*His* birth," said Atherton.

"As what?"

"America's next top model," he said. "I've got no idea. His birth as a star god?"

"Jesus. How does someone get so…?"

"Bat-shit?"

"Exactly. Is that a recognised psychiatric term?"

"No. I think it's dangerous to think of him in those terms. This makes perfect sense to him. A psychological motive is not necessarily a rational one. It's all a means to an end. He cuts and positions these women with accuracy and care. The killings are considered and purposeful in the same way the pyramids were constructed with meticulous precision and skill. Both tributes to the stars."

"If we look at the remaining stars of the Great Pyramid; the constellation of Ursa Minor and Sirius," she said. "If we follow the pattern, I can picture that his interpretation of Ursa Minor would be like the others. Some poor girl torn up into the shape of the Little Dipper, right? But what would Sirius consist of?"

"One star?" Atherton took a large gulp of coffee. "That's a good point. I haven't got a clue. We need to think about that."

"I have been," she said. "I thought if several stars in a constellation equate to several body parts of one woman, what will the brightest star in the sky equate to?"

His eyes darted around the room as he thought. He looked at her, raised his eyebrows and nodded. The closest, she knew, she would get to a complement.

"A grand finale?"

"That's what I thought. Save the best till last," she said. "Or maybe he'll just move onto another constellation."

Atherton was lost in thought. She took her empty mug into the kitchen and then wandered past him, looking out the window once more. After a few minutes, he joined her. On the promenade below, a man took photographs of the view looking back up the Tyne. Atherton followed his line of sight, to the impressive array of bridges that spanned the big river.

Prejean was looking at her phone and he moved closer so he could peer over her shoulder. On the screen was the message: *We Know Who U R*, and beneath it, the constantly rolling loop of Atherton and Prejean in the butterfly house.

"What if there is more than one? A protégé or a spectator?"

"Maybe he's talking about the gods he hopes to join? The stars?" he said. "It's just a distraction. I think we should regard it as one single intent, a single MO. It doesn't matter how many individuals there are."

"It will if they come to that door, Jon." She gestured with her head. He reached out and pushed a strand of hair behind her ear. He watched the glimmer of a smile play on her mouth.

"What is it?" she said.

"Nothing."

"Fine," she said, with a mischievous look on her face.

CHAPTER TWELVE

Callum Brown had come up with the idea of hosting the press conference in the bright, modern vestibule of the station rather than in one of its cavernous meeting rooms. Myers had arranged for the podium to be placed on the landing of the stairs, a mid-point between the ground and first floors. This way, if things were to get awkward, they could call time on the conference and retreat upstairs whilst the media were ushered out. The press wouldn't be offered seats and the whole affair would last no longer than fifteen minutes.

Myers and Amis had drafted and redrafted a statement until it was little more than a series of bullet points. A handful of people had already assembled and Myers noticed Lauren Schloss had made sure she had a prime spot at the foot of the stairs. A TV cameraman had set up a tripod beside her and was already training a small camera up the steps towards him.

Brown's hair was immaculately coiffed and he wore an impressively expensive-looking tailored suit.

"All set?" he said to Myers, touching the back of his arm in the semblance of a reassuring gesture.

"As I'll ever be," said Myers.

Brown took position behind the podium and tapped the microphone once to ensure it was live.

"Good morning everyone and thanks for coming along today. We have a short statement, which will be followed with a very brief question and answer session. For this reason, I'd like to politely ask you all to keep your questions short and on-topic please. I'd like to introduce Detective Chief Inspector Paul Myers and Detective Sergeant Kate Prejean."

Brown stepped away, allowing Myers to step behind the mic.

"Thank you. Northumbria police are appealing to the public for information regarding the abduction and subsequent murder of two local women," said Myers. "Firstly, Miss Ellis Brampton, who was abducted from her place of work at Menshen Insurance at the Armstrong Business Park at approximately 5.20PM and whose body was later discovered in Bottleburn.

"Secondly, Miss Abigail Southern, a nurse from North Tyneside General Hospital, who is believed to have been abducted from her flat and whose body was later found at Coqueton, again in north Northumberland. These were particularly brutal crimes and we are obviously very keen to reach a swift, successful resolution to this case."

Myers took a breath. He heard the clicks from several camera shutters in succession.

"Okay, I'll open now for a few questions…" he began.

"Warren Cox, News Post Leader," interrupted a young bearded man at the foot of the stairs. "Is there a sexual element to the attacks?"

"This is not something we'd like to comment on at this time," said Myers.

"Lauren Schloss, Evening Chronicle." Her piercing eyes levelled straight at Myers. "Is it not true that the police are also reviewing the brutal murder of a prostitute, a Miss Isabelle Lynch in October of last year, and investigating all three as the work of a serial killer?"

The crowd around Schloss bustled slightly and one reporter moved his voice recorder under her face. Myers started to say something, but Brown interrupted.

"The focus of our investigation relates to the murders of Miss Brampton and Miss Southern," he said.

"So you're saying there's not a serial killer at large in our region?"

"To speculate at this point about further activity, which may or may not have links, would be distracting to our current investigation. Do we have any questions relating to the…"

"A serial killer known as the Starman, which sources have revealed to the Evening Chronicle has been taunting the police on social media channels using the name…" she referred to a notepad. "…*Son of Geb*?"

Prejean shot Myers a look of concern.

"We have no comment on that at this time," said Myers. "We hope to appeal to the public for assistance to find witnesses or physical evidence related to the crimes stated."

"Do we have any further questions?" said Brown, looking over Schloss's head, purposefully.

"Can you provide any advice for women in the wake of these incidents?"

"Only to be vigilant. Don't take any risks and continue to take your personal safety extremely seriously," said Myers.

"I think that just about covers it, folks. Thank you very much," said Brown, receiving a few grumbles from the crowd. Brown, Myers and Prejean started to make their way up the stairs.

"Transparent as ever," said Schloss.

"What just happened?" said Prejean as soon as they were out of earshot. She rounded on Myers, blocking his path in the corridor.

"I'll pop in later for a debrief, Paul," said Brown, placing a mobile phone to his ear as he disappeared rapidly up the corridor.

"It looks like Schloss has found a source of information," he said tightly, lowering his voice as someone passed. "And we need to find out who's got the loose lips. My office. Now."

"Two minutes," she said, reaching for her phone. Myers frowned at her but turned to walk away. Atherton's line rang out for several minutes, then cut to voicemail.

Prejean passed the reception where a gaggle of young women remonstrated about something with a beleaguered young officer. The sliding glass doors swished open before her and she stepped out into the cool shadow outside.

"Er…hi," said a voice. Amis stood to one side of the doors, holding a cigarette. "Fresh air?"

"Something like that," said Prejean.

"I don't know if you've come to the right place." She laughed, nodding to the cigarette and taking a drag.

"I used to be a smoker," said Prejean.

"Really? Well done. How long ago did you quit?"

"Couple of years," she said. Amis exhaled and Prejean smelled an aroma that was equally noxious and alluring. "Actually, would you mind?"

"Oh...of course. Are you sure?"

Prejean nodded. Amis took one from the packet she already held in her hand and gave it to Prejean, shielding her lighter from the breeze as she lit it for her. Prejean inhaled and let the smoke out slowly.

"Good as you remember?"

"Bit of a buzz. The actual thing you want is never as strong as the urge to have it, though. Do you know what I mean?"

"You've got that right," said Amis.

There was moment of silence. Amis looked out across the carpark.

"Doctor Atherton...he seems a bit of a character," she said finally, casually flicking a sizeable chunk of ash to the ground.

"He is," said Prejean. "He's a bit much for people sometimes."

"As my mother would say, he has a lot about him."

"He does that," said Prejean. "You know we worked together on the Lee Hicks case?"

"Of course," said Amis.

There was an extended silence.

"We interviewed the whole school, the teachers, the kitchen staff, the caretaker, the parents. We looked at the kids' online activities. Everyone. Atherton was there with his radar on full beam," said Prejean, taking a drag and exhaling a plume of smoke skyward. "Nothing. But Jon also thought it would have been opportunistic. A break in the norm. The kidnapper would have had a window of opportunity to take the boys. If we found that window, we'd find the boys. And that's where we fell down."

"How so?"

"One of the parents at the school had a prior conviction for sexual assault from twelve years previously. He was unemployed and couldn't explain his whereabouts on the day in question. We spent too long on him, when Atherton told us not to."

"Hicks was a shopkeeper, right?"

Prejean nodded.

"A paper-shop the boys didn't often go to." Prejean paused to flick ash from the cigarette. "There were road works that day – only that day – which meant the bus dropped them at the opposite side of their estate, right next to the shop. He told them he had video games in the back."

"Christ."

"When we found them, they were already dead and when they picked up Lee Hicks, he was on his way back from a DIY store with plastic sheeting and a shovel."

"Fucking hell."

"I don't think Jon has ever really got over that. When we found them, I mean. He's always blamed himself, for not getting there in time, but...he was right. We'd got it wrong, not him. I'd got it wrong."

"Ow!" said Amis, dropping the butt which had burned down to her finger. She dropped it and shook her hand.

"Great track record, eh?" said Prejean, who followed suite and ground the cigarette against the wall-mounted ashtray.

*

They heard Atherton's phone ring, the noise drifting through to the conservatory where they sat watching Hannah through the glass. Hannah, in a bright red winter coat, bounced on a large trampoline surrounded by a safety net at the top of the garden.

"Do you need to get that?" said Louise, looking up from her magazine.

"No," he said.

She raised an eyebrow almost imperceptibly.

"We should do this more often," he said. "It finally feels like the holidays have started."

"Speaking of which," she said. "I passed the travel agents yesterday. There were plenty of last minute deals."

"We should book one," he said. "See the new year in somewhere sunny."

"We should. I nearly did, in fact, but I wanted to make sure this police thing wasn't going to drag on."

"I don't think there's much more I can do," he said and smiled. "For the moment at least, I'm all yours."

"We'll have to see if I still want you," she said.

The guilt he'd felt since being at Kate's place the previous afternoon rose sharply once more. He'd returned home, showered as if to remove any hint of potential infidelity. Fortunately, Louise had been out with Hannah. When they'd returned, they'd eaten, bathed Hannah together and gone to bed early. When they'd awoken, it was to a bright winter's morning. She hadn't asked about the case at all, other than his wellbeing. The questions and suspicions had abated. Dabbawal had encouraged an environment of mutual trust and respect. Nothing had happened with Kate, so why did he feel this approximation of guilt? He knew he didn't feel good about it. He knew that much, but he also knew he was high on the psychopathic spectrum; was every emotion muted because of it? It sometimes didn't feel like it.

He watched Hannah play happily. They'd bought the house primarily for the garden, actually forfeiting a slightly larger house for more outdoor space. It was a thin plot, but long, extending over one hundred feet from the back door. It had been worth it, allowing them to have a trampoline, small wooden playhouse and patio, all of which would have been impossible in the yard of their previous 1930's terrace.

He could see Hannah's mouth moving and assumed she was talking to herself, playing a game. She was still bouncing on the trampoline, apparently waving to someone over the fence at the apex of every bounce.

Atherton became aware that Louise had said something.

"Sorry?" he said.

"I said, Gran Canaria," she said. "How do you feel about Gran Canaria or one of the Canary Islands? They get pretty good weather throughout the year, don't they?"

"I think I could get on very well with one of the Canary Islands," he said. He watched Hannah as she waved and giggled. "Would there be enough for her to do?"

"I think so. The one I looked at had a kiddies club," she said. "Would you be happy with that?"

"With an under-qualified, unregistered teenager looking after my daughter's welfare, while I gorge myself on all-inclusive wine?" he said. "Absolutely."

"You have an extraordinary knack for making everything sound wrong."

"Thank you," he said. "Will she be warm enough? It's pretty cold out there."

"She should be. She'll probably be too hot if anything. I'm just happy she's burning off some energy. She's getting hyper about Christmas." Louise opened the door and shouted: "Hannah? Hannah? Come and put your hat back on, sweetheart."

Hannah jumped out of the doorway in the trampoline safety netting and tore down the length of the garden towards them.

"Put your hat on, love. Daddy's worried about you catching a cold."

It wasn't the only thing that worried him. Atherton struggled to his feet, wandered to the top of the garden and looked at his neighbour's house over the fence. There were no signs of life. He could see an empty kitchen and dining room through dirty windows. On the floor of the dining room, he could see a brown co-axial cable trailed over the floor, which had long since parted company with a TV.

Just as he was lowering himself down, he saw something which made him stop and haul himself back upwards: a small patch of grass, a few metres from the fence, which looked as if it had been flattened down by something. He looked back down his own garden to the family. Hannah stuck out her tongue and giggled. He carefully dropped back down and joined them.

"Who were you waving at before, love?" said Atherton.

"The little man in the garden," she replied.

144

"There's no-one there, Hannah. Were you just pretending?" he said, but she had already run off to the lounge. Before long, he heard the inane chatter of cartoon characters from the lounge TV.

*

The swimming pool was heaving with families, an undulating sea of bodies and flesh. Louise held Hannah's hand and walked in with her from the shallow end, where fountains gently sprayed them with water. She still looked good, his wife; attractive and slim, save for a little pregnancy weight she'd never been able to shift. Effortlessly pretty without makeup, she often drew looks from other men. And when he was by her side, he knew what those looks usually said: how did *he* manage that?

The swimming pool was one of the few places he still felt uncomfortable. Without his clothes, people could see the true mechanics of his cerebral palsy; his gait, his skinny, unresponsive right leg and the way his hip swung out uncomfortably to accommodate it when he walked. They stared at him with idle curiosity and he knew how women must feel with all the attention focussing below the neck: *I'm up here, buddy.*

He caught up with Louise and Hannah, play-splashing them as he approached, prompting Hannah to giggle and splash him back. The water felt as warm as blood. A two-tone siren sounded and echoed around the pool.

"Waves comin'?" asked Hannah.

"Yes love, the waves will be on in a minute," said Louise.

Soon, the water began to rise and fall, lifting them up from the floor in unison, before dropping them down once more. Atherton felt people's bodies glancing off his own as they tried to maintain their balance; an arm here, a leg there, as if the pool were simply a mass of these parts, of disengaged limbs and skin in a soup of warm liquid. Louise glanced at him and smiled and he tentatively returned it, feeling as if he was on the edge of something dark and horrible.

Afterwards, they dressed in the changing room, battling for space to move in the tiny cubicle as Hannah played with the hairdryer beside the communal mirrors. When they were dressed, Louise queued for her obligatory post-swim cookie, while Atherton waited with Hannah. His phone rang in his pocket.

"Hi," he said.

"Can you talk?"

Atherton could immediately sense the urgency in Prejean's voice. He looked to the coffee bar. Louise had started up a conversation with someone he recognised from the school playground.

"Yes, of course. What's up?"

"The Chronicle has got hold of details we never released," she said. "Myers has had a fuckin' shit fit. You would not believe the roasting we just sat through."

"Fuck," he said, under his breath. He looked down at Hannah, whose eyes were fixed on the confectionary display at the coffee stand. "What details, exactly?"

"I'm looking at the front page right now," she said. "'Starman Serial Killer on the Loose?' is the headline. Then there are two further pages in the centre. Lots of stuff they shouldn't have known about, including the *Son of Geb* Twitter handle. He's already got two thousand new followers, I've just checked."

"Starman? Great." He looked over again to Louise, who was deep in conversation with her friend. The woman looked towards him and Hannah waved and smiled.

"Any ideas how our man will react to being referred to like that?" said Prejean over the phone.

"I have the feeling he'll quite like it," he said. "It's suitably celestial, is it not? A typical psychopathic trait is rampant egomania. Bear in mind we haven't diagnosed him as such yet, but if that's his disorder, he'll love the attention."

"What about the followers? Myers is concerned about copycats," said Prejean.

"Spectators. Like slow-moving traffic past a car crash."

"So we don't need to worry?"

There was a pause.

"I'd do a review and flag any who appear particularly ...enthusiastic," he said.

"Marvellous," she said.

"He'll like the thought of having a following. He likes to film himself. It's a record, allowing him to re-experience the killings, but the camera could also be seen as a surrogate audience."

"Like the eyes on the wall?"

"Exactly. Is the young lad watching for messages?"

"Mattias? Yes, he's been totally seconded to us now," she said.

"Good. Look, Kate, I'm sort of tied up at the minute. Can I give you call when I get back home?"

"There's more."

"What?"

"They've printed a picture of me and you from the butterfly house," she said. He didn't reply. She listened to background hiss for several moments. "Jon?"

Atherton looked at Louise and her friend. The smiles had now gone and the woman appeared to be telling Louise something of importance. She looked directly at him and her face dropped into an accusatory frown which he hadn't seen for some time. Hannah pulled sharply at his hand and said something which he didn't register. He looked down at her.

"It'll be okay," he said, not quite sure whether he was talking to Kate, the child or himself.

CHAPTER THIRTEEN

Lauren Schloss set down her coffee on a desk that was littered with papers, post-it notes and a parade of identical cardboard cups from the same high street café chain. In the five years she'd been at the Chronicle, she'd never spent more than fifteen minutes at a time there and saw little reason to keep it tidy. She had just sat down and taken a sip before she noticed the man sitting nearby. He stopped chewing and smiled awkwardly. He looked as if he'd been thrown into his clothes from some distance; jeans and a hoodie, over a T-shirt for a band she was unfamiliar with. It was a little casual, even for Chronicle standards.

"Er...hello," she said, finally. "Can I help you with something?"

"Tommy Rowan," he said. "TR Investigations," he added when she looked none the wiser.

"Ah yes," she said and extended a hand. "Nice to finally meet you." He wiped his hand quickly on his jeans before shaking her hand. The guy was a class act. "So how did you get on?"

"Took a bit of tailing, but I got there in the end." He passed her a memory stick on which *TR Investigations* had been rendered in a bad font. She flipped open her laptop and inserted the stick in a USB port on the side. She selected a folder and a bank of image thumbnails appeared. She clicked on the first, so it blew up on the screen: Atherton and Prejean standing at the police station entrance, engaged in conversation, with Prejean's mouth open in speech. She scrolled through a few more: Atherton getting into Prejean's car, another of them sitting in it, Atherton's face partially obscured by the reflection of light on the windscreen.

Schloss looked at Rowan questioningly.

"Keep going," he said.

Schloss scrolled through a few more until she reached a shot of Prejean standing at her apartment window. The next showed Atherton at her side and in the one following that, Atherton stood close to her, their eyes locked in an ostensibly intimate moment.

"Does that do the job?" said Rowan.

"It'll do for the time being," she said. "If you send through your invoice, I'll get that sorted for you. Keep it reasonable and I might be able to get more work for you. I want you on standby. When these two finally build up the nerve to start fucking again, I want photos."

He raised his eyebrows. "Sounds good to me," he said flatly and removed himself from the chair, leaving an odour of fried food behind him.

She clicked through the photos again. The one of Atherton touching the woman's neck was ideal to spice up a bi-line, or to use as leverage for something else. She picked up the phone.

*

They'd argued in the car, of course. Louise's friend had shown her the new *Evening Chronicle* article, which Atherton himself hadn't seen. It made asking about the content rather awkward. As they'd driven out of the swimming pool carpark, she'd turned to her phone, scrolling through the display and he strained to see what she was looking at as they pulled out onto the main road.

"Oh, very cosy," she said after a moment.

He leaned over as much as was safely possible and saw she was looking at the looping video Mattias Klum had showed them.

"We were at work, Louise," he said. "You try and make light of things. It's the only way to deal with..."

"Make light of things? *Make fucking light of things?*" she said. He looked at Hannah in the rear view mirror and chose not to say anything. "Let me just recap here, Jon. I know I'm not worthy of an opinion, but it looks like there's a murderer out there who's started posting pictures of you and your...slut for the world to see. Am I wrong?"

"He's targeting the police not me," he said. "It's an ego thing. He's trying to make a mockery of..."

"Are we in danger, Jon?" she said, clicking off her phone and throwing it back in her bag.

"Daddy, are we in danger?" echoed Hannah from behind in a tired voice.

"No sweetheart, Daddy wouldn't let anything happen to you and Mammy, would I?"

He thought of his visit to the neighbour's garden earlier. A cavalcade of questions marched rapidly through his mind. Was he just being paranoid? There was no way the killer would break cover like that, was there? Were they in danger?

"Ha," said Louise, keeping her voice low. "Everything you say is a lie. A lie."

"Can we just calm down a little. I was going to tell you about it. I just found out myself."

"Oh, was that her on the phone there, Jon?" she spat. He remained silent. There was nothing to be won either way. "An ego thing? I'll tell you who has an ego thing. Running around, pretending to be a cop with a woman fifteen years younger than you. It's pathetic."

"Can we talk about this when we get home?" he said. The drive was only three or four miles, but it seemed indeterminable.

"Oh, we will, Jon," she said. "We will."

They drove past a succession of people laden with shopping bags and a man struggling to offload a Christmas tree from his car. All seemed to serve as a mockery of the silent tension in the car. They returned home and began arguing as soon as they entered the house.

"No shouting, Daddy," said Hannah, wagging her finger at him.

"It's all right, love. Mammy and Daddy are only talking," he said. "Go on and play."

The girl paused uncertainly for a moment and then ran upstairs to her room. Louise looked at Atherton, shook her head and walked away from him. Atherton followed her to the lounge, where he noticed for the first time she'd put up the decorations.

"You're in the paper, Jon," she said, calmly. "And a killer is sending pictures of you and her around for all to see. How humiliating is that? Never mind utterly terrifying."

"It's posturing. That's all it is. Paul said we can have protection any time we want."

"Protection? What does that mean? A couple of coppers sat outside in a car? We don't need this intrusion in our lives, Jon. Not now. This is the last thing we need."

"I know. I know," he said. "Maybe we should book that holiday and get away for a while. We could even spend Christmas away somewhere for a change."

"Maybe," she said. She walked over to the window and looked through the blinds onto the street. She was quiet for the longest time. "If you've been fucking around with her Jon, it's the end of us. Do you understand?"

"Yes." It was all he could say. He turned and left her there, moving into the dining room. As he neared the window, he could hear a humming noise and soon saw what it was: a remote control drone hovering some twenty feet in the air over the garden outside. It was a thin, plastic X-shaped structure with a rotating blade in each corner, a toy familiar to him from adverts on Saturday morning television. He quickly unlocked the door and stepped outside. As he approached the drone, it nimbly darted away and climbed several feet.

"Are you and Mummy friends now?" asked Hannah, who had appeared at his side.

"Yes, of course we're friends, Hannah," he said.

"Would you like a cup of tea?"

"Yes, love. That would be nice. Just go inside now and I'll get it in minute."

The drone returned, hovering just above head height, with a sound not unlike a buzzing mosquito.

"A helicopter, Daddy," said Hannah.

Atherton noticed a small rectangular protrusion on the toy's undercarriage with a circular glass aperture pointing directly at him: a camera. He took a step towards it and it veered back and arched through the air above to the other side of the garden, turning itself towards him once more. Atherton looked around and picked up the clothesline prop, which had been discarded on the lawn nearby. He extended it out in front of him like a spear and took a stab in its direction.

"What are you doing, Daddy?" said Hannah, chuckling.

Again, it veered away and arched above, but this time he was ready for it. He swung, connected with the drone and brought it down, scattering shards of coloured plastic onto the grass. He held it down with the prop until he was able to break the remaining rotors under his foot.

"Have you broken it, Dad?"

Atherton climbed the back fence again, this time swinging a leg over it and falling clumsily into the neighbour's garden. As before, it was empty. He looked through each of the windows, cupping his face against the glass. There were no signs of movement. He rounded the side of the house, found the gate firmly shut and bolted, and when he looked over the top of it, no-one could be seen.

Back in his own garden, Hannah was crouched down looking at the broken drone as if it were a fallen bird.

"Don't touch it, sweetheart."

"Is it sharp?"

"Yes," he said and headed back into the house.

The kitchen phone was not in its cradle and he was on the way to the lounge when he realised Louise was standing by the open front door. She had been crying, eyes watery and red. Outside, he could see a burly man in the doorway, wearing T-shirt and tracksuit bottoms. Standing next to him, was a young lad of around ten, who looked abashed and aggrieved in equal measure. As he drew closer, Atherton saw that the boy held a black remote control device.

"Ah," he said, with relief and rising embarrassment.

*

Sue Cresswell's eyes felt raw. She was overdue a visit to the optician and already knew she needed to update her prescription; too much time in front of one screen or another. Tiredness played a part, but she knew she couldn't leave without examining the camera, which sat in an evidence bag on the lab bench in front of her. It needed to be checked for physical evidence before she sent it off to the tech guys. She rotated the bench top magnifying glass into position and clicked on the built in light.

Finding the end of the tape was no problem, but beginning to remove it with forceps proved more difficult. It was silver duct tape; not a surface likely to yield a print. Also, it appeared that the tape had been cut with scissors and she paused for a moment to note this on the pad beside her. Slowly, she unravelled the tape by pulling with the forceps and rotating the camera with her other hand. Suddenly she stopped, readjusting the magnifying glass. She'd found a hair, an orange tinge to the tip, whiter, almost translucent at the base. It would need to undergo testing, but she instinctively knew it was feline. She'd removed enough from her jackets and skirts at home.

It was a minor achievement – it would unlikely lead to a specific cat – but it made her feel like cheering nonetheless. She understood the attraction of palaeontology, the pain-staking process of uncovering evidence frozen in time.

She discarded the tweezers, knowing these could damage the hair and instead opened a sterile scalpel, using it to ease the hair up from the adhesive until she was able to tease it off with her gloved fingertips and place it carefully into a large glass vial.

She continued the unwrapping process without any further discoveries. As she neared the bare surface of the camera, she discarded her gloves and donned two new pairs, one on top of the other, knowing her own fingerprints could be transferred through a single layer. As she reached the very last section of tape, she noticed the end had not been cut. The edge was jagged and rough suggesting it had been torn, rather than cut...or bitten. Excitedly, she moved to the bench opposite, clicked on the light microscope and rotated the lens down to x10 magnification. Carefully, she placed the tape onto the stage and adjusted the focus until several lightly coloured flake-like structures became visible. Lip cells. She laughed.

"D to the N to the A," she said aloud and slid her chair over to the nearest telephone and dialled the focus room. A male voice answered and she was unsure if it was Rogers or Walsh. "Get ready to love me even more than you do already," she said. "We might just have DNA from the butterfly house."

URSA MINOR

CHAPTER FOURTEEN

He took a bus to be close to her.

He pretended to read the discarded newspaper he'd found on the seat, surreptitiously leaning forward to smell her hair; a mixture of odours from which he could discern honey and apricot. She was so close, her hair like long, dark tendrils mere inches away from his shaking hand.

He counted to ten like Mam had told him, keeping his eyes to the newspaper before allowing himself another glance. This he repeated several times, developing a sense of her each time, taking in every part, piece by glorious piece. Her delicate earlobes, the nape of her neck, a small tan-brown mole just below the hairline. The blemish only made her more captivating. The Japanese called it w*abi-sabi*- the acceptance that true beauty is imperfect, incomplete and, as with anything, impermanent.

He placed a hand under the newspaper and slowly slid it across his knee, imagining not fabric there, but the smooth warm skin of her shoulder. His mind spun off into a wonderful scenario in which he'd reach out and gently touch her neck. She would react, sensuously; her breathing would increase, until she drew the courage to turn to him. And when she did, she would see him, see him, want him and embrace him. Her hair would explode in a blaze of light, irradiated from behind like a seething supernova, and she'd smile at him.

An enormous feeling of joy flooded through his body and he closed his eyes, feeling tears gather almost instantly. Even in the darkness, he felt he could sense her outline in front of him, other senses rising in the absence of sight. He sobbed; a series of long, heavy convulsions that he struggled to control. The bus stopped, he heard the doors open and an influx of air allowed him to smell her once more. He opened his eyes, blinking and wiped them with a sleeve.

She was gone.

He craned his neck as the bus trundled slowly forward and caught a glimpse of her crossing the road towards the riverside, walking confidently and elegantly, before disappearing into the distance. When he finally lost sight of her, he turned to face the front. A single black hair lay over the seat headrest, dancing provocatively with the motion of the bus.

He looked about him, casually assessing the dead-faced passengers as he slowly raised his hand to retrieve it. When he had it, he wrapped it around his index finger into a tight coil, inhaled its odours and then popped it into his mouth.

Just then, as he rolled it on his tongue, he saw it on the bus CCTV screen. He waited for it to scroll through its various views to be certain. Cohen; smirking as usual, near the back, leaning in a dishevelled mess against the window, filthy hair covering half of his face. He was always there of course, the wretch. Loitering and silently observing, at once distant yet omnipresent. He whirled round to stare at him.

Don't mock me, he thought, almost shouted down the bus.

The wretch's smirk receded and the wide forehead nodded knowingly. They were in agreement.

At the front of the bus, he closed his eyes once more and allowed his thoughts to spiral into a familiar and warm sea of fantasy. He felt the texture of the hair play on his tongue one more time before he swallowed it. Then he reached up to press the bell, hoping he still had time to catch her.

*

The imposing Baltic Centre for Contemporary Art sits on the south side of the Tyne, dwarfing everything nearby, including the Gateshead Millennium Bridge, which carries visitors south to its door. Built in the fifties as a working flour mill, it closed its doors in

1981, opening again as a contemporary art gallery twenty-one years and thirty-three million pounds later.

The aboriginal art exhibition was in one of the smaller rooms used for temporary exhibitions and consisted of twenty-five pieces dating from the 1950s to the mid-eighties, each illuminated by a downlight on the stark white walls.

The girl took a seat in front of one of the pictures, a large painting of a snake and a goanna, head to tail, as if about to devour each other simultaneously. It was the colour of Australian desert; a rusty, ferric red into which the forms of the creatures had been scored with a sharp implement. She took a sketchpad and pencil from her backpack and flipped through the pad to a blank page. As she started to sketch, she became aware of someone else in the room.

She had learned to blank out distractions when she needed to. So many of the students on her course just didn't take it seriously. It seemed to be the lifestyle which many of them sought, not the work itself. Not the craft. She felt a certain release that the term was over and she was free to immerse herself in her study without the interference of others.

She sketched a rough facsimile of the snake and goanna, adding in some depth, pattern and shading. Her work was going well she thought, and she could tell her tutor found what she produced interesting. The interpretations of the Aboriginal and Native American styles allowed her to stand out from the pack. Simply put, no-one else was doing this type of stuff. And not only that, her enthusiasm and dedication matched her skill.

The man moved slowly around the room on the periphery of her vision. She stole a quick glance at him, immediately letting her dark hair fall like a veil when she looked back down. She heard her mother's voice: *you should wear your hair up more. Let people see that lovely face of yours.*

The man appeared to be fully absorbed by the paintings, spending several minutes on each. He was slight and neat, with little in the way of hair and a slightly androgynous look. But he wasn't unpleasant looking.

She eyed him up and down. The tight sweater had a company logo and hinted at muscularity. Her eyes lingered for a moment on the rear of his canvas work trousers.

It wouldn't be the first time she'd been attracted to an older man. There was her first year tutor, a man in his mid-forties, whose good looks and gentlemanly charm had affected her. She'd blushed her way through tutorials and peeked at him shyly from beneath her fringe. That little infatuation ended when she'd seen him kissing a fellow student outside a restaurant in town. She'd consoled herself in the bed of an eighteen-year-old fresher from Wolverhampton, who'd complimented her work and didn't return any of her texts or calls, until she'd given up in despair.

The man came closer, until he was standing by the side of the gallery seat. She sneaked another glance, but he was pre-occupied with the painting of the snake and goanna. She busied herself by shading an area, holding the pencil at an acute angle to the paper. Suddenly, he cleared his throat.

"You're g-g...good," he said.

She looked up, nervously flicking away her fringe. He was looking down on her with piercing blue eyes, the semblance of a smile on his mouth, a muscle in his cheek twitching nervously.

"Oh," she said, feeling the blood rise to her face almost instantaneously. "Thank you. Just sketches, you know."

"You've c-c-c..." – his face twisted in frustration – "caught it w-well," he said.

"I like how it's been painted. It's my favourite in here," she said. He looked at the painting again. "I like the fact you can see what's in the snake. Its innards. But more than that. Do you know what I mean?"

He nodded.

"Th-they paint what something *is*," he said. "It's essence. What it c-c-consists of. Not just what it looks like."

"Exactly," she said. She smiled, her teeth a shock of bright white against her olive skin. His face reddened slightly. "It's something I try to get into my own work, you know? To get beyond the aesthetic. I know that sounds pretentious."

"N-n-ot at all," he said. "I think it's c-c-cool."

He smiled at her again, his face a multitude of tics and minute muscular spasms. She laughed nervously and shyly looked back at her sketch for a moment, absently adding a few perfunctory pencil strokes. When she looked back at him, he was staring at the entrance of the room, his face more serious, almost angry. She followed his line of sight to see what was troubling him, but the doorway was empty. Apart from the distant sound of chatter from a far corner of the building, there was silence.

"Uh," he said. "I h-have to go." He began to walk stiffly from the room.

"Okay," she said. "Bye."

He stopped at this, turned and nodded low, almost a bow and left.

*

Later, from his vantage point, he watched the city crawl with life. How they looked like insects, treading their well-worn paths around the city. He let his feet dangle over the edge. Occasionally, he spat, watching gravity catch it; smiling if it connected with one of them and they looked skyward.

As the sun reached its height, above even him, he watched them congregating together to eat and talk, swarming around the cafes and burger bars in unending, babbling droves. Others continued down the streets, those conduits of idiocy. Dithering dots distracted only by the shop windows which channelled them. How oblivious they were to the universe in which they were so irrelevant, incapable of seeing beyond their tragically limited desires.

Eat this. Smoke that. Wear this. Fuck that. Involuntary ataxic responses to stimuli.

Later still, when he was down among them, he felt such an unnatural displacement, a crippling nausea, which heightened with his proximity to them. A young man held out an arm in his path, in the other a clipboard, and said something, the language distant and alien. The man saw his face and the smile dropped in an instant, a stark key-change to the monotony of his simple life. The man stepped back and allowed him on his way.

He wondered, not for the first time, about his decision. He could have already been beyond all this; gone from this tawdry planet. Flown upwards until the planets themselves appeared as inconsequential specks beneath him.

The back of his head itched and he scratched the sticky plaster there. It offered scant relief.

*

It felt good to close the door on the world.

He slid home the two heavy bolts and secured the chain with a sense of relief and contentment. It had been a long day, and when he'd returned, he'd had to wait for the builders to leave. Had to engage the foreman in inane conversation and overstate his happiness that the project was progressing in good time. He was consistently astounded at the capacity of people to talk so much without saying much of anything at all.

No matter. His mask was securely fixed. He could look into their eyes and make them see whatever he pleased. Understanding, sympathy, pathos. There had only been one moment - a throwaway comment from one of the junior members of the crew:

"Fuckin' mad that, innit? What's it for?" the skinny runt said.

The expletive had jarred him slightly and without letting his smile drop, he'd replied, "Storage."

The youth laughed uncomfortably and before long, he left with the rest of them.

The foundations were complete now and he expected parts of the frame to be assembled in the forthcoming days. It was unrecognisable now. Once the show jumping fences had been removed and the years of uncut grass and foliage removed, it had been relatively straightforward to level and start work.

The stables were another issue altogether. Weather-beaten and rotten through in some areas, he still wondered if they could be saved and re-purposed in some way. Another voice told him to tear it down, the stables and the house too. Told him to have done with it all and start afresh. Whenever these thoughts crossed his mind, he invariably thought of his mother and inevitably, arrived at the question: what would she say?

There was a certain cathartic release in the transformation. The further it moved away from how it had been, the better he felt. He could remember waking up to the sound of the horses, the heavy plod of hooves on earth as they were led into the training paddock by his mother. Soon after that, he'd hear Grandpa Harry's boots on the stairs and the thud of his heavy hand on the door: "Time to get up, boy."

Mam would bring in tackle to clean and repair and she rarely changed from her riding clothes. The smell of horse was infused in the place. Through the week, people would arrive – women mostly – to ride in circles around the muddy field, or follow the narrow forest trails around the house. He and Grandpa Harry would stay out of the way, mucking out the stable and laying fresh hay in each of the stalls.

Harry was short, but strong all the same, and not afraid to clip him sharply across the head should he show any hint of disobedience. Old Harry was partially deaf and spoke rarely, but when he did, he would move in uncomfortably close and show the brown tombstone ruins of his teeth, and exhale the stench of stale rolling tobacco.

In the afternoons, Mam would school him from a makeshift classroom while Harry dozed in a reclining chair in the lounge. She taught him to read, write and basic arithmetic, but had as little enthusiasm to teach as he had to learn.

Her long, curly hair was a matted amalgam of fading reds and greys and she wore a standard uniform of threadbare riding trousers and a T-shirt that barely contained her breasts. She walked with a slight limp; a broken leg and dislocated hip. The result of being thrown, back in her youth. She would walk around the room reciting poetry, which – years later – he would recognise as song lyrics.

*

In the evenings, Grandpa Harry would walk to The Black Horse. He'd be left alone with his mother. The TV aerial was always broken, so they'd watch movies on VHS. Historical epics set in far-flung places starring tanned, bare-chested heroes. There'd be sword fights, improbable battles in chariots, gladiators fighting to the death or Christ himself healing lepers and being nailed to the cross.

Mam would lie on the sofa and he would snuggle close at her side. *Cleopatra* was her favourite, recorded years previously from the television, complete with dated adverts about New Year's sales and summer holiday deals.

They'd watch it until he knew the Egyptian queen in every scene; rolling from the carpet in her red and white dress. Looking sensuously up from the marble floor. Lying seductively amongst a bevy of handmaidens. Her nightdress riding up high on a shapely thigh; dressed in duck egg blue, pristine hair and makeup. A black line stretching from each eye to the hairline.

He knew each pensive look, every passionate embrace with Mark Antony and every closed-mouthed kiss with Caesar.

"Am I as beautiful as her?" his mother would ask.

"Yes, Mam," he would say dutifully, and play with her hair as he watched, drinking in the images on the screen.

When he lay in bed awake, a wheeze or a cough would herald the return of Grandpa Harry and the time he spent negotiating the back door told of the number of whiskeys he'd sunk. Soon after, he would hear them, the unusually pleasant tone of Grandpa Harry's voice and the hushed remonstrations of his mother, which would go on for some time. Then finally, after varying degrees of protest, the regular, metallic creak of the bed, which he could hear no matter how hard he pushed the pillows over his ears, knowing none of them would sleep until it was over.

On Saturdays, children would come. Over-privileged brats in brightly coloured fleeces and jackets, chauffeur-driven by their parents in expensive German cars. Mam would give them riding lessons, show them how to groom the horses and host parties for them, using the mobile cabin as a place to blow out the candles on their sickly pink cakes. He avoided them as best he could, shying away to duties either real or imagined, ashamed by his filthy tracksuit and embarrassed by his stammer, which grew to be unmanageable in the company of strangers.

The girls fascinated, but frightened him in equal measure and he would lurk in the semi-darkness of the stables, peeking out at them in the training paddock through a crack where the rafters met the masonry. He would watch them ride, with his hand down his tracksuit bottoms, squeezing himself in rhythm with their movements until he either climaxed or was called away by the throaty bark of Grandpa Harry. At night, he would imagine them in bed beside him, the taste of sweet pink icing on their lips and the soft smooth skin of thighs beneath their riding trousers.

They found Mam on a wet afternoon in September, lying on the kitchen floor with a small pool of vomit beside her. The left side of her face had dropped, with the eye closed and her mouth drooping in an exaggerated frown. He lay beside her and touched her meaty arm, finding it cool and clammy.

He stayed with her until they came to take her away, by which time Grandpa Harry had already retreated to the pub. The funeral was a quiet affair, with only an old school friend and a handful of village regulars adding to the numbers. Grandpa Harry wept openly and dramatically, in an ill-fitting suit, reeking of shit and stale whisky. At one point, the grief appeared to overwhelm him and he reached out, grabbing onto the sleeve of his jacket. By then he was fourteen and had the strength to prise away his Grandpa's fingers and push his hand firmly away, sensing the village women bristle at this in his periphery. But he no longer cared. He listened until the end of the eulogy. Watched the red curtain sweep around the coffin and then he left without speaking to anyone.

The riders stopped coming. The money dried up quickly. He had the Egyptian pottery valued, but found it to be typical tourist-grade stuff and of little interest or importance to collectors. Instead, he sold the horses one by one to neighbouring farms or private buyers. Ten healthy well-kept beasts, in all. He obtained good prices. If Grandpa Harry was aware of these developments, he did not show it. His appearances at the house grew less and less frequent and when they did share the same space, neither chose to speak. Sometimes, several days would pass and he wouldn't be seen at all.

It was early Spring in the following year, when a light frost still lay on the ground, that he saw Grandpa Harry from his bedroom window. He took his time to get dressed and enjoyed a breakfast of tea and toast before he went out to him.

Harry had tried to climb over the stile at the end of the garden and caught his bootlace on the barbed wire that topped the wooden fence. He lay facing upwards, with his boot still caught and his ankle at an acute angle to his leg. His pallor was as grey as the stone walls of the barn and a thick trickle of blood ran an inch or two down his forehead. Harry's eyes were open, red and glassy, but he was clearly still alive. Bending close to his head, he could hear his wheeze with the familiar rattle at the tail end.

He watched Grandpa Harry for a moment, giving him the chance to break over six months of silence, but he said nothing. Slowly he raised his foot, placed it gently across Grandpa Harry's throat and began to apply pressure. The old man's eyes widened and he attempted to raise his arms in defence, but all he could manage was to grab weakly onto his leg.

Gradually, he pressed a little harder, trying gauge how much pressure was needed to cut off the air without leaving a mark. After a few more minutes, his arms fell down to his sides and life left Harry's eyes.

He crouched beside the body and rubbed some mud from the throat with his jumper sleeve, before walking back inside to the telephone. He hadn't spoken for weeks and when his voice cracked, the ambulance service operator assumed it was the emotion.

*

The house was cold. It always had been, even in the summer. He built a small fire in the hearth of the sitting room and when the temperature rose, stripped to his underwear and sat to watch some of the footage from the riverbank.

In time, Cohen joined him, slinking in quietly through the door, where the light from the flames failed to reach, softly singing:

> *Hush little baby, don't you cry,*
> *You know your mama was born to die,*
> *All my trials, Lord, soon be over.*
> *The river of Jordan is muddy and cold,*
> *Well it chills the body but not the soul,*
> *All my trials, Lord, soon be over.*

Cohen repeated it, over and over, smiling whenever they made eye contact, until he stopped and took a seat by the fire. He thought of covering himself, but they were past that now. He felt more comfortable with his body – the strength and appearance – knowing that it put the wretch's slovenly efforts to shame. He knew that beneath the scruffy coat and dark shirt lay decades of inactivity and neglect.

They sat that way for an hour or more, until the footage was finished, watching the flames lick around the logs on the fire and listening to it crackle and hiss. Finally, Cohen pushed the lank hair from his face and leaned forward into the light.

"What's on the agenda?" he said.

CHAPTER FIFTEEN

The crowd had gone, back to their cars and buses. Children tucked into their seats with blankets or duvets to keep out the chill. Jared Crane watched them from the platform, taking the tentative walk through the darkness back to the carpark. He stayed until the final vehicle had trailed its way back down the hillside. He could see the procession of headlights receding into the distance, scintillating as they passed behind the dense fir spruce trees, which lined the track.

Another busy night. The advertising had clearly been taking effect and the promise of a good view of Mars and Venus would have driven even more interest. *Britain's Darkest Skies* claimed the poster. How ironic. The sky above was ablaze, every portion of it exuberantly decorated with stars. *Britain's least light-polluted skies* would, of course, have been more accurate.

Those arriving expecting to find a traditional domed observatory were often surprised to see the pier-like structure jutting out over the rough fell, its two rotating turrets somewhat military in fashion, had they not been constructed with the very same spruce timber which covered the hill. He was frequently amazed at how many people they could cram onto the viewing platform, every head tilted upwards, each eye trained on the heavens above. More impressive still, was how they managed to let each of them have a fleeting glimpse via one of the two telescopes. The children had been ecstatic at the chance of catching a glimpse of Santa doing some pre-Christmas training manoeuvres in the night sky.

Tonight, he'd trained it on the Horsehead Nebula, just south of Alnitak on Orion's belt and had been quietly delighted with the result. There'd been a lot of young ones that night, most simply thrilled to be outside after bedtime, an exotic break from the normal routine, but if it sparked the merest interest in astronomy in just one of them, it would have been worth it.

He pulled the collar of his jacket up around his neck and blew into his hands through his gloves. He felt it worst in his feet. Even with two pairs of thick socks, they felt like ice if he stood long enough, and he'd stood talking to the crowd of visitors for the best part of two hours.

It had already gone eleven. He still had to cycle back to Kielder village, but they never adhered too strictly to closing time at the pub, and he knew there'd be a pint waiting for him if he was lucky enough to get down in time. He'd invited his University assistant for the evening to join him – a plain, but endearing red-haired girl from Solihull – but she'd politely refused and driven herself back to the city in her dilapidated car as soon as the talk was finished. His hit rate on that count was pitiful. At his age – forty-one in a month – he was old enough to be her father and perhaps an invitation to a local pub in the darkest part of Britain was not as appealing as he might have hoped.

He locked the telescope housing and set the alarm on the door. If it was triggered, an audible alarm would sound and the system would automatically text him and a small number of other custodians with news of a break in. He cleared several discarded leaflets from the viewing platform and dropped them into the bin on his way out, closing and locking the gate. He found his bike where he had left it, leaning against one of the legs of the platform and pushed it onto the track. He switched on the front light and spun the bike around so it faced the downward slope of the hill. As he did, the light panned around the small makeshift carpark. A vehicle remained, tucked in at the far end and partially hidden by trees. He turned the bike again and pushed it in that direction. As he approached, he saw it was a white transit van and in the passenger seat was a dark figure. He adjusted the angle of the light and saw the top of a woman's head. He drew level to the window.

"I'm sorry, I'm locking up now," he said. "Can you make your way down to the main road?"

There was no reaction from the figure inside. He unclipped the light from the mount on his handlebars and lifted it up to the window. He saw her, a heavily made-up dark-haired woman, her eyes closed and expression blank. His immediate impression was of someone feigning sleep.

"Hello?" he said. "You're going to have to head off now, I'm afraid."

He followed this up with a polite series of knocks to the window. Immediately, the woman sprung to life. She flew forwards, colliding violently with the glass, her nose bursting in the process, leaving blood and mucus on the surface. She made a noise, an awful hollow sound from her mouth, though her lips remained tightly closed. He quickly realised they had somehow been stuck together, her jaw wide, but lips closed, the skin there stretched and distended.

She made the noise again, an awful, unreleased scream and he was shaken into action, dropping his bike, grabbing the door handle and trying in vain to release her. Then suddenly, from behind, he heard a sound and turned towards it: a man silhouetted against the starlit sky. There was movement, something suddenly swung towards him and connected brutally with his temple. His legs buckled and he went down onto the sharp gravel. Able to lift a shaking hand to his head, he felt warm blood.

As he was swept into unconsciousness, his last image was of the man standing over him. Clenched in his hands were two long sticks, which he pulled apart in a victorious snapping action, the links of the chains between them clicking into place. As the stars above extinguished, he heard the dull sobbing of the woman in the van and all was quiet.

*

Consciousness arrived slowly, each sense coming online in turn and the first sensation was that of pain.

His arms were held out at each side and his hands were in agony. He opened his eyes. He was looking at the floor of the empty observation deck, his hands bound in some way to the timber panels of the south turret. He moved the middle finger of his right hand experimentally towards his palm, a slow painful process, until it connected with something hard, but sticky with blood and he realised the full horror of his predicament; he had been nailed to the wall.

There was more pain in his face, and he remembered the vicious blow he'd received in the carpark. He traced his teeth with his tongue and found a gap where at least one tooth previously resided. There were tooth fragments in his mouth. He went to spit them out, but when he tried to open his mouth, his lips refused to part and he knew they'd been glued shut like the woman's. A wave of terror and nausea washed over him and he slipped back into unconsciousness.

He came to again, unsure if he'd been out for a minute or more, to the sound of footsteps on the deck. The man approached from the darkness, illuminated only by the stars above, dragging the whimpering woman behind him until they were only feet away. Jared saw she was naked, her arms bound behind her back.

He was dressed entirely in black, with a hoodie covering his head. Over his face was a translucent mask through which only the basics of his features could be seen, the eyes marked with thick black lines. He released her and she fell heavily to the floor. The man walked back into the darkness at the far end of the deck, only to emerge again seconds later carrying a bundle in his arms. He turned his back to Jared and crouched down beside the woman, his hands busy with something. There was a glint of metal and Jared saw that he was arranging a series of implements on the deck; knives of varying sizes and a large hacksaw.

The man turned to him and even in the low light, Jared could see there was an unnatural hue to his face, his features difficult to discern. The man placed the flail beside the collection of knives. He took his time arranging the items in front of him, until they were equally spaced, with perfect symmetry to one another. Then he rose and walked to the edge of the deck where a bench was built into the wall. Jared saw a camera had been positioned there on a small tripod. The man checked all was well with it and turned again to Jared, giving him a thumbs-up with one hand.

Jared felt a lurch of terror in his stomach and pulled hopelessly with his hands in an effort to release them, but he was held fast. The man removed his hooded top, revealing a bald head and bare chest beneath. He neatly folded it and placed it carefully beside the camera. He unbuttoned his trousers and removed these too, folded them and placed them on top of the hoodie. Now naked, he walked towards the woman, his body as pallid as his face. He flexed his muscles and stretched his neck a number of times, as if limbering up, then crouched beside the woman. She seemed to sense his proximity and tried in vain to squirm away.

When he stood again, Jared saw he was holding the flail. He came closer to Jared and silently raised his hand to his face, pointing two extended fingers to his eyes. The message was clear: *watch*. He turned and in one smooth action, swung the flail down upon her. There was a horrendous cracking noise and the breeze carried a fine spray of warm blood across Jared's face. He turned his head to one side, unable to look. In his peripheral vision, he saw the headlights of a car ambling along the valley floor. The man arose and approached Jared again. He placed a finger gently on his chin and turned his head so he was facing him once more. He raised a blade to Jared's right eye, tapping it gently on the skin below the lower eyelid. Again, he pointed to his own eyes with two fingers: *watch*.

He wandered back to the lifeless body of the woman. Already, a pool of blood surrounded her head, which appeared black on the deck. He knelt beside her and held the blade high in the air, before plunging it into the body with a hideous slap of skin against skin. Jared watched him work, his arm moving back and forth, as he whispered quietly to himself, words uttered quickly and inaudibly. The man turned to him briefly, the mask marked with blood, a grin visible beneath. He heard a sound not unlike that of a sleepy dog smacking its lips.

Jared felt vomit boil up from his stomach, gushing into his throat and mouth, but it had nowhere to escape. He had no choice but to swallow it down and look on.

*

Myers awoke to the sound of his phone ringing. He picked it up and pressed the red icon to decline the call.

From a nearby driveway, he heard the sound of a car door opening, closing and soon after, that of an engine growling to life. He spread his foot out to the other side of the bed, enjoying the feel of the cool sheet under his foot, but also hoping it might make contact with someone.

Before he could begin to establish his thoughts in the waking world, sleep overtook him again. He could only have been unconscious a few more minutes before the phone sounded once more. This time he took the call, with a grim resignation, listening carefully and replying monosyllabically to the familiar voice. He showered quickly, trying to put an itinerary of actions together; phone calls mainly, those he'd have to make on the drive and those he knew could wait a little longer.

The debacle of the press conference hung heavily on his mind and he cringed as he remembered various details of the previous day. Callum Brown had conveniently disappeared into meetings whilst Myers had been subjected to a barrage of calls from his superiors. Then there'd been an uncomfortable meeting with Prejean in which she'd defended each of the individual members of her team in turn, as he knew she would.

He still had his suspicions. Walsh's money problems were no secret and Myers knew first-hand the pressures – financial and otherwise – of raising a family. When you worked high-profile cases, there were more opportunities to abuse your position than to shine amongst your peers. It was internal swirl and distraction they could do without.

Twenty minutes later, he was in the car, leaving a kettle boiling in the kitchen. When his phone linked to the car's Bluetooth, he steadied the wheel with his forearm and clicked on Kate's name.

"Hi," she said breathlessly over the car's speakers. "Prejean."

"Sorry, have I caught you at a bad time?"

"Just a quick run before I come in," she said. "What's up?"

"There's been another one," he said.

There was a moment of silence in which he heard only breathing.

"Fuck," she said finally. "Where?"

"Kielder observatory," he said. "You know it?"

"I know where it is. Give me half an hour to get back and get dressed and I'll see you up there."

"No, listen...I want you to call Amis, Rogers and Walsh, get them out of their pits and up there. I want you to come with me," he said.

"Where are we going?"

"The Royal Victoria Infirmary. This time, we've got a witness."

*

"Chris?" Prejean held the phone between her ear and shoulder as she pulled away.

"Morning, boss," he said. Prejean could hear the wind blowing over the receiver, muffling his voice. He said something else, but it was lost.

"I'm not hearing you well."

"Is that better?" he said. "We're all here. Site's secure. Sue's lot are doing the business."

"Does she ever sleep?"

"She will after this."

"Is she handy? Can you stick her on?"

There was a long pause and more sounds as the phone was passed over.

"Forensics are us. We never sleep."

"Hey, Sue."

"Did you hear the news? We have DNA from the tape on the camera."

"No way?"

"Very definitely way. We could have a profile in a few hours," said Sue.

"Where are you?"

"En route to meet Myers. Can you talk me through the scene?"

"Same as the others." Sue's voice was a low monotone. "One girl. A mess."

"What's the constellation?"

"I don't know, I..."

"It'll be Ursa Minor. Seven body parts arranged in the shape of the Little Dipper?"

"Sorry, the what? You're cutting out on me."

"The Little Dipper. It looks kind of like the outline of a soup ladle. Can you check for me and text me back?"

"Sure. We have photographers up there now."

"What about the witness?"

"His University colleague found him. He went back down to Kielder for a crowbar to get him off the wall. Poor sod. By the time we got here, there was a little welcome party from the village. The air ambulance took him away."

"Well, if they were on the scene, find out who touched what and where."

"Walsh is doing statements and we'll organise prints while we're at it."

"Good, thanks. What shape was he in?"

"The witness? A right fucking state by all accounts. Hands were wrecked obviously, and he had injuries to the eyes."

"Conscious? Talking?"

"Not enough to make any sense."

"I'm going to see him now with Myers, then I'm coming to you, but text or phone with anything significant."

"No probs."

*

The RVI had changed beyond all recognition since Prejean's last visit.

A new extension had been added, which was a far cry from the narrow claustrophobic Victorian corridors of the original building.

She glanced up at many floors, all of which looked down on a common vestibule containing a café and a small cinema. A man behind a sleek, modern reception desk directed her to the second floor and she headed to a nearby glass-walled elevator.

She found Myers talking to a young, tired-looking doctor, with spots of blood on the belly of her light-blue scrubs.

"...on whose authority?" she heard Myers say as she came into earshot.

"On mine. As ICU consultant, I have a serious duty of care over this patient. Do I need to remind you he's been anaesthetised? He'll not be conscious for several days."

"Days?" said Myers.

The doctor looked up as Prejean approached, sensing further intrusion.

"Ah, Doctor..." said Myers.

"Morgan."

"This is DS Kate Prejean who's..."

"Hello," she said brusquely, cutting him off. "Are we to expect any more of you this morning?"

"Quite possibly, yes. We may need to move him somewhere more secure and have police presence outside his room," said Myers.

"More secure?" said Morgan, crossing her arms.

"Perhaps if we could all talk somewhere a little less public," intervened Prejean.

The doctor led Myers and Prejean into a side room and closed the door behind them.

"We believe your patient could be a witness to a major murder enquiry and as soon as he's physically able, we need to talk to him," said Prejean.

"Is this the Starman?"

Prejean and Myers exchanged a glance.

"Yes," said Prejean. "So you might appreciate our urgency. As soon as he's able to see us, we need to know."

"See you? That's a bad choice of words. Are you aware of his injuries?"

"No. Can you tell us?" said Prejean. "Give us an estimate maybe as to when we can talk to him?"

"His left eye has been removed," she said. "When he was brought in, it was clear there'd been severe trauma and he was in some distress, as you can obviously imagine, so he was sedated before we were able to examine him. When we did, it became clear that his eyelids had been glued shut. We were able to open them using solvent. The right eye is intact and apparently undamaged, but the left has been totally removed. The neurologist is seeing him within the next couple of hours to assess the damage to what remains of the optic nerve and let us know if surgery will be needed, which will then take a day or two to schedule. My personal opinion is that will indeed be likely. If that's successful, when we bring him back around, it will be in stages, over the course of days rather than hours, because of the sheer amount of trauma one could expect from losing an eye," she said, looking from Prejean to Myers. "Does this answer your question at all?"

"It does, thank you, Doctor," said Myers.

"If you need to assign some security measures, then we can talk about that, but otherwise the timescales I've described are the best I can do."

"Understood," said Prejean. "Is there anything in the meantime you might be able to tell us? The weapon used...anything he was saying as he came in...?"

"There was the foreign object we found," said Morgan, a confused expression, passing over her face. "Did no-one show you?"

"No," said Myers.

"Wait here," she said and left the room. When she returned, moments later, she was carrying a stainless steel kidney-shaped dish, covered with a bloody cloth, which was the same colour as Morgan's scrubs. She placed the dish on the bed beside Myers and Prejean and removed the cloth. In the base of the dish was a small fragment of stone with something carved roughly upon it. Both the ring and the bowl were speckled with minute droplets of blood.

Prejean looked at Morgan, puzzled.

"Where did they find this?"

"In his orbital cavity," she said. "In his sealed eye socket."

CHAPTER SIXTEEN

She'd been unapproachable since the incident in the garden. Detached and stoic; always finding an excuse to leave the room as soon as he entered. She'd mumbled something about taking Hannah to meet a friend at a soft play café later, something to which he clearly wasn't invited. Then he'd received the text from Prejean.

"Something's happened," he said in the kitchen, fastening his laces awkwardly. "I need to go out, but I should be back just after lunch."

"Okay," she said, absently, filling Hannah's water bottle from the tap and forcing a smile. He knew they had another session with Dabbawal that afternoon, but there'd been no reminder from Louise. Was it a test?

Hannah, still in her nightie, played happily with plastic building bricks, occasionally raising her eyes to the cartoon on the television. He kissed the top of her head and pinched her side where he knew she was ticklish.

"Daddy!" she shrieked, flinching and giggling.

"You be a good girl for Mammy, okay?"

"Yes, Daddy," she said.

"I'll...I'll see you later then," he said. He waited vainly a short while for a response, before leaving the house.

Prejean's car was parked two streets over from Atherton's house where she'd said she'd be and he was glad Louise and Kate had been spared the opportunity of catching sight of one another.

"Morning," he said, sliding painfully into the passenger seat. "I take it there's some news."

"Lots of it," she said. She looked good; a winter coat with over-sized buttons. "You'd better strap yourself in. We're stopping at the University. Can you ring ahead to Quint? I think she likes you."

"Who can blame her?"

*

The pleasant aroma of hot tea met them as they entered the office.

"Doctor Atherton," said Quint brightly, extending her hand. "I wondered if I'd get to see you again."

He took her hand and she gave up a wide smile, which dropped slightly when she saw Prejean walking in his wake. She recovered it and shook Prejean's hand enthusiastically, before gesturing to sit down.

"Thanks for your time again, Miss Quint," said Atherton. "We have something we'd like you to take a look at, if you don't mind."

"Wonderful," she said, with excitement. "I can't believe I'm helping with a genuine police case."

"You are," said Prejean. "But I need your assurance with regards to confidentiality on our discussion today."

"Oh yes, absolutely." She mimed zipping her mouth shut, locking it and throwing away the key. "I've read about this person...the Starman, in the *Chronicle*. Awful."

Prejean placed the evidence bag on Quint's table.

"What can you tell us about this?" asked Prejean. "I'd prefer it if we kept it in the bag if you don't mind."

Quint picked up the object, flattening down the plastic and rotating it in her fingers.

"Interesting. Where did you find it?"

"You don't want to know. Trust me," said Atherton.

"Well, this is from a stone receptacle, rather than clay, so that would suggest it was made for someone of importance. Royalty perhaps." She turned it over in her hands. "There's an engraving." She leaned over the table, so Atherton could see. "This looks very much like the beginning of a shoulder here..." She changed the angle of the fragment and used her other hand to outline a shape beneath. "With the size, material and marking, my best guess would be that this was from a funerary jar."

"A what, sorry?" said Prejean.

"When the Ancient Egyptians interred their dead, their organs were removed and placed in a jar such as this. One for the liver, one for the intestines, lungs, stomach and so on."

"Nice," said Atherton.

"Oh yes, they had their funny little ways," smiled Quint. "They usually had carved animal heads covering the top of each jar and were decorated with various markings such as the ones here." She looked down at the piece again and examined the engraving. "See this marking here and what looks like the corner of an eye here? Put them all together and you get the mark of Osiris."

"Would this kind of thing be traceable back to a collection? I mean, would it be rare?" said Prejean.

"Well, rare is a very relative term. A first pressing mono copy of the White Album is pretty rare, but I have one, you know? With pottery, you don't have to look very hard in the Nile Delta to dig up examples of pottery fragments, but what you'd commonly find are pieces of undecorated, reddish-brown bowls which they'd made from Nile silt. What you've brought in here? Had it been an intact pot, then yes, I'd say it would – or should, at least – be part of a collection. Something I'd love to see in the Hancock Museum. Just a fragment? Not so much."

"So pretty much anyone could have something like this?"

"I'm afraid so."

Atherton saw Prejean's shoulders drop almost imperceptibly in disappointment. Quint reverently handed the bag back to Prejean.

"Thank you very much," she said.

"Tell me, what did the Egyptians make of eyes?" said Atherton, locking his own with Quint's.

"What did they make of eyes? Lots." Quint giggled. "Eyes were the most important organ, and sight the most important sense. It allowed perception of the real world, whereas being unable to see, meant darkness or death. Being blind was seen as some kind of divine punishment."

"Is there some significance to the left eye in particular?" said Prejean.

"Each eye represents something different. The left eye is traditionally the *Eye of Horus* – that's the one you'll see on all your travel brochures for Egypt and on cheap trinkets when you get there. It represented moonlight and dispersing the darkness of night. The right eye was the *Eye of Re* and represented sun and life." She thought for a moment, looking to the upper corners of the room. "One myth is that Horus and Set battled over the inheritance of Osiris. This one might have a bit of Plutarch in it, though. The ancient Greeks started going to Egypt as tourists from about the fifth century BC and were fed all sorts of crap by Egyptian guides and priests. Not much different from today, actually," she said.

"Who was Set?"

"Brother of Osiris. Horus being Osiris's son, of course. Set plucked out Horus's eye and damaged it. However, it was repaired by...sorry, a bunch of other gods, I forget the detail, and Horus brought the good eye back to his dead father Osiris, who, naturally, ate it," said Quint.

"*Ate it?*" said Atherton.

"Yes. The eye brought him back to life and since then there's been this idea of the eye being the re-establishment of order following a disturbance. It's come to symbolise the guarantee of life and regeneration." There was a long pause where Atherton looked between the two women. "Would either of you care for some tea?"

*

Shades of green melded in Atherton's vision as they whipped past fields and hedges.

"What about the eyeball trick?" said Prejean, changing up a gear and flooring the accelerator.

"What about it?"

"You think he planned to do that? I mean, bring a piece of pottery specifically to do that?"

Atherton rubbed the fragment through the bag between his thumb and index finger. He wanted to touch its surface, to feel whatever the killer had felt.

"No," he said after a while. "I think it might have been a spur of the moment thing. What if it was just something he carried with him? Something he was fond of playing with in his pocket. It has quite a nice feel in the hand, don't you think?"

"If you say so," she said.

"My mother used to carry around a stone she found on the banks of Loch Lomond on her honeymoon, simply because it fit her thumb just so." Prejean waited to hear more. He rarely mentioned his family. "I think he got carried away in the moment and left this in his eye socket as an...artistic flourish."

"He's getting cocky," she said. "Don't you think?"

"He's an egomaniac who thinks he's acquiring greatness and invulnerability with his every action. Yes, he's getting cocky."

"And more likely to make a mistake."

"It's this one," said Atherton and gripped on to the door handle to steady himself as Prejean took a sharp left onto a smaller road.

"You've been here before?" asked Prejean.

"Free ticket from the University."

"You get all the perks."

The road soon dipped and they caught sight of the reservoir, the water a dark, ominous grey. She slowed as they passed by the few buildings which comprised the village and sped up again as soon as they were clear. A brown sign reading Kielder Observatory appeared soon after and they turned off onto a rough gravel track, which climbed the hill and plateaued, before crawling round to its peak. Prejean spotted Rogers's car and pulled in neatly behind it.

Yellow and black crime scene tape had been placed liberally across the wooden steps to the observatory deck and between the trees which marked the entrance to the carpark. Rogers appeared wearing a beige mac, spotted them and raised a hand in greeting. He met them at the steps, lifting up the tape to let them through in the manner a fighter might part the ropes of a boxing ring.

"Boss. Doctor Atherton," he said. "Stick on a pair of those booties and come up."

"How's it going?"

"Good. We're all photographed. Sue's almost printed the entire place."

"Is the body still in situ?" said Prejean.

"Yes."

"Then let's somehow get a tarp over the whole scene, until it's gone. I'd hate a news helicopter to fly over and get a shot. It might just tip Myers over the edge."

"Understood. Just as a heads up, they're running a winter wonderland event on the other side of the reservoir. Might be overkill, but we might need to think about that too," he said. "Let me show you around."

Atherton detected an increased air of authority in his voice; he'd enjoyed a morning of calling the shots in Prejean's absence. They walked up towards the deck and an expansive pool of thickening blood met them at the top step. Beyond, Prejean could see several pieces of flesh, body parts and viscera.

"Just give me a moment," said Atherton, leaning on his knees and taking some deep breaths until the nausea subsided.

"Don't worry about it," said Rogers. "Walsh already lost his breakfast as soon as he got up here."

"I'm okay," said Atherton, though his expression said otherwise.

"Okay," said Rogers. "We have a number of footprints here, as you can see. Don't get too excited by those as we think they're from the guys who rescued Dr Crane. We're getting footwear prints from them all to compare and contrast." Prejean tilted her head to see the body parts from a different angle. "Seven body parts, just like you said. Ursa Minor."

She tiptoed around the circumference of the bloody mess and crouched near the decapitated head. It was a wretched sight. The woman had been as pretty as the others, with dark hair, now matted in blood. Her mouth drooped horribly, almost sorrowfully, into a grimace.

"No signs of any clothes or possessions. Same as the others," said Rogers.

Prejean stood and stepped back, allowing Atherton to take her place. He crouched, leaning on his good knee and lowered himself as far as he could.

"The same make-up job," said Atherton.

"The Eye of Horus," said Prejean.

Atherton nodded. "Where did they find the witness?" he asked.

Rogers pointed to the timber wall of the telescope housing. There were two dark red smudges against the light wood where Crane had been nailed. Atherton stood painfully and began to take a number of shots with his camera.

"Have you seen him?" asked Rogers. "The witness?"

"Not quite," said Prejean. "He'll live, but they're going to keep him under sedation. We'll not get a description for days. Maybe longer."

"Marvellous," he said sarcastically.

Atherton looked out across the valley. He imagined standing in the same spot in the darkness, watching the village and the small series of streetlights lining the street below. Perhaps he would have been able to make out the reservoir in the moonlight, which sat slightly to the left, where the dam carried a road from the north to the south. He imagined cold water running down his naked body, washing the woman's blood and filth from him, leaving him refreshed and renewed.

"He drove up here with her and waited for everyone to leave. He thought he had the place to himself, but he didn't," said Atherton.

"And he didn't like it," replied Rogers.

Atherton looked at him. "I think he's becoming increasingly adaptable."

"You think the astronomy lecturer saw the car?" asked Rogers.

"Possibly, but we're going to have to wait a while to find out," said Atherton.

"Well, more than one of the neighbours reported a white van in the cul-de-sac near Abigail Southern's flat at the nurse's digs," said Prejean.

"This is a working man. Why doesn't he abduct these women at the weekend? Maybe he doesn't have the van on weekends," said Atherton.

"Makes sense," said Prejean.

"We need to look at the staff of the work places again. There's someone who links Menshen Insurance with the hospital...and to this girl." He pointed to the observatory deck.

"Amis has been through them a hundred times. There's no link and there's no-one with a criminal record to fit this profile at either the office or the hospital. We've gone over it, Jon."

"Then we're looking at the wrong list or the list is incomplete. We need to look at it again, or we interview every last one of them. I'll know this man if I see him."

Prejean exchanged a glance with Rogers, who shrugged: *it's worth a try*.

"He knew exactly when Brampton would be leaving the office and be alone in the carpark. He knew exactly when Southern would be off-shift and alone in the flat. There's something that puts him in contact with these girls, allowing him to watch them for long periods without suspicion, and close in on the ones which interest him," said Atherton. His eyes were fixed, oblivious now to the view set out in front of him. He was somewhere else entirely. "We find out what this bastard does and we find *him*."

*

Later, Focus Room 1 murmured with activity. Myers strode in, an errant tuft of silvery white hair sticking up from the side of his head.

"We have a positive ID on the girl from the observatory," said Myers, pushing a photocopied student ID card across the table, with a sigh. "Kaitlyn Thomas, a fine arts student at Newcastle University. Parents are on their way up from Lincoln, god help them. Connie, Chris, I want you to lead the interviews to track her whereabouts on the day she died."

"Sir," said Amis.

The phone in Myers's office stuttered to life with a series of rising beeps. He cursed under his breath and retreated to answer it. Amis watched him lift the receiver to his ear and rub his brow as if trying to massage out a deep-rooted pain.

"Jesus Christ," said Rogers, holding up the sheet of paper and capturing her attention. "Look at her. Twenty-one years old."

Amis shook her head.

Myers re-emerged from the office looking infinitely more spritely than when he went in.

"Stand by your beds," he said. "Kate's coming through with something fairly major."

Almost immediately after saying this, Prejean and Sue Cresswell entered the room at a brisk pace. Sue silently took a seat, whilst Prejean remained standing, placing her battered laptop on the desk in front of her.

"Anyone remember Malcolm Stuyvesant?" said Prejean, plugging a lead into the rear of her laptop. She clicked a button on the remote control and the screen came to life with mugshot photos of a heavy-jowled middle-aged white man. His eyes held a certain innocent, childlike quality, but beneath hung dark, unhealthy-looking bags.

"Yeah, I remember him," said Rogers. "He's a paedo doing time in Durham, right?"

"He was doing time for possession of indecent images of children, three counts of indecent exposure and one of sexual abuse of a minor, but was released in January," said Prejean, breaking into a smile. "Sue's pulled one out of the bag for us. She found his DNA on the video camera left at the butterfly house."

"Yes!" shouted Walsh. The room broke out into spontaneous applause. Sue Cresswell nodded and held one fist in the air like a celebrating footballer. Walsh patted her enthusiastically on the back.

"Not only that, but he's been keeping up with the conditions of the sex offenders register," said Prejean when the volume reduced. "We have his passport, NI numbers, bank details and the change of address which he registered in March."

"We know where he is? So when do we go knocking?" said Rogers, eagerly.

"We need to get the go ahead, but we're looking at a briefing this evening, for an early morning start tomorrow," said Myers. "Well done everyone."

*

Atherton stared at the empty seat beside him, then to the clock and finally to Dabbawal, who smiled sagely, then pretended to be distracted by something in his notes.

"I suppose this is what could be referred to, in counselling terms, as something of a bad sign?" said Atherton. "Last time, she was late. This time, a complete no show."

"Perhaps if we give it another ten minutes," said Dabbawal.

"Why don't we fill that ten with a bit of chat, Dr Dabbawal?" Atherton picked idly at the stitching on the arm of his chair.

"Well, our time today is intended as a working session for the two of you as a couple," he said, holding his pen as he might a dart. "If you feel you'd benefit from an individual session, we can arrange to book one in for you, Doctor Atherton."

Atherton failed to stifle a laugh, causing Dabbawal to raise an eyebrow. It was the most animated Atherton had seen his face.

"Do I feel I would benefit from a session with you? Now there's a question."

"I'm reluctant to start without your wife, but is this anxiety and tension I'm detecting an indication of further problems at home?"

"Ah, see this… *this* is why you're a counsellor," said Atherton.

Dabbawal remained silent and tilted his head slightly in curiosity. It was a standard technique; leave an uncomfortable silence and the client would be compelled to fill it. Atherton resisted and instead pushed himself up from the chair and walked around the room.

"Sorry, if I stay in one place too long, I seize up a bit, Doc. Like the Tin Man." He walked to a wall decorated by Dabbawal's numerous diplomas and certificates. "But as my wife has informed you on several occasions, that's not the only characteristic of his I share."

"I see the analogy," said Dabbawal.

"Let's continue it, shall we? The beautiful, yet whimsical young girl travels on a long journey, taking her heartless companion with her, so they can obtain what they so desperately need in life," he said, passing the diplomas to a series of framed watercolours which complimented the tones of the room. He looked at each in turn, in no hurry to talk.

"Finally," he continued, "by the skin of their teeth, they make it to the guy who can solve all their problems and he gifts him with a heart, so he can feel love and compassion, like normal people."

Atherton ran out of wall, so turned back to the room and found himself right at Dabbawal's desk. "However, instead of an all-powerful wizard, what they find behind the curtain..." Atherton flicked a chrome desk toy, "...is a little fat shyster."

He looked at Dabbawal and smiled. The councillor smiled with his mouth, but his eyes said something rather different. Atherton looked back to the wall; a view of a quaint, typically English fishing village, but the light fell in from the nearby window in such a way that he saw more of his own eyes reflected in the glass. Behind him, a familiar alarm chimed.

"Time's up," said Dabbawal.

"I know," said Atherton. He walked towards the door and had his hand on it, ready to turn.

"He didn't need a heart, Doctor," said Dabbawal. Atherton didn't turn. "He had one all along."

Atherton opened the door, exited and closed it gently behind him, knowing with all certainty that he'd just had his last session.

CHAPTER SEVENTEEN

He rang the doorbell again and cradled his face against the glass of the bay window to peer inside. He saw the back of the armchair and a shock of white hair standing proud of the backrest. Finally, the bulky frame rose and waddled slowly out of sight, appearing moments later at the frosted glass of the front door. Atherton heard a mumbled complaint as his father wrestled with the latch, until the door finally opened and he emerged, blinking his puffy eyes.

"Hi, Dad," said Atherton.

"Oh, hello stranger," he said, suddenly more animated at the sight of his son. He smiled, showing his remarkably well-preserved teeth and ran a hand through his hair, a deflated white quiff, the way Elvis's might have gone had he lived. He threw open the door.

"Where's Mam?"

"Shopping and gabbing," he said. "Five minutes of one and two hours of the other."

Atherton followed him through the narrow hall to the back room, where the French doors looked out onto the garden. The smell of home hit him hard; years of tobacco smoke ingrained into the very fibres of the teak furniture and a recently cooked meal, probably fish pie. Also, his father's own odour; the earthy tones of his body, the petroleum jelly he used on his hair and the barest hint of aftershave.

Michael Atherton took his seat, allowing the automatic footrest to swing up under his corduroy-clad legs. Behind his head, an erstwhile table doily took the brunt of the grease from his head. On his chin was several days' growth of silvery-white stubble. A small table-top Christmas tree stood on top of the sideboard beside him, with a row of remote controls beneath.

"She'll be back soon with any luck and we might get a cup of tea," he said.

"I'll make some in a bit, Dad. How have you been?" His eyes shot involuntarily to the oxygen bottle beside the chair.

"Not so bad, son," he said. "I hardly use that thing."

"Use it when you need it," said Atherton. "That's why we got it, Dad."

"Oh aye," he said, looking down at his beefy forearms. The top two buttons of his check flannel shirt were unbuttoned, revealing wrinkled yellowed skin, like a window cleaner's chamois leather. "I do son, I do."

Atherton noticed dirt beneath the fingernails of his calloused, sausage-like fingers.

"You've been working in the garden?"

"Hey, you never miss 'owt, son, do you? Just tidying it up a bit. There's not much to do at this time of the year, but it gets me out."

"Looks nice anyway, Dad."

"I should have got that grass cut one more time before the end of the summer, but I'll just have to live with it now."

His eyes fell onto a collection of framed photographs on the sideboard, faded from decades of sunlight: Atherton as a child, standing awkwardly in school uniform, a graduation shot where the photographer had caught him in the midst of a palsy-fuelled gurn, and the wedding, Louise and him, both fresh-faced and glowing. Behind them all was a large certificate from the coal board, recognition, to go with the emphysema, of Michael's twenty-five years underground.

"So, how are you, son?"

The question itself served to make him more conscious of his leg and of the numbness in his face.

"Good, Dad," he said. "Glad Christmas is here."

"How are those two lovely ladies? Why haven't you brought them today?"

"They're fine. Full of busy." Atherton wiped some saliva which had collected at the corner of his mouth.

They heard the front door click open, followed by the rustle of shopping bags.

"I've forgotten your shaving foam, Mike," said his mother.

Atherton looked at Michael, who rolled his eyes and gripped the arms of his chair as if bracing himself for something. She appeared suddenly at the doorway, in a long white and black hounds-tooth coat.

"Jonny," she exclaimed and he stood to hug her. "How are you, my love? Has he made you a cup of tea? I bet he hasn't."

"We were hanging on for you, sweetheart," said Michael.

She tutted and broke away from him to look at his face and ruffle his hair.

"Still a handsome wee devil, are you not?" She'd changed her hair; still the same long bob which had endured through the years, but now with some light streaks which softened her face. Her pale blue eyes, insightful and loving, looked into his.

"Put him down now, Barbara," said Michael.

"Hush yourself. Something's on Jonny's mind. I'm going to put the kettle on and hear all about it," she said and left the room. Atherton heard the sound of the kettle being filled.

"Did you get to the butcher's, Barbara?" shouted Michael.

"Yes," she shouted back, with a flat, impatient tone.

"There's never 'owt in the house, Jon. She's got that big, black fridge the size of an Edwardian wardrobe," he said, leaning towards him conspiratorially. "There's never anything in the bugger to eat, though. Nowt but condiments."

"I can hear you, Michael Atherton," she said tersely.

He laughed and was out of breath almost immediately, but when Atherton started to get up from his seat, he held up a hand to stop him. He coughed a number of times and seemed to settle.

"She'll never change," he wheezed.

"Luckily for you," she said after a moment. She appeared soon after carrying a well-worn tray which Atherton could remember from the few occasions he was allowed to watch TV at teatime, lying fully stretched out on the thick fireside rug, which was scarred with holes from wayward fire embers. "I just don't see the point in getting loads of shopping in when there's just the two of us," she said, pouring the tea. "Anyway, I like things fresh."

"Aye, but what if we have visitors and we have nothing to offer them but bloody mayonnaise?" said Michael, with a smirk.

"Ah, hush, Mike," she said. "Save your oxygen."

"She just likes to get away from me as much as she can," he said, raising his eyebrows accusingly.

"Who can blame me? Bloody man," she said. "How are things with you, Jonathan?"

"Fine, Mam," he said. "Staying out of mischief."

"Rubbish. I have to read about you in the paper to find out what you've been up to," she said, handing him the obligatory plate of ginger snaps. "And you never ring me back, whenever I call."

"I know, I'm sorry. There's been so much..."

"How's that little treasure of mine? She'll be excited for Santa, no doubt."

"She's on another level. Louise has her all over the place at the minute. You know; play dates with friends and so on, just to keep her occupied," he said.

"We'll be seeing you on Christmas day?

"Of course, we'll get the morning out the way and come straight over."

"Great. And how's Louise?"

"Just fine, Mam," he said.

She looked deep into his eyes. Not the usual general sweep, but a more focused invasion to see if she could detect anything of interest. He smiled, but it was clear she'd already bookmarked his marriage for further discussion. Satisfied, she let her eyes drop and he felt his heart sink with them. He watched her sip her tea.

What is it you want me to say? he thought. *She might be leaving me, Mam? Because she doesn't trust me. Because I couldn't help her when she needed me. But mainly, because she knows it'll be easier to live without me.*

"And what about you? I hope you're more help than someone I could mention." She poured Michael's tea, handing it to him with a smile that was heavy with sarcasm.

"Well, I try, but I've been a bit occupied," he said. Barbara raised an eyebrow slightly and Atherton felt a rush of blood to his ears. "With the police."

Barbara shot a glance at Michael, who had pulled himself up to attention, the prominent tendons of his neck like that of a tortoise.

"I read it in the Chronicle, Jon. Do you think that's wise, after last time?"

"He's a big lad, Barbara," said Michael, managing to convey some authority in his voice, before subsiding into a long wheeze.

"What does Louise say about this?" said Barbara.

"Not too much, but it'll pay for a holiday, so she'll be happy about that part, I expect," he said.

Barbara took a sip of tea, as if to vanquish the tightness from her lips. Atherton sensed a question hanging over them, which thankfully dissipated. "It's only for a few days, Mam. Just in an advisory capacity. I think you picture me booting in villains' doors with a warrant card in my hand. It's not like that; they use me like they use a library."

"No, son," she said. "I picture you in therapy and left in pieces with your family trying to put you back together again."

"Barbara, come on now," said Michael.

"That'll not happen, Mam."

"These evil people you study and the horrible things you have to see...they all leave their stain," she said, putting her cup back on the tray somewhat dramatically. "Like tea on a china cup. You don't notice it building up, then one day, it just doesn't wash off. I only say these things because we love you," she said. "Be careful what you put in that head of yours, because whatever you put in, you'll never get out."

"I know, Mam, I know," he said.

She slapped her knees as if to mark the subject as closed. "Right. Now, I don't know what your plans are, but there's a chop in the fridge for you if you'd like to stay for something to eat? There are a few other things in there amongst all the condiments." She stood and made an eye-poking gesture at Michael with two fingers.

"Better do as she says, son," he said. They sat in silence for a while, listening to the familiar sound of cupboards opening and saucepans rattling. "Howay son, let's take a look up the garden."

Michael struggled to his feet and stood tentatively for a moment in battered tartan slippers before opening the door and walking out into the gardens. Atherton followed, unsure how much to help him. "We might try some courgette next year, if the slugs give us half a chance."

The garden was long and thin with a well-manicured lawn. Leading to a gravel path was a flowerbed with raised brick trenches at either side, containing an array of winter vegetables in various states.

Michael sat on the side of one of the trenches. He spotted a stone, which he fished out and threw up the garden. He smiled and Atherton was now close enough to see the blood vessels on his father's nose, spreading out across his cheeks like a miniature road map. Old memories effortlessly dropped into Atherton's mind.

Growing the leeks had felt like a military operation. He had an image of his father cradling a leek like a sleeping child, walking it slowly from the trench to the aluminium bathtub. He would lay the leek in the lukewarm water, the blanched portion submerged, the green leaves above. Slowly and purposefully, he would run his fingers through the roots, as if it were the hair of a lover. Then, with a knitting needle, he'd tease the dirt from the hard to reach places. With a cotton bud, he'd clean the point where the leaves met the barrel (the small clitoris-like nub known as the button). Inside the house, he'd lie it on a pillow on the dining table, and polish the white portion using milk and a soft cotton cloth, rubbing in small precise circles until it shone, as shiny and smooth as Venetian marble.

"She just worries, you know. We both do," said Michael. Atherton looked back down the length of the garden and caught his mother watching them from the kitchen window. "It never goes away. You'll find that. It's just the things you worry about that change."

Atherton nodded. He thought of Hannah, how she had taken up permanent residence in his mind. His thoughts jumped back to the afternoon they'd watched her on the trampoline in the garden. He'd happily kill for her – he realised – if anyone threatened her. He'd happily die.

"With you, it went from, 'will he be able to walk?' and 'will he be able to talk?' to 'will he make friends?' and 'will he get bullied?'"

"To 'will he ever move out?'" added Atherton.

"Well, we did wonder that too," said Michael, laughing. "What were those kids' names at school?"

"You remember them, Dad."

"Of course I do. I wanted to know if you still did."

"I remember everything."

"Those bastards. It was hard to know what to do. We wanted to protect you, but not so much that you couldn't do it for yourself," he said. "She found it hard, Jon. We tried not to let on we were worried, of course. That's the bloody trick. In fact, we probably threw you into things a bit heavily to be honest. Me more than your Mam."

"It hasn't done me any harm, Dad," said Atherton.

"You're right there," he put a hand on Atherton's shoulder, where it stayed briefly. "I'm not talking about the books you've written and all that, proud as I am. I'm talking about you, Louise and Hannah. You're doing a good job."

Michael stood and kicked the pebbles around on the ground, evening them out beneath his feet. He glanced down to his wife, now absent from the kitchen window and walked to the shed. He opened up a shallow wooden box, which was mounted on the wall, that Atherton knew contained his gardening gloves and secateurs. He pushed aside the gloves and pulled out a battered box of cigarettes. He took one and a disposable lighter from within.

"It's our right to worry about you," he said, sparking up the cigarette and inhaling deeply. "Just as it's your right to do what the hell you like."

He sent out a plume of smoke into the air and smiled at his son.

*

Atherton sat up abruptly in his chair when he heard the key in the lock, followed by the sound of Hannah's rapid footsteps on the wooden floor of the hall. He wiped a trail of saliva from his chin, realising he must have dozed off where he'd sat.

He'd reigned himself in to a couple of glasses of his mother's white wine, but it had still been enough to knock him out almost as soon as he returned home. On the TV, he saw overhead pictures of the observatory, the deck covered by a large white tarpaulin and surrounded by a wreath of bright green trees. He clicked it off, just as Hannah bolted into the room.

"Daddy!" she shrieked and ran to him, throwing herself across his knees. She thrust a picture in front of him; a lion with a multi-coloured mane drawn in felt-tip. "We're going on hol-i-day," she said in a sing-song voice.

"Are we?" he said.

Just then, Louise passed the lounge doorway. She glanced briefly at him before snapping her head back and continuing to the kitchen, carrying several shopping bags which rustled against the hall walls as she passed.

"Yes," said Hannah. "Mammy bought me a new pair of shorts and a dress and sunglasses."

"That's brilliant, love," he said. "You'll have to try them on and we'll have a fashion show."

"Mam," she shouted, wiggling off his lap and running after her.

He stood up, rubbed his eyes and walked slowly through to the kitchen where Louise had dropped the shopping bags on the table. She looked up at him silently, then went back to the letter she'd been reading.

"Gran Canaria?" he asked.

"Yes," she replied, offering a thin smile.

"When?"

"We leave tomorrow morning," she said. "Two tickets."

"Ah," he said. "I see."

"I've booked a taxi to the airport, so you needn't worry about that," she said. She walked to the table and began to organise the bags on the table.

"You'll be safe," he said. He couldn't bear the thought of them leaving, but the prospect of them staying felt worse.

"Exactly. Plus I want Hannah to have a proper holiday this year."

"And if the police no longer need me, can I join you? Before Christmas?"

She looked up at him incredulously and took a while to answer. "I think we could both do with a little time apart so you can decide what's important to you."

"Yes. Yes, of course," he said. "Let me drop you at the airport, at least."

"If you must." She grabbed the bags and waited a moment for him to step aside, brushing past him. A moment later, he heard her feet on the stairs and later again, the sound of her voice in hushed tones as she spoke on the telephone.

SIRIUS

CHAPTER EIGHTEEN

It was less of an awakening, more of a realisation that she was already awake. The bedroom blinds split dull light into blades which cut across the wall above her head. Kate placed her finger at the edge of one, watching for long moments as its position changed with the passing of time.

After a while, she sat up at the side of the bed and let her arms hang loosely down towards the floor. She'd ditched the evening wine in favour of green tea, which hadn't helped, but a full night's sleep would have been unlikely anyway. Her final thoughts before sleep had been of her father and it felt as though he'd just left the room. The memories were poor and broken; the stale smell of his aftershave on his shirts, the timbre of his voice and the semblance of his profile, faded and re-imagined through time. He'd read to her; Roald Dahl, Enid Blyton and comic books, changing his voice to fit each character. When it was time to settle down, he'd whisper; *Night, night, sleep tight, don't let the bedbugs bite. Wake up bright in the morning light, to do what's right...* and he'd let her finish; *with all my might.*

Her eyes felt sore and gritty, and time precluded the chance of further rest. She showered quickly and sat at the kitchen table, with a coffee that lacked in flavour, looking at Malcolm Stuyvesant's blank expression on his file photograph. She checked the time and knew she needed to get moving, but picked up her phone with uncertainty.

"Fuck it," she said and pressed the call button.

Atherton answered with a sigh.

"Hello," he said, his voice a low rumble.

"Jon, I'm sorry for calling so early," she said. There was a pause where she imagined him looking at a clock or wristwatch.

"It is. To what do I owe the pleasure? Not another one?"

"No," she replied. "Is it okay to talk? Louise is she..."

"It's okay. Trust me," he said.

"Sue got a DNA match from the video camera. We're arresting this morning," said Prejean.

"Jesus. You're kidding? Was someone going to tell me at some point?"

"Yes, I know. I'm sorry. We had a long briefing last night and by the time we got finished, I didn't think I should ring."

"So," he said, after a brief pause. "This guy has a record?"

"Malcolm Stuyvesant," she said. "He was convicted of..."

"I remember him. Child molester from a few years back."

"That's him."

"No," he said, firmly.

"What?"

"That's not our man," said Atherton.

"We have his DNA at the butterfly house crime scene, Atherton."

"You could have him covered in blood doing the Lambada at the crime scene and I wouldn't believe he was the right guy."

She sighed. "Feel like telling me why?"

"Other than what's in my profile? Does anyone read my hard-thought notions on this stuff, Kate?" he said. "The man we're looking for is average to above average intelligence, with a passion for astronomy. Malcolm Stuyvesant has learning difficulties, am I right?"

"Apparently, but you also said the killer may have a history of sexual assault. Am *I* right?"

"You are. I said he may do. He's harboured these thoughts for a while, but this isn't some bumbling half-witted monster," he said. "He's a precise, thoughtful individual."

"We need to follow the evidence. If it comes off a blank, at least we've tied it off."

"If you say so," he said, flatly.

"Look, I need to go," she said, reaching for her jacket. "I'll call you later."

"Adieu," he said and heard the line click dead.

*

The sky was grey, as if mirrored by the gum-speckled pavement below. Any semblance of light was still low in the east, and any that had cleared the horizon was shrouded in a thin veil of cloud. Squad cars blocked the road at either end of the terraced street, with the armed response vehicle tucked out of sight several hundred yards away in a neighbouring street. There were ten of them in total; six to go in through the front, four of them already at the back.

"In position," a voice crackled over Prejean's headset.

She glanced up and down the street and found it empty, save for a dog walker, who was quietly ushered in the opposite direction by Rogers. Beside her, Walsh gave a supportive nod. She checked her watch, feeling a sick and giddy excitement: 5:55AM.

She raised the headset to her mouth, pressed the button and said simply, "Okay."

Three officers approached rapidly from each side, keeping low to the walls and hedgerows of the neighbouring gardens, holding their weapons close to their black, armoured chests. They advanced up the path in single file, the front-runner – and largest by far – carrying the *Big Key*, a metal battering ram, with his gun slung over his shoulder. They assembled either side of the front door.

"Rear?" said a voice over Prejean's headset.

"In position," came the rapid reply.

"Go," she said.

The officer nearest the door nodded to the others, aimed the ram squarely at the lock and swung. The heavy door gave with a single blow. The ram was cast aside and the men swarmed into the house.

"Come on!" shouted Walsh, leaving his position behind the car and running forwards, with a speed that belied his paunch.

Prejean followed, covering the distance in no time. She entered the hallway and saw black uniforms moving rapidly up the narrow staircase and into rooms at the rear of the ground floor. Presently, she heard the noise of an extendable ladder and knew they were already in the loft.

"Upstairs clear," said a voice over the radio.

"This door, this door," said Walsh, standing next to an officer who was trying vainly to open the door to the lounge, using first the handle, then his shoulder. When it failed to budge, he ran towards Prejean.

"Back, back, back!" he said and hurried back down the narrow hallway, forcing her to retreat in the process, until she found herself outside again.

He scooped up the discarded ram and ran back in. Prejean remained outside and attempted to look through the window at the point where the filthy curtains failed to meet. Inside, it was dark. The features difficult to discern. But there was a sudden movement which drew her eyes to one corner of the room.

She could see Stuyvesant sitting there, looking back at her with wide, frightened eyes. He was naked except for his shorts, which were all but covered by the overhang of his substantial pale gut. When he saw Prejean, he shouted something at her, his eyes bulbous and earnest. He shook his head franticly as Prejean heard the ram connect with the door.

" *Wait!*" she screamed, turning away from the window just as it shattered.

The explosion ripped out the windows, sending shards of glass outwards into the street. Prejean felt a sharp sting to her cheek and was thrown to the ground. She pulled herself up, using the wall for support, aware of warm blood on her face. Her hearing was all but gone, replaced with something akin to background tape hiss, with the wail of car alarms the only thing audible.

Suddenly, Rogers was in front of her, saying something, shouting. It took a moment for her to realise what it was: "*Lie down! Lie down!*"

She shook off his hands and dashed into the house. A heavy cloud of plaster dust made it difficult to see. The locked door was all but obliterated, leaving only a few shards of wood in the frame. The officer lay on the ground unconscious against the wall, his neck cocked at an awkward angle.

Walsh lay beside him, wheezing and rasping as if trying to clear his throat. She knelt down and he immediately reached for her, clawing and scrabbling desperately with one hand, his eyes wide and panicked, his other hand clasped to his throat.

"Ambulance!" she yelled to the figure beside her, her own voice distant and muted. "Call it in. Now! Officer down!"

She tried to remove Walsh's hand from his throat. "Let me see, David." She pulled his hand away and saw a fragment of wood the size of a table knife, impaled in his neck. Dark red blood pulsed out from the wound. "It's okay, Walsh. Help's on the way," she said, looking into his eyes. She placed her hands at either side of the wood and applied pressure, trying to stem the flow. "Stay awake, Walsh. We got him. We got him."

"He was shouting a name," whispered Walsh with effort.

She hushed him and wiped some blood from his cheek.

"Don't talk," she said. "Just hang on, Walsh."

"Ma...Matthew Bank," he said. "He was saying something...couldn't hear most of it, but he said...Matthew Bank."

"Matthew Bank. Got it. Just chill now. Help's coming," said Prejean.

He nodded, weakly, the corners of his mouth twitching into a smile. A deep gargling noise came from him and blood frothed up at his lips.

"He's choking," said Prejean. "David, we're going to roll you over."

Rogers helped to push him over onto his side and they saw where the shard of wood protruded from the back of his neck. Rogers clamped his hand there and they both held him. Interminable minutes passed, while Prejean whispered words of comfort, until she felt a strong hand on her shoulder.

"We'll take him from here," said the paramedic.

She staggered out into the street where two ambulances and several squad cars now stood. She pushed her way past clusters of people, vaguely aware that Myers was among them, and walked down the narrow alleyway. She leaned against the wall and sunk down into a seated position, making balls with her fists until the blood became sticky, then dry.

Eventually, Rogers found her and he stood for long moments in her peripheral vision, with Prejean unwilling to raise her head.

"He's dead," said Rogers, finally.

"I know," she said.

CHAPTER NINETEEN

Outside, the street had begun to stir modestly. A house a few doors down was having a new drive put in and Atherton was awoken by the sound of the men through his open bedroom window. Their words were out of earshot, but their gruff voices intermingled with the remnants of a tenuous dream. He enjoyed the reckless vacancy of semi-consciousness for indiscernible minutes before reality stole him back.

Atherton let his limbs spread to the far regions of the bed, simultaneously enjoying the freedom of movement, but missing Louise's warm presence. After a while, he rose and plodded heavily down the landing wearing only his pyjama bottoms. He stopped to look in on Hannah's room with bleary eyes. The bed was made, her toys tucked neatly away into brightly coloured plastic containers. A menagerie of faces looked out at him, with glassy, sightless eyes.

He ran a bath. Atherton preferred baths to showers. Osram had written a compelling essay once on the psychological aspects of this choice, with an analogy of the womb and amniotic fluid. Consequently, his baths were often spoiled by the thought of Osram watching over him and taking notes.

Downstairs, he clicked on the kettle and picked up his phone, absently scanning his messages. There was nothing from Louise. Nothing to say they'd arrived safely, or that Hannah had been okay on the flight.

Nothing at all.

He flipped up the lid on his laptop. He refreshed the screen and selected a news site from his favourites. The item was vague:

*Police are investigating an explosion which killed two men
in the west end of Newcastle. The blast occurred in the
early hours of the morning, causing substantial damage to
a property in Wainwright Crescent and killing two men,
including one police officer, neither of whom have been
named at this time. Several others were injured, though
none are thought to be serious.*

Lauren Schloss's name stood above the piece in bold. He was
reaching for his phone again when it rang. Kate's name flashed up
on the screen.

"Hi," he said. "Are you alright?"

"Hello," she said, flatly. "Can I come around? I'm in the next
street."

"Of course," he said.

"Where's Louise? Is it okay?"

"She's away for a few days. I just read about it in the news. Just
get here."

"What about the neighbours?"

"Fuck them."

He heard the line go dead and began to bin a few empty food
packages. He straightened the cushions and threw a pair of shoes
into the cupboard under the stairs. He had time to don a T-shirt
from the basket; laundered but not ironed, before he heard a gentle
knock at the front door.

"Hey," she said and attempted a smile. Her eyes looked heavy
and red. The fine cut on her face bisected her cheekbone.

"Ouch," he said. "Come in."

He couldn't help but look over her shoulder as she entered.

"Neighbours?"

"Like I said, fuck them," he said. "What happened?"

"Walsh is dead," she said.

"Oh, Jesus Christ," he said.

They walked into the kitchen, where she folded her arms and
hovered uncomfortably by the counter. She quickly took in the
room: the furnishings, the décor, the family photographs and he

watched her closely. If it were Louise, he would have known what to do. He'd hold her, she'd cry and then she'd talk and he'd listen. He didn't know what to do with Kate.

"You want some tea?" he said tentatively.

"Better make it coffee," she said.

He clicked the kettle on again. She sat and let her head fall back onto the chair, with her eyes closed. The kettle had boiled before she spoke again.

"I keep seeing his eyes. Just...the shock and the fear. The helplessness. Like a child. I wanted to be the one to tell his wife, but Myers wouldn't let me. He sent me home, Jon. So here I am." She snorted a weak laugh.

A rolodex of possible responses scrolled through Atherton's mind. He was aware of his habit of repeatedly self-editing before he spoke, to the point where it would come out sounding exactly as it was: rehearsed.

"I'm sure you did everything possible, Kate," he said finally.

"I did fuck all of any value," she said, opening her eyes to look at him. "Just watched him bleed out all over that pervert's carpet."

"You were with him."

"I'm sure that'll be a huge comfort to his boy."

He added milk to the coffee and gave it a cursory stir, before handing it to her.

"He was doing his job, just like you were. It could have just as easily been you." His eyes met hers briefly. "Are *you* okay?"

"Yes," she said. She placed the coffee on the table beside her. "And Stuyvesant isn't even our man, is he?"

"I don't think so, no," he said.

"You don't think so? I hope Myers opened with that when he explained to Penny Walsh why her husband is dead."

"That's not fair. I told you my professional opinion. Stuyvesant was incapable of these killings."

She closed her eyes again.

"You want to know why I'm here, Jon? I know that Myers is on the verge of taking me off this case, if he hasn't already. I know my team is in bits and has no confidence in me. But you're immune to all of this, aren't you? You don't have much in the way of feelings, what with your position on 'the spectrum'." She made quotation marks in the air. "When we have more time, I'd love to know if you gave a shit about me when we were fucking, but whilst Myers is floundering, and before the media start baying for my resignation, I'd like me and you to go and *end this*, like we did the last time, for better or for worse."

He looked at her eyes, unflinching and obstinate.

"Okay then," he said. "For better or for worse."

*

"So this is what happens when you mix an explosion with the human body," said Rick Gibson, who used a disposable biro to raise a charred piece of material from the chair.

Prejean turned away from him when he spoke, leaving Atherton nodding in exaggerated awe. She'd heard that Gibson was an arsehole and hadn't been disappointed. Gibson had no doubt been briefed on the circumstances of Walsh's death, but it was hard to tell, given his apparent glee at being let loose on the crime scene.

"This is a dentist's chair, right?" said Atherton. The cushioning had been almost completely burned away, exposing the metal carcass of the chair. "But what's this?" He pointed to the makeshift scaffolding at the rear of the chair. There was a drill attached to it. The plastic casing had melted into long plastic stalactites, but the drill bit remained virtually untarnished, passing through a hole in the chair's headrest. "That doesn't look like standard dental issue to me, Sue?"

"I doubt it," said Sue, preoccupied with another side of the room.

Atherton looked at the charred casing and followed the line of the bit through the headrest.

"Torture?" he said.

"Looks like it," said Sue. "What do you think?"

"Hmm," he said.

"Basic pipe bomb," said Gibson, holding out a charred fragment of pipe. "You can pack something like this with gunpowder, match heads, whatever you want; it'll do the same job." He ran a gloved finger down the black residue on the interior of the fragment. "I'd say this was most likely nitrate fertiliser, probably soaked in petrol."

Sue nodded, but attempted to project the body language of someone who couldn't care less. Atherton picked up on it: Sue disliked Gibson, but respected him. Prejean kept looking out through the splintered doorway to the patch of blood in the hallway where Walsh had died.

"Tripwire," said Gibson, pointing at the small metal eyelets, which had been secured to guide the wire on the skirting board beside the door. "Probably a simple mechanical trigger; pull the wire, create a spark. Boom. Like flicking a lighter." He turned again to the centre of the room where the mangled dentist's chair stood. Stuyvesant's body had been removed, but pieces of blackened blood and flesh still hung from it, like meat on a long-neglected barbeque grill. He crouched behind the chair and peered into its ruptured base. "Looks like he stuck the pipe in this spot right here," he said, pointing to an opening. "It's enclosed, so it would further intensify the explosion. The brunt would travel up through this part of the chair and through the path of least resistance; the victim."

He gestured with his hands. Sue looked out onto the road. It had taken hours to remove all traces of the body, meticulously marking and photographing numerous locations. The explosion had ripped him in two, sending his legs to the far side of the room and leaving a hollow cavity where his intestines used to be. They'd even collected pieces from the gardens of the houses across the street.

*

Myers surveyed the solemn faces around the table, trying to gauge the depth of the mood. Prejean was ashen-faced and Atherton stared at her with intense curiosity. Rogers wore a frown, staring into the middle distance and tapping incessantly on his notepad with his pen. Mattias Klum appeared to occupy a default setting of nervousness. Sue was simply tired, her eyes bloodshot and heavy. It was Amis who looked at him first, her dark brown eyes a little puffy and swollen, but she offered him a tight-lipped smile, which galvanized him into speech.

"I want to thank you," he began. "All of you. For everything you've put into this case." He looked at each of them in turn. "We've lost a good officer and a great mate. I'd urge you to take advantage of the counselling services which are available to you all. In a civilised world, we'd have time to grieve him, but we don't. Not for the moment. We owe it to Walsh...to David, to tie this thing up thoroughly and meticulously."

"Tie this up?" said Atherton. All eyes fell on him. "Let's not be under any illusions here."

Rogers looked from Prejean to Atherton and back again before he spoke. "Stuyvesant *was* the Starman, right? DNA doesn't lie, does it? You said the killings would follow the constellations; Al Nitak, Alpha Draconis, Ursa Minor and the final one would be different. Something..."

"Something to mimic Sirius," interrupted Amis. "Brightest star; a huge flaming ball of energy in the sky. That explosion seemed a fair interpretation to me. It looks like a swansong."

"No," said Atherton, firmly. "It doesn't fit."

"Wait," said Amis. "Doesn't fit the evidence, or doesn't fit your profile?"

"It doesn't fit either," he said. "We have three victims, all killed in the same meticulous way, following Ancient Egyptian astronomical beliefs and leaving almost no physical evidence. Does that sound like Stuyvesant to you? A semi-literate child molester who..."

"Who had years inside to dream this all up maybe?" said Rogers.

"This is a man who was caught on CCTV masturbating in bushes, who kept the underwear of his victims in his bedside cabinet. The most significant Starman evidence we've found so far?

Stuyvesant's DNA on the tape. Right where we were supposed to find it."

Myers raised his eyebrows, but said nothing.

"Starman has all the arrogance to film and message us, build up a following of...how many, Mattias?"

"Ten-point-three thousand," said Mattias, immediately.

"...but doesn't leave us – or them – with a goodbye?"

"So you're saying that Starman killed Stuyvesant? Sacrificed him to put us off the scent?" said Rogers.

"I think he killed him to take the *piss*," said Atherton.

"It's an insult," added Prejean, her voice low. "He's mocking us."

"Stuyvesant wasn't tied. Are you telling us he sat on that bomb and waited for it to go off?" said Rogers.

"Yes," replied Atherton.

"That's ridiculous. Why?"

"Fear. Because he was more afraid of what would happen to him if he didn't."

Rogers puffed air slowly from his lips and looked up at the ceiling.

There was an enduring silence.

"Okay," said Myers. "If we're to go with this, we need to get back to Stuyvesant's lodgings, pursue the possibility he was being held captive, and murdered. We need to close out any leads on Matthew Banks; widen the search, interview any and all men of that name. While we're doing that, we need to fly under the radar. As far as the media are concerned, Starman died with Stuyvesant."

"We ran Matthew Banks through the system," said Amis. "Quite a common name. Thanks guys. We have a total of nineteen in the North East area. Only three had a criminal record of any kind. Two of these were guys with traffic offences, the third for tax fraud. No charges or cautions for anything of a violent or sexual nature. They're well behaved, your Matthew Banks."

"Okay, thanks Connie. I'd like you and Chris to work through the list. Talk to them. See if they have alibis for the observatory, butterfly house and Bottleburn dates. Look for vans on driveways..."

"Size seven shoes? Got it," said Amis. "Come on, Chris."

Rogers clearly didn't like being given an instruction from Amis, but picked up his jacket from the back of his chair, threw it over his shoulders and followed her out the door.

"I just don't get it," said Myers. "Why would he change his MO, unless it was to kill himself? If this doesn't represent a conclusion, what does it represent?"

"The end of a chapter," said Prejean.

CHAPTER TWENTY

"Jared Crane is awake in hospital," said Myers. "They've been bringing him round slowly. They're not overly keen on letting us in to see him, but I've managed to get us ten minutes."

"Is he *compos mentis*?"

"That remains to be seen. You've got an appointment to see him at 2PM today. Expect squeaky-arsed hospital execs in the room. Keep it brief and go softly-softly, Prejean."

"Sir," she said. Prejean followed his eyes to Amis, who was talking on the phone in the focus room. "We're working on the probability that he uses a van and did so at the observatory. Assuming he took the A69, there's an accident blackspot camera eight miles away. I've asked Rogers to log all the potential suspect vehicles in and out in a four hour window."

"I'm sure he thanked you for that."

"He was overjoyed."

"And you?"

"We're going to interview Mrs Henderson, the landlady of Stuyvesant's place," she said.

"Good," said Myers. He finally turned to look at her and saw that her steely look of determination had returned, although the liberal use of foundation failed to hide the cut on her face. "That reminds me..." He walked to his desk, opened the top drawer, removed a business card and handed it to her. "This lady will be getting in touch."

Prejean quickly read the card.

"Counselling. Sure," she said.

"Mandatory, Kate," he said firmly.

She raised the card to her forehead and used it to salute him. As she headed towards the door, her phone rang.

"I'm calling with an update on Matthew Banks," said Amis. Prejean could hear traffic in the background. She looked at the clock and realised it was already rush hour. "We split the list and we've seen seven of them, between us. We don't have anything so far. One of them is sixteen and another eighty-three, so we've prioritised and left them until last."

"Happy for you to prioritise, but due diligence on all of them, please," said Prejean. "Bank might not be the killer himself, but he could be an accomplice, or linked in some other way."

"Sure boss, but this is going to take a while," said Amis.

"I have some things to do, but after that, let's see if I can take some of that list off your hands," she said.

"We'd appreciate it. Catch you later?"

"You will. I'll be in touch, Connie," said Prejean, tapping her phone to disconnect.

Atherton watched as she swept up her long, brown hair into one hand and transferred a band from her wrist to make a ponytail, which she pulled tight to her head.

"What?" she said, catching him watching her.

"You're still hanging on to this idea of some sort of accomplice?" he said. "Two killers?"

"I think it's possible," she said.

"Highly unlikely," said Atherton. "There have only been a handful of cases like that on record. I think this is a shy little lone wolf."

"I said I thought it was possible, not probable," she said. "Once you write your profile, you stick to it, hmm?" He looked away and she sensed he'd taken an affront. She walked around the table and into his line of sight. "I wasn't having a go there, Jon."

"Oh, you weren't talking about Lee Hicks?" he said tersely.

"Fuck, no." She put a hand on his forearm. "I just don't want to get blinkered. I think we have a bunch of random data points which we need to bring together. So random, we might be looking at two suspects, rather than one."

*

Prejean mounted the kerb with some force. Atherton steadied himself with a hand to the dashboard.

"Are you okay?" he said,

"Tip top," she said, wrenching up the handbrake.

"You can't ride around with all this angst inside you, Kate. You'll explode like a dead whale on a beach," said Atherton. "Couldn't Rogers or Amis have done this?"

"I've sent them back to look at the statements from Menshen and do cross-checks with the hospital contractors," she said. "Your idea, I believe?"

"It also keeps them out of the way, doesn't it?"

She looked at him with weary eyes.

"There is that," she said.

The office was above a motorcycle showroom in the west end of town and Prejean had pulled up, perilously close to a long line of bikes parked diagonally on the road. Outside, a large board displayed numerous flats for rent behind a glass screen, but there was no other obvious signage. They climbed the steps into an open-plan office with walls clad in varnished pine.

A large woman in a black cardigan was speaking on the phone with her back to them. She turned and raised her eyebrows in acknowledgement and gestured to a beaten leather couch in the corner of the room. Beside it, an old wire-haired crossbreed dog looked up with some interest from a dog basket, which looked in better condition than the couch.

Atherton followed Prejean's lead and remained standing.

"Tell them we've got pictures of the carpet before and after they moved in," said the woman in a tired tone and then listened for a moment to the answer. "Well, they don't know that."

Prejean cleared her throat.

"Look, I'm going to have to go. Call me back later."

"Mrs. Henderson?" asked Prejean.

"Yes, hello," she said, reaching out a small, freckled hand which Prejean shook. Henderson looked at Atherton, decided a handshake either wasn't appropriate or worthwhile and nodded instead. "Please, sit down."

"Thanks for seeing us. I can see you're busy."

"Sixty-five properties in the city centre. Most of them student accommodation. There's always someone moving in, someone moving out or" – she gestured to the phone – "quibbling over bonds."

"We'd like to talk about the house on Wainwright Crescent."

"Yes, of course. I've had tenants die on me before. I've had to break down the door and get them removed, but I've *never* had an explosion. That's a new one."

She reached for a pack of cheap cigarettes, removed one and lit it, exhaling a thick plume of smoke, which loitered above her head.

"Can't be very good for business," said Atherton.

"No," she said, smiling. "It's not, and the insurance company take a lifetime to cough up of course."

"How well did you know the tenant?"

"Barely at all. I generally get to know the bad payers quicker than the good. He was good."

"You know Malcolm Stuyvesant was a convicted paedophile, released from a five year prison term?"

"I didn't at the time, but your colleague mentioned it when he was here. The young lad. I told him I took the usual ID stuff for my paperwork, but I don't exactly run a CRB check on everyone who answers an ad, you know what I mean? If they can pay, they can stay."

"No, of course," said Prejean. "We understand, but we just wanted to ask a few general questions."

"My memory's pretty good when it comes to people living in my houses," she said. "Shoot."

"Stuyvesant took up accommodation at Wainwright Crescent in March this year, right?"

Henderson turned to a computer on her desk and put on some reading glasses which had been hanging around her cleavage. She moved the mouse with a talon-like hand and made a number of clicks.

"Yes. Cheque cleared on the fourteenth of March and he moved in on the twenty-fifth."

"And did you show him around the house yourself?"

"I did," she said. "You meet plenty of strange people doing this. Plenty of nice ones as well, mind, but I think he was a little strange."

"And could you describe Mr Stuyvesant?"

She looked up and to the left as if the answer might be pasted to the ceiling.

"He was pretty...average, I think you'd say. Let me think."

Prejean reached into her bag and pulled out a large image of an obese, middle-aged man with an unhealthy pallor and several days' worth of stubble.

"This is Malcolm Stuyvesant," said Prejean.

"Wait, this isn't the fella I rented the house to," said Henderson, looking from one face to the other as if she were the victim of a practical joke.

"No, we think someone else rented it from you using Stuyvesant's details and let him live there," said Prejean.

"Why would he do that?"

"It's part of the ongoing investigation. We're just examining some possibilities," she said. "But what we really need is a description of the man who did meet you with regards to renting Wainwright Street."

Henderson stubbed out the remains of her cigarette and seemed to be reaching for another one before raising her hand to her face to stroke her chin in thought.

"He was short, for a bloke. About my height."

"Which is?"

"Five foot five. I think he was late thirties, early forties."

"Hair?"

"No, he was bald."

"Bald as in clipped really short or bald as in bald?"

"I mean totally hairless. It made me think he might have that...what do you call it?"

"Alopecia?" suggested Atherton.

"Aye, that's it," she said, pointing at him.

"And what about his eyes?"

"Light. Blue or green. I can't remember which."

"Can you remember his hands?"

"His hands?"

"Did he have a wedding ring? Did you shake his hand? Did they feel rough?"

"I can't remember no ring. I did shake his hand though." She thought for a moment. "I think maybe he had a working man's hands," she said, giving in to the temptation of another cigarette. "He was wearing kind of work clothes, too. It made me think he'd come straight from work."

"Overalls?"

"Not exactly. He had on those work trousers with lots of pockets."

"Did they have any paint on them? Plaster or dirt?"

"Not that I remember."

"And did you see what he was driving?"

"No. He was outside when I got there and I didn't see him take off."

Prejean continued to write notes, but fell silent for a moment.

"He had a stutter, didn't he?" said Atherton.

"How'd you know that?"

Atherton smiled.

"You don't happen to know if he was called Matthew do you? Matthew Banks?"

"I'm sorry, but I've never heard of Matthew Banks," she said. "I have a *house* on Matthew *Bank*, will that do you?"

"Excuse me?" said Prejean.

"A two bedroom semi on Matthew Bank, Gosforth," she said. "Nice views of the dene. More for the professional market."

Prejean looked at Atherton, eyes widening.

"Can you tell me the name of the tenant?"

Henderson shrugged.

"Sure," she said and turned back to her computer screen.

"Here we are," she said, finally. "Thirty-four, Matthew Bank. The tenant was a Mr Oliver Sirus...and he began tenancy in...June, last year."

"Osiris," said Atherton. "He's a fucking comic genius."

Henderson's glance told him she wasn't keen on the language.

"Thank you, Mrs Henderson," said Prejean. "Jon, we're going to have to wrap this up and get Myers to organise a warrant and armed response unit to go in."

"Or I could give you the keys?" said Henderson. "I've seen how you lot *go in*."

"We can do that?" said Prejean.

"Well, the tenancy agreement lapsed two months ago and it's been empty since," she said. "It needs redecorating. When my lad went around to check it, he said it had a bit of an odour. Some of them do."

*

The man wore bulky bomb disposal armour; a green suit, with a visored helmet, a thick black plate over his chest and a collar which rode up over the shoulders almost to eye-level. Armed response officers held positions behind him in the small front garden of the house. He knelt at the open door and ran his gloved hand across the floor and doorframe.

"He's checking for wires," said Rick Gibson into Prejean's ear. "It's only useful to an extent. There could be explosives under the floorboards, remotely activated..."

"Do you mind?" said Prejean, leaning away from him. He stepped back from her and Atherton smiled to himself. "How's the back lane?" she said into her radio.

"Nothing," replied Rogers, cutting through the static.

The armoured man stood and made a step into the hallway. Suddenly, a ginger cat bolted past him and out into the street. Several of the armed response team levelled their guns at it instinctively, before letting them drop.

"Rick," said Prejean. "Make yourself useful and grab that cat, will you?"

Gibson looked at her for a moment in disbelief and then at Atherton.

"Don't look at me," said Atherton. "My cat-catching days are over."

Gibson dutifully scampered after the animal.

The bomb disposal officer disappeared from view and several minutes passed.

"Okay, fellas," he said over the radio finally, and the armed men poured into the house.

Atherton tapped Prejean's shoulder and pointed up the street, where the road had been cordoned off with barriers and a squad car. She could see Lauren Schloss, easily identifiable by her large mane of dark hair.

"Great," she said.

"She's here awfully quick, wouldn't you say?" said Atherton. "She's had a tip-off."

A further fifteen minutes passed until the men reappeared in the street.

"Okay, we're clear," said a voice over the radio. "But proceed with caution."

"I'll be proceeding with bloody nothing but," slurred Atherton.

The inside of the house was sepia, coloured by decades of cigarette smoke as if the wallpaper itself were a lung, filtering dirt from the air. They moved from the hallway into a lounge containing nothing but a single wooden dining chair that faced the window. Atherton stared at it intently as if by doing so, it could conjure up someone sitting upon it. Prejean slid open some French doors which split the room and recoiled at the stench.

"Nice," said Rogers. The rear room was littered with cat faeces and in the corner was a pile of empty cat food tins.

"We need to see if Sue can get a match from here to the cat hair she found on the camera tape," said Prejean.

"I'll call her," said Rogers, pulling his phone out and dialling.

Atherton followed Prejean out of the room and up the stairs, which creaked with every step. As they approached the top, there was a muffled thud from one of the rooms beyond. Prejean looked back at Atherton and held a finger to her lips before extending her baton with a flick of her wrist. They walked across the semi-lit landing to a large door, which was slightly ajar. Prejean nodded at Atherton and he returned it, his breathing becoming more rapid and shallow. Prejean held the baton above her head, ready to strike, and kicked open the door.

Another cat screeched and tore past them down the stairs.

"Fuck me," said Atherton.

"What's the matter?" shouted Rogers. A moment later, they heard his feet on the stairs. "Are you okay?" he said entering the room.

"Just another cat," said Prejean.

"I knew it. There's nothing here," said Atherton. "Why would he..."

"I wouldn't quite say that," said Rogers and nodded at something across the room. Atherton and Prejean turned to a small empty fireplace surrounded by a simple wooden mantelpiece.

On top was a glass jar containing a clear liquid and at the bottom, as if staring out at them, was Jared Crane's eyeball.

*

Jared Crane watched impassively with his remaining eye as they entered. He was sat upright in bed, with a number of plump pillows behind him and an intravenous drip feeding into his wrist. A heavy dressing covered the left side of his face and his hands were bound across the palms with bandages. Two well-worn plastic seats had been positioned at the side of the bed and the lights appeared to have been dimmed somewhat.

Atherton and Prejean sat down and a nurse, who had followed them into the room, moved a tray away from Crane and wheeled the table out of his way. She positioned herself on another chair near the foot of the bed.

"Thanks for your time today, Doctor Crane," said Prejean. "We know you've been through a lot and we really do appreciate it."

"No problem," he said. His voice was soft and his mouth curved into a weak smile.

"I was wondering what you can remember about your attacker?"

"I didn't see much of his face." Crane's lip shook a little as he spoke. "When he hit me, the lights from the observatory were behind him, so I could only see a silhouette. Then, when I came around on the platform, he was wearing a mask."

"What kind of mask?"

"I don't know...like a doll's face. What do you call those things?"

"A *Pierrot*?"

"Yes, except it had black around the eyes and here..." He drew an imaginary line from his eye to his ear with his bandaged hand. Atherton wrote something into a moleskin notebook he'd balanced on his lap.

"Can you tell us any more about him, physically?" asked Prejean.

"Well...ah...he was bald. Quite short." Crane looked away suddenly. "Do you think I could have a glass of water, please?"

The nurse poured water from a plastic jug into a small beaker and helped to raise it to his lips.

"Thanks, I can do it," he said.

When he struggled to place it on the bedside cabinet, Atherton reached over and took it for him.

"This can't be pleasant for you to relive, Doctor Crane," said Prejean, tentatively. "But would you be able to tell us some of what happened next?"

"What happened next?" said Crane. He ran his hand across the bedclothes and gripped the edge of the blanket. "What happened next was...he made me watch." His voice cracked a little. "And when I couldn't watch anymore, he did this to me." He gestured to the dressing on his face, with an over-sized, bandaged hand. "He cut

me, until I thought he was going to kill me and I passed out...and
I..." A tear breached his eyelid and ran quickly down his cheek.

"I think we should leave it there for the time being, don't you?"
said the nurse, with a finality that suggested negotiation would not
be a possibility.

"Of course," said Prejean. "Thank you so much, Doctor
Crane."

Crane nodded, his face giving way to a succession of facial tics.
Atherton pocketed his notebook and he and Prejean rose. Then,
when they were at the door:

"One thing I did notice was...he had a plaster on the back of his
head...just here," said Crane. He demonstrated the position on his
own head.

*

Atherton could remember the bar from another era, when a
permanent fog of cigarette smoke hung in the air and the
dilapidated jukebox would click over on a seemingly endless series
of 45s from the eighties. It had since undergone the inevitable
transformation to a gastropub, with the old dark fittings replaced
with lighter shades of purposefully distressed wood and hipster
paintings. He followed her to the furthest snug from the door,
where she settled into a seat and said only, "Gin."

He hung his coat over the back of a chair and turned towards
the bar. She grabbed him suddenly by the forearm.

"Thanks, Jon," she added.

He nodded.

"You want some food? Maybe you should eat?"

"Later," she said.

"Okay."

When he returned from the bar with their drinks, he prodded
at the teabag in his cup with a wooden stirrer and pretended to be
interested in the specials. A smiling waiter placed wooden boards
with burgers and chips in small metal pails on a nearby table.

"What is all this about serving food on bloody chopping boards and roof tiles?" he said. "What happened to plates?"

"You're going to do this, are you? The small talk?"

"It's the talk I'm best at," he said.

"Well, isn't that a shame?" She smiled, sarcastically. "So, Stuyvesant gets out of prison and our man befriends him, maybe even pretends to have similar interests to him, to get close and gain his trust, then uses him as a decoy when he feels he needs one."

"A patsy? Leaves Stuyvesant's DNA at the scene and it sends us off the wrong way giving him plenty of time."

"Time for what?"

"I don't know. That's what worries me."

*

"I want a divorce," said Louise. There was a drawn out silence, during which Atherton could hear Hannah playing in the background. He heard Louise exhale and felt a clammy sweat rise on the back of his neck. "It's not working, Jon. Is it?"

"Louise..."

"All of the counselling and all this time. This is what it comes down to."

"You know I love you, Louise. We've spent months unravelling ourselves in front of a stranger, so you know this."

"I know that's what you tell me, Jon," she said. "But why don't I feel it?"

The question hung unanswered. Atherton transferred the phone from one ear to the other.

"I know I find it hard to express myself with you sometimes. I sometimes have to...compartmentalise," he said.

"It's not that you compartmentalise, it's the fact that I really believe you don't give a fuck, Jon."

"I am the way I am," he said. "Can we talk about this?"

"We are talking about this," she said. "That's all we've ever done. Gone over it and over it until we've fooled ourselves everything is okay," she said. "I've had enough of that. I don't want to fool myself anymore. I want to do something about it, not just talk."

"What if I jacked in the job?"

She snorted derisively.

"You know, Jon, it probably doesn't help our marriage that you're spending more time with *her* than your own wife, but it's made me realise that there's no way back for me. It's broken."

"If it's broken, it can be fixed," he said. He heard Hannah murmur something in the background.

"We're going in a minute, love," Louise said to her. "Can you get your things together in your little bag?"

"Can I speak to her?" said Atherton.

"Of course."

A pause, then: "Daddy."

"Hello gorgeous," he said.

"We've been to the beach three times," she said excitedly. "And we're going on a bus to a water-slide park."

"Oh, that's brilliant Hannah. Is it hot?"

"It's quite sunny, but a little bit windy," she said.

"You make sure you let Mammy put all your sun cream on, okay?"

"Okay, Daddy," she said. "Mammy says Santa will know where we are, even when we're on holiday. When are you coming?"

"I don't know, love. Daddy has to finish a job, then I might be able to come out to see you."

"Hurry up, Daddy," she said.

"I will, darling," he said. "Listen, you look after Mammy until I get there, okay?"

"Okay. Bye, Dad," she said.

"Goodbye my love," he said. There was the noise of fabric against the receiver, then Louise cleared her throat. "Is everything alright there?" he asked after a moment of silence.

"It's fine. It's beautiful, actually. Not very busy, but she's made a friend already."

"How about you?"

"I'm not here to make friends, Jon. I'm here to think," she said coldly. "I should go now. She wants to go out."

"Louise...Louise, please just stay in touch, okay? Let me know when you're coming home."

"I will," she said. He heard a click. Atherton placed the phone on the table and pressed two fingers hard onto his forehead, where an impressive ache had developed. A moment passed then he rose suddenly, throwing over the table and spilling everything on it to the floor.

Transcendence

CHAPTER TWENTY-ONE

Mattias Klum flicked rapidly through the tabs on his internet browser. He'd set up a number of searches to pull out key words and phrases pertinent to the case: 'Starman', 'Son of Geb', 'Osiris' and the places and dates of the three killings. These searches drew in a huge number of comments. He electronically snipped and saved examples that seemed representative of the general public's sentiment; fear, confusion and bad jokes. His eyes flicked across the characters on the screen, until he'd read every word, then he scrolled back up, refreshed and started again.

It was like a tic. He paused to swig from his mineral water and looked around the room. The faces of Izzy Lynch, Ellis Brampton and Abigail Southern looked back at him from the boards standing across the room.

Myers was in his office, talking on the phone, but looking out at Amis, who was sifting through a pile of files on her desk. Mattias took another long swig, rubbed his eyes and replaced his glasses. He scrolled across the screen again and something caught his eye almost immediately. The profile of *@SonOfGeb* appeared almost as before: the badly cropped Egyptian picture, the digits representing the ever-increasing number of followers and the few messages sent so far, but there was one crucial difference. The 'following' number, which had displayed '0' for so long, now said '1'.

"Fucking hell," he whispered to himself.

He moved the cursor so it hovered over the single digit and clicked. The profile appeared and he recognised the photo immediately. As he read the name, a chill fell over him. He looked up.

"Er...can you come and see this please?" he said. Amis carried on working. "Come and see this," he said, louder. "Please."

Amis pushed back her chair and joined him at his desk.

"What is it?"

"*Son of Geb* is following someone back," he said.

"Who?"

"Me."

He raised his finger to the screen and Amis read the name: MATTIAS KLUM.

*

"What do you mean, he's 'following' you?" said Myers. "Sorry, I'm not really what you'd call up to speed on social media."

"He's friended me. He sees my updates. Whatever I post, he now sees," said Klum.

"It means he's watching us watching him," said Amis. "Of all the thousands of people out there, he's only following one person, who happens to be one of our team. He knows who we all are."

"Fuck," said Myers. He reached for his phone and lifted it from the cradle, only to replace it moments later.

"We need to think about how he's come by this information," said Amis.

"You think whoever's doing this knows someone inside Northumbria Police?"

"We need to consider that possibility," said Amis. Myers's eyes darted around the room as he thought.

"Mattias, I'm sorry about this and we'll do everything to ensure your safety isn't compromised," began Myers. "Connie, can you get Prejean and Atherton in here? We need Atherton's perspective on this."

"Sir," said Amis, leaving the office at a pace.

"Mattias, do you have family? I mean, who've you got at home?" said Myers.

"I'm single," he said. "I share a house with a bunch of other people in Jesmond. There are five of us."

"Okay," said Myers. "Let me get my head around this. Just because he's following you online doesn't mean he knows where you're based geographically, right?"

"He'd have to do some digging around, I think," said Klum. "All of my social profiles just state Newcastle and I don't have geography set up on anything. I don't like anyone knowing where I am particularly, never mind a serial killer." He laughed nervously.

"Good," said Myers. "Let me make a few calls, if you'll excuse me."

"Another thing," said Mattias. Myers replaced the phone for a second time. "I follow him. He follows me. This means we can send him messages, if we want to, which no-one else can see."

"What do you propose? That we use you as bait? There's no way that's..." started Myers.

"I'd be happy to do that," interrupted Mattias.

Amis had returned with Atherton and Prejean, and everyone looked at him.

"Well, happy's not *quite* the word," said Mattias, "but I'd do it, if we could catch him."

The possibility hung unaddressed in the air for several moments.

"That's commendable, but we're not asking anyone to do that," said Prejean.

"It wouldn't serve any purpose," said Atherton. "He'd know that any attempts to make a rendezvous would be a trap. He'd just enjoy watching us dance."

"What then?" said Myers.

"I don't know," said Atherton.

*

"Kate," said Myers. "Sorry, do you have a minute?"

"Sure," replied Prejean. "We need to talk about how we get help for Mattias on the social monitoring front."

"No problem," he said, although his face said otherwise.

As Prejean entered Myers's office, he was rotating the poles on the blinds for privacy.

"That's never a good sign," she said, closing the door behind her.

"No," he said. "Please, take a seat, Kate."

"It's okay, I'll stand," she said, folding her arms.

"I'm sorry. I have to take you off this job, Kate." He sat on the edge of his desk and tried to adopt a relaxed poise.

"Well, Paul..." She sighed and looked at the floor. "I wouldn't expect them to do their own dirty work. Was it that pointless PR fucker?"

"There've been a lot of discussions going around about the press intrusion..."

"That's not my issue, Paul," she said, raising her voice slightly, trying to control it. "I didn't ask to join this shit. *You* asked me."

"Because you're one of the best we have and I knew..."

"We're so close to catching him. Don't you feel it?" she said.

"Yes, but..."

"But fucking what? We have a description, a link to a convicted paedophile and a property we know he rented for over six months. We could be arresting this bastard tonight and you want to take this away from me now?"

"I don't want to take anything away from you. I want you to have this, but other...*parties* think the press intrusion has become oppressive. I think this is why they want you off now, before we do make an arrest."

"What?"

"It's becoming too much of a circus for them, Kate."

"For them? For *them*? Who the fuck *are* they?" she shouted. "Was it that pointless cunt, Callum Brown? Paul, really? Is this what we're all about now, public relations? He's not my boss. He's not even your boss."

"That doesn't come into it," said Myers. "He has influence."

"He has a suit and a gob, Paul."

"Things have changed. Social media scares them. It used to be that we'd get the job done and who gave a shit if it got a bit messy?

We'd tidy it up and put a smile on our faces. Justice would be seen to be done and life would go on. Now, no-one will talk to us without waving a phone in our faces, ready to push it viral if we say or do the wrong thing."

She sighed.

"Oh, fuck this," she said and left the office, pushing past Atherton, who'd just entered the focus room.

"Good afternoon," he said, steadying himself against the nearby desk.

When she returned, minutes later, she was wearing her running gear: black training tights with silver reflective flashes on the ankles and a bright yellow running jacket.

"What's going on?" said Atherton.

"What's going on is that I've been taken off the case, Jon," she said, removing her phone and keys from her bag, before hurling it into the bottom draw of her desk. She put her phone into a sports armband, which she pulled up high on her arm. Atherton glanced at the closed blinds of Myers's office. Rogers and Amis did a poor job of looking busy nearby. Outside, a window cleaner leaned out from a cherry picker and thumped the window with a heavy cloth, a noise that momentarily distracted Atherton.

"You're kidding me? We're closing in on this bastard. We could find him anytime."

"Exactly. They don't want me around to embarrass them when he's arrested. Can you believe that?" she said. "Has Myers not summoned you yet?" She made eye contact with him for the first time.

"No," he said.

"Well, I wouldn't be surprised. Expect a little chat," she spat. "We can't have the department bandied about in the local rag can we?"

She began to leave and he grabbed her arm. She turned to look at him, her eyes dropping to his hand, which he quickly removed.

"What now?" he said.

"Now, I'm going to run home and on the way, I'm going to buy at least one bottle of wine, probably two," she said. "See you."

*

Prejean had just left the building when she heard Rogers's voice.

"Kate? Atherton told me. What's going on?"

Prejean turned quickly, grabbed Rogers by the neck of his shirt and pushed him against the wall. He felt her knee in perilously close proximity to his testicles. The two nearby smokers were unsure of whether to intervene, finally choosing to withdraw a couple of metres and watch the spectacle unfold.

"I thought it was Walsh," she growled.

"What?"

"You *know* what. Lauren Schloss got to the butterfly house and Wainwright Crescent and fucking everywhere else almost before we did, you arrogant bastard. How much does she pay you?"

He looked away.

"I *knew* it!"

"Please, can we just talk?" he said. "Inside?"

"You want to give her a call with a story? Tell her I just fucking quit," she shouted.

"Kate?"

"Oh fuck off, Chris," she said and put in her earphones as she descended the steps to the street and broke into a jog.

*

She ran. The quayside promenade was largely deserted and she was glad for that, feeling the anger dissipate the further she got from the station. The music helped. She'd learned long ago that slow, unfamiliar classical music suited her best. Anything too fast and she found herself unrealistically trying to keep pace.

She left the riverside and veered up to higher ground on a smaller track, feeling her thighs burn in complaint. Soon, she was surrounded by trees. The only sound was her breathing, which she could occasionally hear over the strings on her headphones. The track plateaued beside a heavily graffitied stretch of exposed sewerage pipe and between the trees, she could see the dark river, meandering eastwards.

The track rose once more, through a shady copse of sycamore, until finally, she saw the dilapidated bench. She paused, resisting the urge to sit down, and instead pulled at her running top to let in some cool air, which felt welcome against her perspiring skin. She placed her hand on her hips and breathed deep, looking upriver to where the Gateshead Millennium Bridge – the eye, as it was known – stood mid-wink to let a boat through to the west.

She was about to start running once more when she felt a firm hand grab her ponytail. She felt a sudden sharp scratching pain on the right of her neck.

"And...relax," said a voice close to her ear.

CHAPTER TWENTY-TWO

Mattias Klum's laptop pinged, alerting him to a new message from *@SonOfGeb*. There was no text in this one, just an image, which appeared as a thumbnail. He clicked on it and it expanded to fill most of the screen.

"Guys," he said, feeling his heart rate increase rapidly. When it seemed no-one had heard him, he yelled: "Guys!"

His shout filled the room and everyone stopped what they were doing and looked at him. They quickly gathered around his screen. There was no mistaking the person in the picture; no lighting or framing trick to bring her identity into question. It was a shot of her head and shoulders. Her eyes were closed, but her cheeks still flushed from her run.

"He's got Kate."

"She was just here," said Amis. "She was just *here!*"

Atherton felt as though the floor had been removed from under his feet and all that was left to do was fall.

*

The storm arrived a day later than the weathermen had predicted, rolling in from the west and blanketing everything in shade. Cumulonimbus clouds towered high above, like an oppressive boot heel poised to come down on them all, like so many ants.

Atherton stared at the table in front of him, absently rotating the plastic coffee cup in his hand and feeling the fading heat of its contents. He was all too aware of the movements of the others around him, but he chose to ignore them and they left him to his thoughts.

Suddenly, something collided with an almighty thud against the window, causing him to spill his drink. He looked down to see young blackbird lying motionless on the narrow concrete ledge below.

"Shit," he said quietly and shook coffee from his hand with a flick of the wrist.

Something occurred to him then, and he reached out to touch the cool glass. Rain began to fall, hitting the windows gently at first, but building in ferocity, until it was as if handfuls of grit were being thrown at it.

He looked across the room. "Connie?" he shouted, getting to his feet.

"Hey," she said. "What's up?"

"Do you know who cleans the windows here?"

"Not personally," she said, looking confused.

"Please humour me," he said. "Can you call someone who'd know?"

"Sure. Hold on." She referred to a list of numbers and dialled. While she talked, Atherton wandered to the boards displaying photos of the victims and looked at the women. "Okay, Jon," she said, after a short while. "We use a company called O'Dean's Corporate Cleaning."

"And who does the same for Menshen?"

"Let me have a look at the spreadsheet. The name doesn't sound familiar though."

Atherton returned to Amis's desk and watched as she opened a spreadsheet and then a search window into which she typed 'O'Deans' before pressing enter.

"No. Not used by Menshen," she said.

"Are we sure? If they don't do it, who does?"

"I don't know. Let's see," she said and tapped windows into the search box. "Here we go...No, it says they use someone called JLM Management for maintenance and cleaning services, so..."

"Maybe they're a service management company who deal with cleaning the interior, emptying bins and so on. Who cleans their windows from the *outside*?"

"This is meant to be the full list," said Amis, holding her hands up to the screen. "This is everything."

"Everything paid for by Menshen. Maybe the windows are done by the business park's contractors. Is there someone who can find out?"

She blew air out the side of her mouth.

"I suppose so. Just a sec," she said. Amis found Douglas's number and dialled. "Hi, this is DC Connie Amis. Sorry to bother you again, Mr Douglas, but I just wanted to ask a quick question...yes, I'm fine thanks...I just wanted to confirm which company cleans your windows...yes...not the interior. Yes, the spreadsheet is very thorough, but I just wanted to clarify this one point...Okay. Thanks."

She replaced the phone in its cradle and looked at Atherton. "He's calling back. Okay, what have you got on your mind, Doctor Atherton?"

He locked her with his eyes.

"This guy is all about seeing, right? Watching," he said. "His calling card is the Eye of Horus. His victims are all physically of a type and he finds and studies them before he takes them, yeah?"

"Yes," she said, though her eyes suggested more convincing was required.

"Menshen's office, where he watched Ellis Brampton. The hospital, where he watched Abigail Southern. The Baltic gallery, where he watched Kaitlyn Thomas. All big buildings covered in glass and he's been staring in at them like pretty fish in an aquarium. He's a wallflower and always has been. He feels like a...like a supporting character in his own life."

"The van," she said.

"Hmm?"

"Jared Crane said he saw Kaitlyn Thomas in an unmarked van in the observatory carpark," said Amis.

"Exactly. But do you know what really made me think he's been watching through windows? He knew exactly when Kate was running home instead of driving like she sometimes does, because she was wearing her running gear in here. He *knew* she'd be alone on her training route and it'd be the perfect time to take her, because he was watching us and watching her. Watching us, through that fucking window." He pointed to the wall of glass.

"Jesus Christ," said Amis. The phone rang and she picked it up. "Hi, Mr Douglas. Yes, thanks. No, that's everything, thank you so much. Goodbye."

"O'Dean's Corporate Cleaning?"

Amis nodded, eyes widening.

*

"Okay, just run through it again please, Jon," said Myers.

Atherton leaned forward from the back seat, so Myers could hear him better, whilst Rogers shifted up a gear and the Audi roared down the street. Amis struggled to balance a pile of files on her knees whilst talking to someone in quiet tones on her phone.

"O'Dean's window cleaning is common to all of the victims in some way. I think he's an employee of the company," said Atherton.

"And we just bowl in and start firing questions?" said Myers.

"We don't know how much time we have, do we?" said Rogers.

"Everything fits," said Atherton. "He's our man. Trust me."

"So what's the plan? Have you considered that if you're right, he might well be on the premises?"

"Well, that's why I thought I'd bring Newcastle's finest with me," said Atherton. "We have Jared Crane's description to work with."

"Short and bald? That's half the men in the North East, Jon," said Myers, sounding increasingly exasperated. "What if we go in half-cocked and compromise everything by showing him our cards?"

"We don't have many cards to show, Paul. That's the problem," said Atherton. "If I can look this man in the eye, I'll know him. Trust me."

There was a period of silence whilst Myers mulled this over. Rogers overtook a bus, pulling in with seconds to spare as the oncoming car blared its horn.

"What could he do if he's cornered?" asked Myers.

"I'm not sure," said Atherton.

"Marvellous. Connie, place a call to have armed response on standby."

"Sir," said Amis and lifted her phone once more.

"Okay, boys and girls," said Rogers, pulling over to the side of the road. "We're here. Are we doing this or what?"

All eyes fell on Myers and he nodded. They vacated the car and walked across a forecourt which was crowded with white vans to a small one-storey building with 'O'Dean's' displayed on a brown and beige hoarding above. They followed Myers through the door and a young, bespectacled receptionist looked up in surprise. Myers flashed his warrant card.

"DCI Paul Myers. We just need to ask you a few questions about one of your employees," he said.

"Oh...of course," said the girl, and got to her feet, her face quickly reddening. "Which one?"

"Good question," said Myers. "Do you have photographs of each of them?"

"Er...I'm not sure that I do," she said and looked from one side of her desk to the other as if the answer might present itself there.

"What about copies of their driving licenses, when you insured them for the vans?" said Amis.

"Oh, yes...you might be right. They'd be in...oh hold on." She wandered from one filing cabinet to another. "This is them."

She pulled a battered document pocket from one of the drawers and handed it to Myers.

"That's a great help. Thanks," said Paul. "Atherton, you're up."

He handed the file over and Atherton immediately pulled out all the documents and began sorting through them on a nearby table.

"Keep that woman away from me," whispered Atherton. "If she interrupts me, I might just strangle her."

"Sure."

"I should probably tell my boss you are here," she said.

"Of course," said Rogers. "I think you should, but can I just ask you something?" He took her over to the window and began asking a series of random questions about the vans outside. Amis joined Atherton at the table.

"Is this the 'no' list over here? Let me see," she said.

Atherton moved to make space for her and dealt several more documents onto the same pile, each with a black and white photocopy of a driving license stapled to the corner.

"Too young...too hairy...too black. No offence."

"None taken," she said. He rifled through another handful and pushed them to one side, then he stopped. He showed Amis: a bald man in his mid-thirties staring out with dark eyes, the smile on his face bordered on arrogance. He took the sheet and strode over to the receptionist.

"Tell us about this guy," he said, holding it in front of her. "Please."

"Oh, that's Carl," said the receptionist. "Carl Cutler. He's been with us for at least four years. That's how long I've been here and he was already..."

"Can we have an address for Mr Cutler?"

"I'm not sure if I can..."

"You can...sorry, what's your name?"

"Linda."

"You can, Linda. This is unbelievably important and time really is of the essence here," said Atherton. "We could go away and come back with a warrant and lots of sirens blaring loudly, but we'd rather save you from all of that. We think there may be issues with national security. Do you know what I mean by that, Linda? Do you have his address here?"

"Well, it should be in their files. The lads are paid by BACs, so it's not like we send their payslip home, but we ask them to give us a contact address in case of emergencies. Just a minute," she said, and moved to a set of drawers behind her workstation, finally producing a thin yellow folder with Cutler's name hand-written upon it. She opened it and handed it to Atherton.

"Shit," said Atherton and held it up to the others.

"The address is Matthew Bank," said Amis. "That bastard again."

*

Back at the station, Atherton sat alongside Mattias, looking at the message feed on the monitor.

"Hey, Matty," said Amis, approaching the desk.

"Hi," he replied, not taking his eyes from the screen.

Amis set a sandwich and a cup of coffee down in front of Atherton, before taking the seat opposite.

"Thanks," he said after a moment during which he looked as if he might have protested.

"Carl Cutler doesn't have a record, but we have a name and a National Insurance number. Everyone leaves traces. We'll have his address in hours," said Amis.

"That could be too late," he said. He took the lid off the coffee and shook in some sweetener.

"One of his workmates could lead us straight to him," she said.

"Or we may have simply scared him into killing Kate quicker," said Atherton.

She was taken aback by his bluntness. "Don't think like that, Jon," she said.

He shot her an angry glance and Amis prepared for a verbal attack, but Atherton appeared to rapidly regain his composure.

"Then what do you propose we do?" said Atherton. "We have him gloating in this social media shithouse, but we're not doing anything about it."

"You think you know enough about Carl Cutler to say you can engage with him, without accelerating his activities?" said Amis, leaning across the table towards him. "Because, it didn't sound like it to me."

Mattias shifted uncomfortably in his seat between them.

"Come on, guys," he said, quietly.

"I think the time to out-psyche the psycho has passed," she said.

Atherton's eyes burned back at her and he suddenly arose from his seat, jarring the table and tipping over the coffee. Mattias righted the cup, but not before it had spilled most of its contents.

"I'm sorry," said Atherton. "I think I'll just...get some fresh air."

Amis watched him leave, before finding some tissues to mop up the spillage.

"I'm sorry, Matt. Maybe some fresh air is what I need, too. By that, I mean a cigarette," said Amis. "You want to join me?"

"I don't smoke, but thank you," he replied. He listened to her receding footsteps and realised he was now alone in the room.

There was a high-pitched pinging noise, an alert from the social media monitoring client and his eyes shot to the screen. There was nothing new on the feed monitoring public *@SonOfGeb* activity, so he flicked from one column to the next, searching the rows until he found it: a message, not in the public arena, but one sent privately. He clicked it open. There was a photograph of Atherton, clearly taken by himself in the dimly-lit street outside the station. A series of messages followed showing the sender as Mattias himself.

> **You:** *It's Atherton. I'm alone. I know you've been watching my decline. With your permission, I'd like to bear witness to your transcendence.*

> *@SonOfGeb: Yes.*

> **You:** *Send me a rendezvous point.*

> *@SonOfGeb: Your parents' house. Twenty minutes, or I'm going in.*

Mattias stood up and read the screen again as if doing so might change it. He'd been at his desk the whole time, so how had Atherton done this?

He delved into the pockets of his jacket, which hung over his chair, searching each one without result. He picked up the desk phone, his hand shaking as he dialled.

"DSI Myers? It's Mattias Klum," he said. "I'm sorry. I don't know how to explain this, but basically Doctor Atherton has stolen my phone and is privately messaging the Starman."

CHAPTER TWENTY-THREE

Atherton slammed the taxi door and crossed the pavement into the shopping precinct that he remembered well from his youth. Three teenage boys lurked in the shadow of a newsagent where he'd once had a short-lived job. One smiled and said something to the others before drawing on a dog-end and laughing. Atherton ignored them and made his way past the shop fronts; the hairdressers, the pizza shop and the post office, before emerging at the other side into his parent's estate.

He moved as fast as his body would let him, but he was already out of breath and his hip ached painfully. He turned the corner and struggled up a slight incline.

When he rounded the bend, he could see his parents' house and he looked in all directions. The street was free of cars and quiet. The light in his parents' bedroom was already on and as he approached, he saw his mother walk past, carrying something in her arms.

He quickened his pace, expecting the appearance of a white van at any moment. He reached the open front gate, just as the bedroom light went off above and he leaned against the post to catch his breath, until he finally conceded and sat on the low brick wall which encircled the garden.

He slid a hand into his pocket and was about to retrieve Mattias's phone, when he saw it at the far end of the street. The van. It edged forward, so that the front peaked out from behind a wall and Atherton was certain he could see the silhouette of a man behind the wheel. A pause, then the van turned the corner and as it rolled slowly towards him, the full headlights were switched on. Atherton shaded his eyes.

The van pulled up beside him and came to a stop, with its engine ticking over for several moments. The window rolled down. Atherton caught a glimpse of the man inside; dark clothes, a bald head. A hand appeared from the van window and passed him an envelope. On it was scrawled: INJECT ME. Atherton opened it, revealing a small plastic syringe, containing colourless liquid.

He took a moment to glance back at the house. He pictured them and felt grateful that they were oblivious to his predicament. Then he rolled up his sleeve and picked up the syringe.

*

Thoughts passed in and out his head like a conveyor belt of possible realities, each briefly presented for consideration, before yielding to the next.

In the end, one simple thing coalesced: the cold. It brought him back rapidly, enveloping him and he tried to curl his body into a foetal position, but found his limbs tethered. His teeth chattered uncontrollably against something in his mouth. There was the taste of metal and he felt the bar tentatively with his tongue, running its length from one side of his mouth to the other. He moved his head, trying to make out something from the blackness and saw a chink of light; not much, merely an area above, which was simply less dark than the rest. It disappeared from view as he turned his head and he realised something was restricting his sight, affording him a narrow corridor of vision, something not on his eyes, but beside them, blocking his peripheral vision: *blinkers*.

He dropped his head to his shoulder and felt the base of the bridle which had been fixed tightly to his scalp. Breathing deeply, he tried to control a wave of nausea, fearful he would choke if he vomited. There was the dawning realisation he'd been stripped. The damp ground beneath him emanated cold up into his knees and shins, and a draft blew over his bare shoulders and neck. With his elbows, he felt the waistband of his boxer shorts, thankful for this minor dignity.

With his bad knee protesting painfully, he shuffled first to one side, then to the other and found the rough wooden walls which contained him. It was a stall, perhaps five feet wide. Locating a corner, he hunkered into it and sat, shivering and trying to shake the effect of the drug.

He kept an eye on the small, lighter area above. In time, a pinprick of light came into view; a single star in the night sky above the building. He watched it for interminable minutes, until it had long since tracked out of sight. It was possible he had slept for a while, but his eyes flicked open when he heard a sudden and sharp clicking noise.

A row of fluorescent strip lights hanging on chains flickered to life in the apex of the corrugated iron ceiling. The sudden light was blinding, but he tried to take in his surroundings as rapidly as he could: a stone floor and wooden walls, each as grey as the other. In front of him, a hinged door hung some two feet off the ground.

His wrists had been tightly bound with dirty brown rope, which dug into his wrists leaving the flesh of his hands with a blue, deoxygenated tinge. The rope was attached to a thick rusty chain, which was padlocked to a large ring secured to the side of the stall.

Atherton listened intently, but there was only silence. Then he heard the scrape of a shoe turning on the floor and the sudden boom of something striking wood nearby. Two further loud knocks sounded and an even longer silence followed.

"L-little pig, little pig," said a quiet, almost distracted voice.

Footsteps scraped against the floor, getting louder and louder, until Atherton saw a pair of feet in light brown leather sandals appear at the gap beneath the door. He retreated back as far as the chain would allow. A hand appeared at the top of the door and Atherton heard a bolt slide back.

"L-let me in."

The door opened slowly and Carl Cutler stood before him. He was a middle-aged man of less than average height, wearing a white robe and a bright red belt, which had been wrapped around him several times and tied loosely about the waist. His skin was the colour of death; an unhealthy dark green hue. As he moved forward half a step, Atherton could see he had makeup on his eyes, thick black lines leading from the edge of each socket towards his ears. The eyes twinkled with intelligence and as he drew even closer, he could see that as well as being bald, he was entirely without eyebrows, eyelashes or any other discernible facial hair.

The man stopped and stepped back out of the stall, smiling to someone unseen.

"You were r-right. He's awake," he said.

The smile broadened and he raised a hand in acknowledgement, before turning back to the stall. Atherton's eyes dropped. In his hand was the flail; two thick wooden rods separated by a short length of chain. He saw Atherton watching and rattled it playfully. He moved towards him once more and took hold of him by the bridle, angling his head one way and then the other as if assessing the purchase of a piece of costly livestock.

"Not afraid? Good."

He pulled the bridle down towards the floor and Atherton sensed a huge amount of strength in his arm. Atherton leaned down as far as he could, until he collapsed to the ground. The bit jarred roughly in his mouth and he felt sharp fragments of tooth against his tongue. The sole of a sandal pressed down on his neck, pinning him to the floor and he heard Cutler unlock the padlock and unthread the chain from its fixing on the wall.

He took hold of the bridle once more and dragged Atherton awkwardly behind him. They followed the series of strip lights, passing several identical stall doors and out into a small courtyard, lit by a single lamp, which hung precariously from a nearby post.

A narrow track took them past more out-buildings and a dilapidated portacabin. Dazed, Atherton scanned the landscape for potential landmarks. There were none; no streetlights, no houselights, no headlights. Only the silhouettes of trees lining the horizon.

Cutler let go of the bridle, but kept a tight hold of the chain, keeping the length short, yanking it hard whenever Atherton lagged behind. The farmhouse loomed above them, like a huge pebble-dashed monolith. A single light from a room above cast a rectangle of orange light onto the ground below. As they passed through it, Atherton noticed a large bloodied dressing on the back of his tormentor's head. Cutler pulled hard at the chain and Atherton stumbled pathetically to the floor, his knee buckling painfully beneath him. Cutler grabbed him by the hair and pulled him up until they were eye to eye.

"Lame," he said, looking down at Atherton's emaciated limb, the *L* a long drawn out noise which took several attempts to enunciate.

He strode off, with Atherton staggering behind and turned away from the house and onto a poorly lit road lined with tall Juniper trees.

They hadn't walked much further when Atherton saw it; simply a glimmer of light at first. Something in the field to the right of the road. But as they approached, he could see the size of it. A glass structure, with triangular frames and a soft light flickering within.

They came to a break in the trees and a ramshackle gate and he saw it in all its majesty: a pyramid, perhaps fifteen feet at its peak. Atherton could see the doors were open and resting upon the walls of its nearest face.

Cutler murmured a tune to himself as they crossed the field, his eyes fixed on the rich display of stars above. When the chain was slack, Atherton moved his wrists in an effort to loosen the rope, but it was useless. As they entered the pyramid, he felt a welcome blast of warm air upon his skin. The wood-burner stood at the far side of the pyramid, and provided the only light. Beneath his feet was grass – the field itself – and Atherton could smell the strong odour of earth as he was led across the dark grass and thrown down beside a cattle stone.

Cutler threaded the chain through a thick iron ring on the stone and clicked the padlock in place. He strode to the burner, threw on a couple of logs from a small pile and stoked the flames with a poker, which he left leaning against the log pile. He walked casually back to the stone and sat on an upturned horse trough, which was the only other thing in the pyramid. He possessed a fluid, almost graceful way of moving, as if time was abundant, and even the slightest gesture should not be cheapened by haste.

Cutler fixed Atherton with his deep black eyes.

"You must be where it is darkest to best see the light," he said, with a smile playing on the corner of his lips. "This is perhaps unfair. Should I take it off?"

Cutler moved towards him and took Atherton's head gently in his hands, looking deep into his eyes as he unbuckled the bit and threw it down. "No biting now, Doctor."

Atherton felt the tension on his jaw release immediately and he rotated it a couple of times. He ran his tongue along his teeth, finding a place on the upper left where they were jagged and broken.

"I wouldn't dream of it," said Atherton. "Is this the bit where you tell me how alike we are?"

Cutler laughed.

"I don't think so. Do you?" he said. "You're no different to all the others. As much as you'd like to be. Bound by convention. Tied to obligation. You want to be with DS Prejean so much, but you won't give in to that, will you? As if your obedience was a virtue. No matter what the *Evening Chronicle* says."

"And you *are* different?"

Cutler opened his arms wide, palms upwards to display his splendour.

"They'll write about me. *You'll* write about me," he said.

Atherton wondered vaguely if this might mean Cutler would let him live.

"I promise you, I will not," he said. "Why are you even interested in me?"

"Have you ever seen anything so horrible, you couldn't look away?" said Cutler. "That's how it was with you." He smiled a sickly grin. "You have everything a man could possibly wish for, but there you are, sniffing around DS Prejean, playing p-policeman, desperate to mess up your life by any means necessary. Another middle-aged fool, sliding across car bonnets to impress a woman. Aren't you tired of it? T-tired of all the pretending? Are we risen apes or f-fallen angels, Jon? I rather like to think that I-I'm the latter."

"So this is the plan? You're going back to heaven?"

"Yes. You see, w-when you're dying it takes away the fear and it leaves only focus."

"You're dying?"

"I dare say you already guessed this, Jon." He touched the dressing on the back of his head. "*Anaplastic astrocytoma.* The tumour isn't far in, but it's inoperable. They tell me it's the wrong shape. *The wrong shape.* I wonder what the right one is?" He laughed briefly. "It gets bigger, the deeper it goes, like a c-cone."

"Or a pyramid?" said Atherton.

Cutler smiled again.

"W-w-what would you d-do, if you weren't afraid?" he said. "Would you leave your wife for Kate?" There was a silence. "Come on, Jon. You're going to be dead soon, you might as well get involved."

"I made a choice to stay with my wife."

"But where is she? She's gone, hasn't she?"

"Yes. Yes, she has."

"I have to say, I'm n-not surprised," said Cutler. "It had to happen sooner or later. The babies in the nest always push out the ones they think aren't normal and neither of us are normal are we, Jon." Atherton wanted to look away, but held his gaze. "Gone with your lovely daughter, too. They must be a huge miss. I came to visit you one day, you know. Watched you from the house next door."

"I thought so," said Atherton.

"Yes, I watched you," said Cutler, moving closer. "But you didn't know I came back, did you?"

Atherton stared incredulously. Cutler snorted a laugh.

"I stood in your hallway. So close to your wife I could smell her delicious skin. She was very trusting, very accommodating." He giggled. "All you need is a money belt and people think you have a right to knock on their door. She paid me for windows I hadn't even cleaned, Jon. Do you leave this woman in charge of the housekeeping budget? I hope not."

"Bullshit."

"Is it? Your daughter was there. What a sweet thing she is. I ruffled her hair," he said and mimed touching Hannah's head. "I nearly did it, Doctor Atherton. I almost closed the door behind me and slit both of their throats."

"And why didn't you?" said Atherton, seething.

Cutler didn't answer, but smiled cruelly.

"And what about poor Kate? Sad, needy Kate, stuck on the sidelines of her own life, accepting only the love she thinks she deserves?"

He looked suddenly to his side. Atherton followed his gaze, but there was nothing there except the flickering shards of light and dark cast by the flames of the fire.

The wood on the fire crackled and hissed, and Cutler's face was lit on one side by the light from the flames, whilst the other stayed in darkness. Atherton leaned with his back against the stone and tried hopelessly to twist loose the ropes on his wrists.

There was a sudden thudding noise. Atherton looked at Cutler, but he was stationary, eyes transfixed to the stars above. Atherton heard the noise again, followed by the sound of movement and a muffled cry. His eyes dropped to the upturned trough on which Cutler was sitting.

"I think someone is waking up," said Cutler, smiling.

He stood, turned slowly and flipped over the heavy metal trough, with no small amount of effort. Prejean looked around her, eyes wide with panic. She was naked, save for her underwear and was bound by rope on her ankles and wrists. Her knees, elbows and shins were scratched and bloody.

"Oh my dear," said Cutler, warmly. He reached down and cradled her head in his arms, as if he might kiss her, then jerked her head roughly to one side so she could see Atherton.

Atherton watched her eyes shift from fear, to despair, to some kind of acceptance within the space of a few seconds. A single tear tracked down her dirty cheek. Her makeup matched Cutler's; her eyelids a shimmering blue which scintillated in the firelight.

Cutler crouched and unrolled his collection of knives. They reflected light from the flames onto the dark ground. The fire crackled and spit, and a smoking ember tumbled out of the burner and rolled on the grass.

Atherton made sure Cutler wasn't looking; saw he was busy organising his shiny toys around him. With his eyes locked upon Cutler, Atherton reached out towards the burning coal, and with his fingers outstretched, brushed its hot surface. He tried once more, pushing his body away from the stone with his feet, feeling the rope tighten and bite into his wrists. This time he got a finger on it and he tentatively moved it towards him until he was able to grab it.

The ember burned his palm, but he had it and he shuffled back until he was leaning against the stone once more. He dropped it in front of him. It was still smoking and when he blew upon it, he saw a faint glow. When he blew again, it burned a little brighter and Atherton pushed his bound wrists down upon it. He pulled his wrists apart, twisting them in opposite directions and feeling the rope give a little as its fibres began to burn and split.

He looked at Cutler who was kneeling over Prejean, but with his eyes trained on that same empty corner of the pyramid, quietly mumbling. Atherton wrenched at his wrists; it felt as though they might snap before the rope did. He looked at Kate whose eyes flicked rapidly between him and Cutler. She gave him a minute, almost imperceptible nod of encouragement.

"Are you ready to bear witness, Doctor?" said Cutler, finally turning to look at Atherton, who let his arms drop loosely in front of him. "It's hard to look away, isn't it?"

Cutler smiled, showing more gum than teeth, before turning back to Prejean. He picked up the flail and took a standing position over her.

Atherton twisted his hands apart, feeling the skin burn and break. Prejean squirmed on the ground, like a landed fish in a hopeless attempt to move away from Cutler. Atherton gave a final twist to his wrists and suddenly he was free. He got to his feet and staggered towards them, just as Cutler swung the flail back.

Atherton caught it in the palm of his hand and gripped it tightly. He threw himself at Cutler and wrestled him to the floor.

Atherton was on him in an instant, hands tight around his throat, slamming his head back against the ground. Cutler squirmed beneath, and punched Atherton in the side several times and wresting his weak arm away. It was enough to unbalance him. Cutler pushed him off and bounced quickly to his feet. It was only then that Atherton saw the small, curved blade in Cutler's hand. Atherton's side was slick with warm blood, which pulsed out through several dark slits in his skin. Cutler smiled and flicked blood from the blade with a snap of the wrist, before hurling himself forward. Atherton somehow dodged the knife and threw his fist at him. It glanced off Cutler's cheek, but it was enough to send him toppling over onto the grass. His robes flew open and it took Atherton a moment to register what Cutler was wearing beneath; countless plastic pipes encircled his waist, with numerous fuses projecting out like insect proboscises. He removed the robes altogether and threw them to one side.

"Are you coming with me, Jon?" he asked. Then he shouted to someone over Atherton's shoulder: "Is it time?"

Atherton held his hand over the wounds to his side, wondering how much blood he'd lost and what could be damaged beneath. From the corner of his eye, he saw movement; Prejean twisting to undo the rope that bound her ankles.

"What did he say, Carl? *Is* it time?" said Atherton.

Cutler's eyes remained focussed on the same empty corner of the pyramid.

"There's nothing there, Carl. Don't you see? He doesn't exist. Your subconscious has manufactured him, but I can help you."

Cutler appeared bemused, but remained silent. Behind him, Prejean worked furiously, rubbing the rope against the overturned trough.

"He could be a manifestation of your fears over your illness."

"*All my trials, Lord, soon be over,*" sang Cutler, quietly. "*All my trials, Lord, soon be over.*" He repeated it like a mantra.

Prejean approached silently behind Cutler. She grabbed his hand and twisted it at the wrist, causing him to drop the knife. He reacted quickly and turned to punch her with his left fist, but failed to connect. Prejean stepped in with her rear foot and unleashed a side-kick to the ribs, which sent him reeling towards Atherton. Atherton grabbed him around the torso, clamping Cutler's arms to his sides. As he struggled to control him, Atherton could smell the contents of the pipe bombs; a pungent smell of ammonia.

Prejean snatched up the knife and held it to Cutler's throat, her hands still bound by rope.

"What now?" gasped Atherton.

"Get him down."

Atherton awkwardly kicked the back of Cutler's knees until they buckled and he fell forward to the floor. Atherton pinned him down, putting all his weight through his knee on the small of Cutler's back and twisting his arms up behind his back.

"Over there," said Atherton. "The rope."

Prejean took the rope from by the cattle stone and brought it to him.

"You're bleeding," she said.

"I'd noticed."

Atherton bent painfully to tie the rope as tightly as he could around Cutler's wrists and flipped him over. Cutler's eyes bulged from their sockets in fury. Atherton punched him heavily; once, twice, three times until his body relaxed, his eyes rolled back and he was unconscious.

When he was confident Cutler was no longer moving, Atherton slumped weakly to the ground. Prejean immediately retrieved Cutler's discarded robes and draped them over Atherton. She turned his body so she could see his bloody side with the light from the fire.

"Press here, as hard as you can," she said. She placed her hand over his and pushed down on the wounds. With his free hand shaking, he wrapped the robes around her shoulders and pulled her close, feeling her warm skin against his body.

"Stay awake, you lazy bastard," she said and he mumbled something in reply. "What did you say?"

"I said, is this our first proper date?"

"I fucking hope not," she said and pulled him tighter. Off in the distance, she saw a procession of lights speeding along an unseen road. "Cavalry's coming. Be here soon. Don't be a dick and die on me."

"I honestly have no intention of that," he said.

She cradled him from behind and felt his head fall heavily against her shoulder. His body shivered against hers and she pulled him tighter, watching the lights grow larger.

"I'm sorry," he said.

"What for?"

"Take your pick," he slurred.

She thought she could see movement silhouetted in the field outside and hear muted voices. She waved her hand in their general direction, aware that she might be more visible to them than they were to her. Someone shouted, a gruff instruction that she couldn't decipher, but recognised as Myers. She felt a rush of relief at the sound of his voice: their discussions in the clean, warm confines of his office felt as if they'd occurred weeks ago.

"Here!" she shouted, waving her hand once more. As she did so, her eyes dropped to Cutler, prone on the floor and realised that his eyes were open. "No. Atherton, he's awake!" she shouted.

Cutler rolled to his side and struggled awkwardly to his feet. Without looking at either of them, he ran across the pyramid, stumbling once, and staggered on towards the wood burner. Prejean was right behind him, pausing only to pick up one of the knives from the roll that still lay on the floor beside the upturned trough.

"No!" shouted Atherton. Struggling weakly to his feet. "Leave him!"

Cutler reached the burner. Without pausing, he dropped to his knees and pushed his head and shoulders through the open door and into the flames. Prejean reached him, grabbing the rope that bound his wrists behind his back and tried to pull him away, but he held fast. As he began to burn, she heard him scream. One of the fuses around Cutler took light and hissed violently, sending sparks in all directions.

Just then, three men burst through the door: Myers, Rogers and an armed officer.

"No, don't come in!" shouted Atherton. Staggering towards them, still holding his bloody side. "He's rigged with explosives!"

The armed officer, shocked at Atherton's appearance, raised his weapon and took aim, until Myers firmly pushed it away.

"No, no. Get out!" he shouted, catching all three with his extended arms and pushing them out of the door, where they all collapsed in a heap.

There was a tremendous explosion. The noise was deafening. Atherton felt a burning sensation on his back and heard the sound of glass shattering. He tried to sit up, but Rogers held him back.

"Kate?" he shouted. There was no answer and as the smoke cleared and sections of glass continued to fall, all he could see was the charred remains of Cutler's body.

CHAPTER TWENTY-FOUR

The music was at odds with the décor. A ballad from the nineties, which he couldn't quite place. The pews, wall panels and lectern were all teak veneer and the floor was covered in a dark red, heavy-pile carpet. A large cross hung over them, suspended, somewhat precariously, by a number of steel wires. The place smelled damp, the result of being heated only when it needed to be.

The coffin lay upon a rolling aluminium conveyor, giving it the feel, Atherton thought, of a factory production line. Roll in, roll off. He couldn't stop himself from staring at the coffin and wondering how the occupant looked now.

"Do not mourn, for I am but a pilgrim on these shores," said the vicar. "And before me is a ship, a vessel of beauty with full sails. So it will bear me across the ocean, to the edge of the horizon and beyond. Then you will say, 'he is gone, he is gone' – but gone where? Gone from your sight is all. And just as sure as the ship which bears me is constructed of love; the bow, the mast, the stern, there are others watching it arrive and they are gladly shouting 'he arrives, he arrives'. This is dying."

He closed the book and the room was silent, until he gestured for the congregation to rise. Louise helped Atherton to his feet and once up, he put an arm around her shoulders to steady himself.

"Thanks," he whispered. He glanced around and saw Amis, sandwiched between Rogers and Myers. She nodded to him.

"We now commit this mortal body to be consumed by fire. Earth to earth, ashes to ashes, dust to dust. And we beseech thine infinite goodness to give us grace to live in thy fear and love and to die in thy favour, that when the judgement shall come which thou hast committed to thy well-beloved Son, both this our brother and we may be found acceptable in thy sight. Grant this, O merciful Father, for the sake of Jesus Christ, our only Saviour, Mediator, and Advocate."

There was a mechanical noise and a thick red velvet curtain swept slowly around the coffin, hiding it from view. Atherton heard someone crying nearby.

"I've got to get out of here," whispered Atherton. "I'm sorry."

"Do you want me to come?" Louise answered.

"No, I just need air," he said.

Several heads turned as Atherton made his way up the aisle and out of the chapel. Outside, he leaned back against the cool stone wall, took several deep breaths and loosened his tie. He looked east, across the headstones and angels to where the dark blue sea met the horizon.

"Couldn't face it either, eh?"

Atherton looked around. Prejean stood beneath the chapel's portico in a black dress smoking a cigarette.

"I thought you gave those up?" said Atherton.

"Another passing flirtation," she said. "It'll pass."

She took another drag and then stubbed it out beneath the sole of her shoe. He noticed the dressing peeking from the edge of her long sleeves.

"How are you?"

"Healing," she said and shrugged. "They tell me there might be a little scarring, but not much. They're going to see how it goes and if I might need a graft."

"I'm sorry, Kate," he said. "I could have got to you. Maybe got you out the way quicker."

"Yeah, but you saved the other three, didn't you? It's okay. Basic maths, right?"

"Yeah. Maths," he said.

"It's my own fault I got burned. I just didn't want him to get out of it. He deserved to stand trial. To have eyes on him for a change. For people to know what he did."

"He deserved to burn," said Atherton.

"Maybe," she said. "I never thought I'd be happy to get back under that trough."

"They should roll them out in the middle east," he said.

The music from the chapel suddenly increased in volume as the door opened and Walsh's family emerged. Atherton and Prejean retreated to give them space as people lined out to give them their condolences. They watched for a while as people took turns to hug or kiss Walsh's wife, whispering words of support, wiping away tears of their own.

"Are you going to the pub with the others?" he asked after a while.

"I don't think so," she said.

"When are you going back to work?" he said.

"Not for a while. I don't know," she said. "I feel like milking this one for all it's worth."

"Good plan," he said. He saw Louise walk out into the sunlight and stand, looking uncomfortable amongst the crowd. Myers stopped and said something to her and she replied smiling.

"How about you?" said Prejean. "What's next?"

He sighed and looked at her. Her eyes dropped to the grass.

"I have absolutely no idea," he said. He saw Louise looking his way. "Let's stay in touch this time. Okay?

He smiled at her and waited for her to look at him.

"Sure," she said.

He left Kate there and walked across to Louise and put an arm around her waist. She turned to look at him with red eyes and offered a smile.

"Paul says they're going on to a pub somewhere," she said. "Do you want to go?"

"I'd just as soon the two of us got out of here," he said.

"Alright," she said. She reached into her jacket pocket, pulled out some sunglasses and put them on.

Atherton looked back to Prejean, but she was already gone, walking up the street and lighting another cigarette.

If you enjoyed this title, follow Obliterati Press on Twitter and Facebook for details of forthcoming releases.

@ObliteratiPress

https://www.facebook.com/ObliteratiPress

Also, be sure to check out our website for regular short story contributions.